The House of Zebulun:
A Dwelling of Honor

The House of Zebulun:
A Dwelling of Honor

Jan Harding Chapman
2015

Frist Printing: 2015

ISBN-13: 978-1517189587

ISBN-10: 1517189586

Jan Harding Chapman
Anna, TX 75409

Acknowledgements

Thanks first of all to my husband, Don, who has given me a wonderful life along with a multitude of others that he has given so generously to. Only God knows what he has sacrificed.

I owe so much to my sister, Juanita, who provided so much of the facts of our history and remembrances in this book.

Were it not for my talented, faithful daughter, Shannon, this book would have never been possible.

To my grandchildren, who inspired me to write a "Brief Little Family Tree" of our history. Who would have thought it would be as long as "Gone With the Wind"?

The Storyteller

This is a story told by a storyteller. It is the story told to my children of their past family. So gather together my children, and learn this tale told to me. It is a tale told to me by other storytellers in my family. I cannot tell you exactly what their faces looked like. Yet, I dimly see the lines in their faces in the faded light of the past ages - faces in the soft light used in a by-gone age, perhaps that of a tallow candle or smoky oil lamp.

Out of the midst of the past their voices come to me with voices passed down from the storytellers' before them in their families. Most were not aware that they were leaving a legacy with their words; not aware that they were telling the tale of their lives to generations to come. Not aware that they were passing on the legacy of those that had gone before them.

Some read this sadly, because you have not heard such a story. Your past and the people thereof, for whatever reason, have not left behind your history or story. To you it is mystery. I therefore give you this challenge: a hero's challenge. I ask you not to take up the sword, but the quill. Take up the quill of a storyteller. This will be the sword of your family's future. You will become the one to begin the family legacy. Your family looks to you!

You are the one who will write, in blood, your story. I say blood because it will be written only with the bloodline of your life lived. If you do not stand as their storyteller, who will? Should you know nothing of your past, for whatever reason, you stand with clean pages to write to those coming after you; the story of your life. You have no heroes, nor villains with which to contend with in your blank pages. You will know that those little ones that would sit at your knee will have only the pages of your life that you are now writing daily.

What an awesome challenge is that! How can they have a story to tell without yours? So let the story now begin!

If you are one of the older ones in your family, tell them they will want to know these things later. Speak your story out on the winds so it might survive. Now as I write my family stories, there is much I wish I had asked of those that went before me. Those around you now will wish the same in their future. They just don't know it yet.

To those that have the stories of your family, I ask you to not let them fade. We all have family stories that need to be told - good or bad, happy or sad, exciting or boring. (Those probably were the most blessed of people.) To those who will live in the future they will be as precious as gold.

This admonition I give you: If you do not tell your story, and the stories told before you, you will fade from this earth to never be heard of again. You will no longer be! It will be as if *you* never existed nor those who went before you.

STORYTELLERS ARISE!

Oh that I had in the wilderness a lodging place for
wayfaring men! - Jeremiah 9:2

LITTLE SARAH'S BATTLEFIELD

Endlessly, the gruesome battles went on. How long had she heard the smothered groans of America's people at war? How long could she stand this never ending graveyard they called a battleground? Brothers in different blue and gray battle array fighting one another. Never ceasing cries had become, unbelievably to her, the background music of her day. The moans went on relentlessly: the sounds of piercing pain, the cries of torment, the cries for help, the cries for death! The worst cries were the cries for Mama. This was the thing that would cause her husband to turn his body away from the surgery table and she would see his back heaving with the sobs he tried to keep silent. These were children on this grisly and overwhelming battlefield!

The horror of her day was that she and her husband helped produce the screams, in the vain hope they were helping the tortured to survive. As a doctor and nurse team, it was their daily task to bind up the crippling wounds.

She and Zebulun Wheeler Ingrahm had married when Sarah Elizabeth Stanton was 20. Zebulun being a physician and she a nurse, they seemed to be quite a match. They were definitely not your normal couple. That was in 1860. A year later the civil war broke out and they both enlisted for service. He was in the eighty-third infantry, and she enlisted as an army nurse in the same regiment. Both would serve during the entire war.

How weak she felt at times. Her small frame, not even five foot tall, had learned to help an orderly hoist corpses off of tables so they could move on to help the living. Many times, with what seemed the last ounce of her tiny strength, she must roll huge men in delirium and keep them pinned to a table until fastened to what seemed like a torture rack to them. Many times she not only prayed for them under her breath, but for herself, that she would not go from the tent to run and take her place with the screaming and moaning of those waiting outside.

It was getting harder to hide the secret that was hidden in her body. The nausea was now impossible to hide. Her husband although sympathetic, had dismissed it as being the sickening sights that shocked even him. He had suggested she go home. After all, this had been a volunteer mission on her part. Many women came to the war to help in the place where their own community's regiments were, but not where she had been. She had been allowed to attend her husband these last few days in the actual surgery field tent.. He had been short-handed and it had been needful. This was not her normal place for she belonged with the Sanitary Corps with the other women.

Washing, cooking and whatever skills that would help not only the cause, but the people of their communities was what women usually did in service in what was called the Sanitary Commission. Comforting, sanitizing and cleansing wounds, and attending the comfort needs of the wounded warriors, was her normal charge, being a nurse. She was seeing how these unsung heroes of civilian women made enormous contributions to the war effort. She knew it was a new thing being allowed by this present President. How she admired him for his wisdom and compassion.

Nothing was more important to her than relieving and helping the suffering on the battlefield, but because her husband was a doctor, she was allowed to come into the place of surgery. It was to this cause she had come. Should she reveal the secret that lay within her, she most certainly would be sent not only out of the tent, just when he needed someone to help him, but he would definitely send her home. It was for this reason, she struggled on, but it was getting harder. She didn't know how much longer her secret would be hidden. Until now, she had squared her shoulders and went on. Leaving her husband she had married so shortly before the war was unthinkable to her young mind. Yet, attending him in this surgery tent was affecting her mind more than she imagined it would.

She saw splintered bones of every kind that needed to be removed or repaired. She saw her husband cutting through those bones with teeth gritting effort. There was the yanking of swords from the wounds before they could be tended. There were limbs thrown aside like so much garbage. Some screamed, some groaned softly, some cried like babies, and some prayed, waiting for death. Blood not only had soaked through the soldier's clothing, but dripped on, and many times drenched hers. The dirt floor of the tent was stained as if it were some kind of dirt and blood colored floor covering.

She consoled herself thinking, "They will survive. They will live. I have helped. I am helping." Over and over she tried to reassure herself that the butchery that was being performed would produce a life later on that was better than death, or the slow gangrene, or the horror of carrying a mangled body part with them the rest of their lives.

She tried to comfort herself with the thought of "after the war pictures" in her mind. She pictured them being in the arms of loved ones and carrying on a life, and of holding their children in their laps. She used these thoughts to transfer her mind from the brutality of the cure being done on that awful table that would help them survive. Sometimes, the screams drowned out her thoughts and she wanted to throw her body over their pitiful bodies and cry out, "No more. No more", but this could not be. Her husband had warned her of what her behavior was to be. Even in the midst of blood and confusion she was to stay a nurse's course or leave the hospital tent.

Now in the midst of all that assaulted her soul, a gentle moment would come. She had stepped outside the stifling tent during a lull at her husband's suggestion. The shrill, early April wind bit into her face. The cold air gushed through her hair, pulling at the nurse's bonnet that she wore. The dead, charred trees looked barren against the terrible landscape. Even the cold air, though, felt better than the stifling, stinking air in the surgery tent.

As she turned to go back in, she glanced to the place where the fallen dead had been placed. A movement had caught her attention. Among the bodies she had seen one body, pale as death, move. Her heart cried out in sympathy.

How young he was. He was covered already with the whiteness of death. How awful to lay still alive among the hundreds of piled dead. He was groaning softly. His sword lay beside him and he was still clutching it.

Overwhelmed by the brutality of battle, and this young death seeming so unfair, she knelt at his side. She gently squeezed his hand to let him know someone was there. His soft, young hand was shaking. His pale face turned to her with grateful eyes. He was struggling to say something. She bent low to hear his words. Weakly, with all the strength he could summon, the too young soldier asked, "Is the war over?"

Gulping back the terrible lump in her throat and the tears stinging her eyes, knowing that heaven forgave her, she squeezed that bloodless hand and said, "Yes my brave young warrior. Thanks to you we won."

His young blue eyes stared into hers for what seemed a long time, smiling, until the life left his gaze.

She did not know then that unto the end of her days she would remember those eyes and she would link them with another pair of eyes she would see momentarily. She removed the sword from his hand and laid it by his side. Gently, she folded his battle soiled hands together as if in prayer up under his chin. She whispered a short, wordless prayer for his soul and for the mother that was waiting for him to come home.

She arose slowly, looking on that now peaceful face. She wiped her tear-stained face with the rag that she used in the tent to wipe sweat from her eyes. She turned and squared her young shoulders to walk back to the needs of the hospital tent, expecting to see her husband.

As she entered the tent flap, to her surprise she encountered a man in white; a glistening white. How the purity of that white stood out in the contrast of all the filth that surrounded them. The stranger's gaze into her eyes was so startling, that she froze with the wonder of this encounter. She was shaking. A gentle hand was put on her trembling shoulder. With that touch came an indescribable peace and strengthening. Without saying the words, a "well done" came from his indescribable eyes. He looked her directly in the eyes and said, "The war *is* over." Joy flooded her being and although she was not sure if this heavenly being was real, this Union girl immediately asked the inevitable question. "Who won?"

Shaking His beautiful head sadly, he said, "No one won." She turned to look around the tent to see where Zeb was. They were the only two in the tent. Zeb obviously had gone outside for a break too. She turned to the stranger with another question on her heart. To her surprise he was gone! The jolt of this encounter shook her to her very core. She would always remember the stranger in white!

Suddenly she heard a loud horse whinny! Then the sound of hoof beats! Why would there be a horse whinny in a tent? She suddenly jerked awake! She was in the wagon! The war was over! They were mercifully heading home at last. She had fallen asleep! It was all a dream produced by the horror she had seen in the war!

Then she remembered the beautiful visitor who had come to her. The love that was in his eyes; the soft touch of his gentle hand still seemed to be on her shoulder. Her heart glowed with that warmth again as before, now as she thought of him. He was no dream! His silent "Well done" resounded still in her being.

How good it would be to be home at last. The Donaldson Tennessee Regiment in which they had served together would become a memory, but this would be a part of their lives that could never be forgotten. On the journey that lay before them she would at last reveal her secret to her Zebulun. A child would be born to them in this year the Civil War had ended. With great joy they turned the wagon toward that blessed place called home.

DAYS OF TRIBULATION OVER AT LAST

It had been a long, long war, but now it was over. Some of the nation rejoiced as many mourned. The losses were indescribable. Sarah and Zebulun rejoiced as they started the long journey home. It would be cold in early April and the ride would not be an easy one. Sarah had been accustomed to cold weather. As a young girl she had seen bitter weather in Oneida, N.Y. County. When she was fifteen, her family moved to Knox County, Illinois. So having endured those northern winters, this early April was not considered too cold. However, back home, being able to sit in a house with an iron stove and a fireplace with a carefully kept roaring fire with piled high blankets was a far cry from riding in a wagon. Even back at both the primitive forts she had been stationed at, Fort Donaldson and Fort Henry, there had been a pot-bellied stove.

The first part of the journey by wagon to the train station was not to be a long one, however it would be the hardest part to endure. Once at the train platform they would be leaving the horses and covered wagon at the livery stable. Arrangements had been made ahead through some army staff that needed to pick up the wagon at the town depot to use it to return back to the fort. The nights, sleeping on the bedsprings in the wagon were not easy. A fire helped to keep the wild things away that would be lurking in the dark unknown wilderness around them.

At times Sarah would get off the high wagon seat during the day because she became stiff. Her muscles started to cramp after a day because of the rough wagon ruts. They found themselves walking more and more rather than endure the wagon. Of course there were many things for Zebulun to do. Starting with the axe and cutting firewood was just one thing when they stopped in the evening. She of course got out the coffee pot from the wagon and put the skillet on to prepare the evening meal. They also had some jerky with them. She was prepared for the meals before she came, should there not be any game. The army rifle was not only a comfort against the wolves, coyotes, and all that they felt threatened by, but meat was a treat when a rabbit or squirrel or possibly a pheasant appeared. They had filled a wooden barrel full of water before they left, but they were careful to ration the precious liquid. The hope was to find a place to camp near a creek or river.

Always in their thoughts was the hope there would be no spring snow as could happen the further north they would go. Blizzards came up quickly and many unfortunate people's bodies were not found until after the spring thaw. They had been able to secure two buffalo hide robes early in the war, but many nights they huddled together shivering. Knowing what the poor soldiers on the field of battle had endured, they felt well off. They wore the scarves around their necks and ears that Sarah had knitted and they, of course, had heavy overcoats before they started the journey, which they had during the winter war time. Zebulun wore the woolen socks that she had knitted for him in the spare time she had back at the fort. There were no exotic foods, but the big heavy pot, and the iron skillet did well for their cooking needs. A steaming pot of coffee seemed as heavenly ambrosia after traveling all day until the light was going and it was time to stop for the night. After battleground fare their simple food seemed enough.

For the first time in years they were able to talk to each other without the background of the war going on. There was much talk about the war. The discussion about the Appomattox Courthouse surrender of Lee to Grant had been started quickly and spread in every detail by those who witnessed it. Since they had been stationed at Grant's camp when it all happened, there were those who witnessed it almost first hand. Others had at least been in the group that had been assigned to accompany General Grant to Appomattox Courthouse when the surrender took place. Sarah had Zebulun repeat to her each word he had already told her before, that those who witnessed that historic scene were more than willing to repeat. He said those that had been there talked about how handsome Lee's uniform was right down to the sword with a gold-inlay scabbard on that day of the surrender. They had observed that General Grant, on the other hand, was muddy with wrinkled clothes. They said that General Grant had generously allowed Lee's enlisted men to take home their horses for spring planting. Afterwards, they said Grant's men shared their ample rations with the hungry Confederates. They were moved when they told that many, after they had eaten, shook the confederate hands, while crying.

It was not until later that Zebulun and Sarah would find out that the Union armies had literally destroyed the Confederacy and that nearly everything was demolished. They heard that nearly one in three had paid for the secession with their lives making the taste of that victory bitter. However, Sarah and Zebulun rejoiced in one great thing: the most significant thing to them was the Union armies had destroyed slavery. To them that was what the cause was all about.

The thing they knew first hand was that hundreds of thousands of Union troops had been maimed and crippled. They later were to hear that 360,000 Union soldiers died. It had been a hard and bitter war and many wounds, beyond the physical ones, that had to heal.

The saddest one of all later was the assassination of the gentle giant who would die in the name of freedom of an oppressed people. They, in their great joy, were yet to hear of that terrible thing to come that would cause a nation to mourn. All they knew at that moment was that there was no more war for them and the joy of a new baby was on their horizon. It was on that joyful trip home that Sarah shared the news that there was a baby on the way.

Not only had Sarah kept her secret until after the war was over about the baby, but she never told Zebulun she knew the war was over before he did. Many times on that ride returning to Illinois, her mind was on the stranger. She never told Zebulun about the visitation. She never knew why she couldn't but it was to her too precious a thing to share even with the closest one to her: the one she called husband.

As they journeyed on their way, they encountered what they considered the most fearful thing on that trip. As they were on what was the last part of their journey to the train, there standing in the distance looking at them was a handful of Indians. With the stories they had heard, this caused Sarah's heart to thump in her chest. They were standing in a clump of trees on a small hill near the horizon. The men mounted their horses when they saw the wagon. Zeb reached for the rifle, but carefully kept it out of sight. There were a couple of women with the group of men. One grabbed a young child by the hand. The small boy was transfixed and looking at the contraption being pulled by the horses. She hoisted him up behind one of the men. "Sarah, sit still and just look ahead as if they are not there," Zeb said as he looked straight ahead. He forced himself to keep his own gaze fixed. As they continued on in a normal pace, the men turned their horses with their eyes steadily upon them. One started to move his horse a few steps toward them.

Sarah's heart was racing. "Oh, Zeb, they are going to kill us!" she quietly said. Zebulon said, "Sit still and be quiet. Keep looking ahead." She did as she was told. Her mind was spinning uncontrollably. "Keep your gaze ahead, Sarah," he repeated. She complied but she could hardly breathe. To come through the horrid war unscathed and to die like this, she thought. She wanted to cry when the next thought came, Oh my poor baby. She kept looking straight ahead. Another brave approached them, following quickly to catch up with the first. The first one stopped his horse in front of the wagon. Zeb knew nothing else to do but stop and smile. He felt as if his lips were pasted to his cheeks but he held steady. Both men walked their horses slowly around the wagon, leaning their heads over to see what the wagon held. One pulled the flap on the back of the wagon aside, looking in. As one neared Sarah's side of the wagon seat, he leaned over and grabbed the hem of her colorful, wool dress, lifting it up, revealing her wool leggings and her high top laced shoes. Zeb's hand twitched as he was getting ready to lunge for the rifle. Still he held steady. The man looked curiously at the fabric, rubbing the material between his forefinger and thumb as if the warm material was a novelty to him. Sarah's heart was pounding in her ears. "Dear God," she silently prayed to herself. "Please God" was her unfinished prayer.

Suddenly one man grunted something to the other, and whirling their horses around, they trotted back up to the trees to their waiting party. Sweating now, Zeb cracked the reigns and though everything within him wanted to run like a banshee, as they said in Sarah's old country, he methodically and naturally drove the team off. Something in him wanted to wave a friendly type wave, but something else in him said, "Let sleeping dogs lie." Neither one of them breathed freely until they were over the top of the hill and well out of sight. Sarah looked over her shoulder for a long time, her body was shaking uncontrollably. When they were sure that no marauding war parties were coming after them, they both began to laugh uncontrollably. Zebulun started thanking God in a way that Sarah had never heard. She too joined in the thank you chorus.

Upon seeing that she was still trembling, Zeb put his arm around her. He said, "All is well now. Don't worry." However, she noticed he was not driving the horses at the leisurely pace he had been before the encounter.

Just as they arrived at the town, took care of the horses and wagon at the livery stable, and stepped upon the train platform to board the train, the first few snowflakes started to fall. As the train started slowly to move, Sarah looked out the window, and said a prayer of thanks under her breath. She prayed a prayer of thanks for the safety of the journey that was behind them, and a plea for the journey ahead. God's great hand had been upon them, there was no doubt. This tiny woman knew that if she could, with God's help, face a Civil War, she could face anything. Well, maybe, she thought, anything except Indians!

*Sarah Ingrahm's Army Nurses Pension Certificate
dated 1892*

THE BATTLE CONTINUES

At the station platform Zebulun made sure that everything was on the train that was to accompany them on the last part of the journey home. He double checked with the station agent, and made sure none of their bags or parcels were left on the platform. They found their seats, and Sarah wearily settled back in the wooden seat that they had secured on the overcrowded train.

In this transition time of the war from the battle-grounds and army camps, space was at a premium for soldiers returning home on trains. Men took passage on tops of the overfilled trains. Every boxcar and available inch was allowed for this country's heroes. This was never permitted before but these were disoriented times. Some soldiers had to be driven off the train's cowcatchers.

These were times for weary men to get back to the home place that they had dreamed of for so long on those horrific battlegrounds. *Hail the conquering Hero* was the mood of the day for Union troops and *When Johnny Comes Marching Home Again* was the song of the day. Woe to those of that day that had a Johnny that didn't come home. People waved and joyfully cheered for their war heroes as they passed by.

Some stood and paid homage, but yet cried for the ones they knew were not coming back and the ones they would not see again and yet had no idea where their body lay. Many still held out hope, not knowing for certain whether their loved one would return to them or not. They were waiting and hoping daily from some word of their sons, fathers, or husbands.

As the train so slowly made its way toward their destination, Sarah realized what a toll the long struggle had taken on her. Her body, which was very much feeling the discomfort of the baby within her, was feeling every inch of the hard bench, every lurch of that ancient engine, and the stench of the smoke as it penetrated the passenger car. She did not realize that the young face, that was so youthful when they married at the age of twenty, had matured as much as it had. Her careworn cheeks were tight from the war diet that had been provided as meals. There were light lines on her face as a result of the anxiety of mind she had suffered through what had seemed to her an endless ordeal. The war had taken away the youthful look she had, and she was now a mature woman. She was still a young, attractive woman, with no gray in her dark brown hair, but not the very young girl that had embarked on a very strange honeymoon that would be named by history as the Civil War. Neither she, nor Zebulun, had expected the long, grueling war to last as long as it did.

Soon she would find it was a long, tedious ride to Galesburg, Illinois. Reading the war stories, the effort involved for the troops getting to the regiment they are assigned to, or getting back home is seldom considered. With the baby being born in the year the war was over, the journey must not have been an easy one for Sarah. On the train journey, as she gazed out the window, there was much time for her fluttering mind to wander over the past years of the war. Remembrances we could never imagine played over in her mind. What a dark period, what anxiety of mind she must have suffered, what phases of fortune and misfortune she must have witnessed to be replayed in her memories. How the terrible scenes would have to be shaken from her thoughts purposely. She would turn them to the joy that was before her of the arrival at their home and the adventure of the beginning a new family and all the excitement ahead that was hers.

As the "Iron Horse," as the natives of the land called it, chugged along, she could see no longer trees and hills, but flat land stretching ever onward. This frontier land opened up to the sun. It seemed flatter and flatter the closer they got to home. At times there were cloudless skies, and at times there were dark, threatening, and ominous black clouds billowing against a cool plains sky, which seemed to be the way in the prairie land in the spring. As the chilly winds beat against the little struggling train, Sarah wrapped her heavy woolen shawl tightly around her shoulders, and reached over and gently tucked in the woolen blanket over her sleeping husband. She studied him, as he restfully slept uninterrupted for the first time in a while. As she gazed at his dark hair she noticed there was some gray forming at his temples and some slight wrinkles in his forehead. She wondered what had caused this man to be the man he was. She saw such a strength and honor in him. She tried to put the words together in her mind. He had such goodness of character, it seemed to her. She had seldom seen him angry. As she thought of that, she realized the few times she had seen anything approaching anger, it was on behalf of someone else being taken advantage of.

He had a way of making her feel ashamed of some of her judgment of others, without verbalizing her being wrong, simply by suggesting maybe there was reason for their flaws. As she searched for the words to describe this man that she was so happy to have, two words surfaced in her mind. The words were integrity and honesty. She had such an admiration for the way he carried himself with what seemed to her like honor. He was indeed an honorable man, she thought to herself as she watched him sleep. Of course, she did realize she was prejudiced for she was very much in love with him.

Suddenly, as the train jolted and started to slow down, Zeb awoke and sat up to see what was happening. Both turned their head to see a station platform pulling into view. They were pulling in to one of the little towns along the railway track. The train slowing down noisily, revealed crowds of people standing on the platform. Some of the people were waving banners of a homemade kind, and others were looking expectantly for someone on the train. Suddenly coming to a noisy halt, there were a few soldiers rising to get off the train. Struggling to get down the aisle as fast as they could, they had joy and expectancy on their faces. As Sarah and Zeb watched out the window, they saw the different reactions of those on the platform. Behind those peering into the train expectantly, there were those with their backs to the train, looking at some kind of lists posted near the rail office. There were joyful shouts of others with waves, and hugging of those waiting, as they met their loved ones. There were those with serious looks on their faces who were still looking, expectantly hoping to find the person they were hoping to see.

A railroad employee had gotten a mail bag off the train and took it quickly to what must have been the railroad master. Some of the crowd gathered around him, watching him as he opened the bag. He took out some sheets of paper that had obviously been put on the top of whatever mail had been placed in the bag. Going to a notification board near the door of the railroad office, the man posted a list, as many of the people on the platform crowded around him to see. As he struggled to get out of the way of the crowd trying to see if their loved one was on the death notification, he took the rest of the mail bag into the station. Zeb and Sarah were looking out the windows watching jubilation over reunions and disappointment from those who would be there every day when the train went through, searching for their loved one. Some of those bravely waved their banners to cheer on the train even though it had not brought their loved ones yet.

Just before the train pulled out they heard another sound. These sounds made the congratulatory ones die out. Crying, moaning and sobs came from those who were reading the list that had been posted that day. For some that waited that day, the war's end had come too late. They would not return to the train station in expectation again.

As their train pulled out of the station and on through the little village, Zeb said with tears in his eyes, *"A voice was heard in Ramah, lamentation, weeping, and great mourning. Rachel weeping for her children, refusing to be comforted, because they are no more."*

"What?" asked Sarah.

"It's a verse from St. Matthew," replied Zebulun. "It's about the slaughter of the innocents."

"Oh," said Sarah, although she did not recognize it.

As she turned her face out across the endless plains, she may have seen a scattering of natives. Surely a black, winding train must have crossed their paths before. What a strange appearance to them it must have been at first, after all those centuries of wilderness and the peaceful solitude of only nature, she thought. Not only had it frightened them but their buffalo, as well. It is quite possible Sarah and Zebulun may have seen small herds of these shaggy, lumbering, brown creatures that could have not that long ago in this vast American prairie, made the ground shake when their great herds ran. They were on their way to sad extinction. Even the train they now traveled in brought their demise. Sarah knew nothing of that woeful story.

These natives had seen villages of these strangers springing up one after another. They would see them dot the whole great hunting land of theirs, from the big water to the big water. They would eventually see these strange men's "villages" cover their land.

Now they had knowledge that these strangers had put on strange battle clothes and fought one another. They had learned they carried two flags. They were flags of two warring tribes. They sounded strange horns before they slaughtered each other. Some of the men of their own tribes said they piled up many dead men. Some were just left scattered. Now they heard it had stopped. Two of the greatest war chiefs had met. They had smoked the peace pipe, so it was said.

Sadly, the Indians were caught up in the great epic that would cause this war for those that had come to their country. Many of them were forced to take sides and be part of the war that went on. Their lives would never be the same afterward. Extreme relocation and changes were their lot in this great place that had formerly been their open hunting and grazing land. They themselves had been called either Union or Confederate and an effect of this war of these white men was to change the Indian way of life forever. This was the fate of the Native Americans that were unfortunate enough to be in the pathway of this Great War.

Not knowing this, as Sarah looked out on the sprinkling of Indians, she remarked innocently to her husband how fortunate they had been to not have been involved in the war and that they had not been a part of the conflict between the north and the south. How fortunate they were to have to take no sides in the war, she said.

"That's not so," he said, shaking his head, "I have heard the Indians lost farms, homes, land and all their cattle. They are going to have to begin the task of re-building their lives just as we all are. There was misery and destitution to Indian communities in 1860 in the Indian Territories. Their houses were burned and laid waste just as much as the white war zones suffered. Many of them were compelled to fight in the war or fought for their own reasons."

What Sarah and Zebulun did not know was just as their lives were being affected in the year of 1865, so the tribes that had been delegated to what was called the Indian Territory then, that just as Lee had surrendered to Grant, so they had to surrender. Peace had to be worked out and worked together to work out friendly relations with the United States Government. There was a meeting in the Choctaw nation. The Indians who had joined forces in the war claimed the right to surrender their forces separately.

Principal Chief Pitchlynn surrendered the military forces of the Choctaw Nation on June 19th in 1865. Four days later General Stand Watie surrendered the Cherokee, Creek, Seminole, and Osage troops. On July 14th, the Chickasaw troops were surrendered by Governor Winchester Colbert. On the same day, the Battalion of the Caddoes was disbanded. Their people had a great job of rebuilding their lives. Many, considered refugees, had to remain in camps waiting for all terms to be officially decided. Of course, the word Caddo was but a strange word to Sarah at that time, not knowing how many times she would repeat that word before her life was completed.

New treaties, as a result of the settlement of the war, caused harsh terms to be given to the Indians, and new ways of living at the end of the summer. Part of the treaty was the plan for each Indian nation to give up its lands in western Indian Territory for the settlement of other tribes. The eastern half of the Indian Territory remained the country of the Five Civilized Tribes from that time.

Each of the treaties of 1866 had three provisions which were similar: first, Negro slavery was abolished and the freed slaves were to be given rights of citizens in the Indian governments; second, Right of Ways of construction of railroads were granted; and third, An intertribal council made up of representatives from every tribe and nation should organize as one government within the boundaries of the Indian Territory.*

Of course, Sarah had no idea of all these things. She had no idea how the war that separated America affected the Indian Nations of America that had taken sides in the war. She certainly didn't realize how that would affect her life in the future.

As Sarah passed scattered solitary houses, she saw people that later would be called pioneers. These people were trying to build lives on this lonesome prairie land. They were all new people on this frontier wilderness that was spreading out. Some still spoke a mother tongue from a foreign land. In these days of early pioneering, English was the most important subject in the little schools among the new places that were springing up.

Finally, day after endless day, and mercifully, as her body could seem to protest no more with the pain in her joints, muscles, and the sharp pains from her continually moving child, the train slowed down at their final destination. Now it was just a brief ride from the station. They should be home just before dark.

Joyfully, they stepped down from the wagon that brought them from the station. Sarah couldn't restrain herself from starting to unload the wagon, as Zeb paid the driver, even though her husband objected. They were home at last, to their wonderful little house. Cold, abandoned, and lonely as it was, sheer joy filled Sarah's heart as she entered the place they called theirs. The board floors, not dirt ones, seemed as a palace floor to her. The familiar homemade furnishings seemed so welcoming. The calico curtains on the windows seemed to be banners that would be in the court of royalty. The dust everywhere could soon be done away with, but how awesome the word home. How sweet the words "Sarah and Zeb's home." There had been times she doubted she would ever see it again. It was just as plain as all frontier homes were, but to her eyes it was such a thing of beauty to her that tears filled her eyes.

Zebulun gathered up some of the wood that still rested where they left it and quickly put it in the fireplace. The kindling they had left in the box was still there. Sarah tore some paper off of a package they had carried with them on the train, and used her lit candle to fire it, to put under the kindling. The kindling might be years old, but still it had been dry and it burned.

"That will be one of my first chores in the morning to see about firewood," Zebulon said. "I'll get a small bit to see us through the night," he said as he went out the door. "I hope there is some still in the shed. I wouldn't be surprised if someone had not taken it even though Mr. and Mrs. Reynolds said they would keep an eye on the place." He added, "Their house is so far away from here, it would be hard to watch the property carefully."

Sarah took a rag and dusted off a few things that they would want to use that night, for it was late. She thought to herself that oil for the lamps would be on her list of things to get at the general store in the morning. She arranged the candles as she needed them. The table was the first thing she dusted, because it had been her dream to fix themselves a hot cup of coffee and sit at their own leisure and drink it together. For tonight it would be brewed over the wood in the fireplace and tomorrow they would see to getting the old iron cooking stove filled with wood. Tonight, though, the dream she had pictured in the army camp so many times was to be reality. She pulled the carefully dusted table near the roaring fireplace, and set on the wiped clean, tin coffee cups that had set so long in the cabinet awaiting their return. Just as she picked up the pot to pour the hot coffee into the cups, Zeb came in the door with enough firewood to keep them warm through the night, remarking on his surprise that it was still there.

The fireplace must have looked inviting to him too, for he put the wood down, took off his coat, hanging it on the hook and then walked over to the table. He pulled two of the heavy oak chairs in front of the fire place, and after picking up a cup off the table, sat down putting his hands around the cup of steaming brew. A contented smile was upon his face. Without saying a word, he smiled at Sarah and leaned back in his old familiar chair. Sarah smiled, pulled her shawl around her shoulders and joined her husband. When she sat in the chair he had placed there, he pulled his chair close to hers, and put an arm around her shoulder. They sat there long into the night, neither saying anything, contentedly staring into the fire, each seeing their own visions in the leaping flames.

Then they finally started to talk, sharing heart things that had been too risky to share in a time of wondering if they had any future. Zeb told her of things he planned for their future should they survive the war. Dreams he had for their life together, his exciting dreams and plans unfolded. Her heart sang with the joy of life together in a land of peace. Contentedly, she listened. In the rosy glow of the fireplace, they rested. Even little Clyde Francis seemed to be resting in his own house.

Clyde Francis Ingrahm was born in Galesburg, Illinois, November 6th, 1865. Being a Civil War baby, born the year it ended, the date was easy to recall by all. Since the baby was born alive and survived to an old age, we can assume the birth went well. Sarah was born in the year 1840. The child was born in 1865. Therefore, Sarah was 25 years old when the long restless little Clyde made his appearance. This was an unusually old age for a lady of that time to birth her first child.

For Sarah Elizabeth and her small baby Clyde, historical events were still ahead in the destiny of both. A future still marked with adventure not many women see. As with us all, not knowing her future, Sarah had no idea of what crowning achievements, and what tragic sorrow the future would bring her.

LIFE AFTER THE WAR

Shortly after the birth of little Clyde in 1865, the couple moved to Davenport, Iowa where Zebulun opened a practice in what was the main area of the town. It seemed a practical thing for Sarah to fill the need of his assistant and so she and little Clyde joined Zeb in his office. They had found a house slightly out of town in the country that fit their needs. It was not long before the couple realized that a doctor's office was no place for an exuberant little boy who needed to run and play. Sarah's duties were constantly pulled away from the patient's need and it was obvious that a place with sick people was no place for their little boy. Very disturbing things were there in the way of patients being brought in with terrible wounds, and the sounds of patients in deep pain were distressing to the child. They had discussed Sarah remaining at home and hiring a nurse to assist at the office, but needless to say in an early frontier town a medically skilled person was not to be found. Another factor faced was the money issue being not plentiful for a new doctor in the town. It seemed the problems were getting too big to ignore.

The answer to the problem came in the meeting of new people visiting the office with a minor physical problem. As it turned out, the two visitors to the office were new neighbors who had moved into the community just down the road from the Ingrahm's house. Mrs. Hawthorne accompanied her daughter, Lydia, to see if there could be any relief for the teenage daughter's ear ache. After a short examination, Zebulun administered some very simple things to relieve the pain and made his suggestions of home application to help the ear canal. He gave the patient some Willow Bark tea to lessen the pain and sent home oil with the instruction of how to warm it and apply it.

In the process of taking down the information on the new patient, Sarah took note of the address being near them. "We are neighbors," Sarah warmly told the two, "You moved into the old Hastings's house. You will have to come visit us some time."

While the conversation was going on, little Clyde did something not uncommon for such an outgoing boy by climbing up in Lydia's lap. Sarah apologized to the young woman as she started to remove the boy. Lydia said while smiling down at the curly headed boy, "Think nothing of it. I not only have little brothers and sisters that I have taken care of, but I have been taking care of children since I was thirteen in other households."

"It's wonderful that's your attitude," Sarah said with a smile, "But I'm afraid not everyone will welcome a child in their lap when they are very ill. It has become such a problem that I am considering staying home with him, and the doctor is looking for someone else to help him here at the office. I'm afraid nurses are not too plentiful though," she laughed.

"I hope you don't think I'm being too presumptuous," Mrs. Hawthorne interrupted, "But I would like to make a suggestion. It would seem more practical to have someone to come to your home and care for the boy. That way you could remain at your husband's side as his nurse at the office."

"Yes, it is a good idea and I agree that would be a solution. However, I have never known anyone that would do that," Sarah said as she handed her son a toy to distract him.

"Should you be interested in that idea, I can't recommend my daughter highly enough. That is exactly what she did in the last place we lived. She stayed at the children's home in the daytime and also did household chores. The people she worked for were quite disappointed when we moved away."

"Thank you for the idea," Sarah said, "But we've never thought about leaving Clyde. I'm quite sure that Zebulun would not want to leave his son with someone." Then she laughed, "I would almost be afraid to suggest it to him." She added quickly, "I'm quite sure Lydia would be quite trustworthy though."

After some neighborly conversation and the usual country invitation to come and visit, the two arose to leave. As they were going out the door, Sarah asked a question, as an afterthought. "Lydia, what's your age?"

"I'm seventeen," the seemingly shy girl replied. As she lifted her head up to Sarah and looked her squarely in the eyes for the first time, not being distracted by the child, she noticed how beautiful her eyes were. They almost looked violet they were so blue.

Sarah suddenly said, "Mrs. Hawthorne, I would have to speak to Dr. Ingrahm first, but we might be able to use Lydia for the housework you mentioned. I certainly could use some help in that area. The fact that we are neighbors, makes it very tempting to think about hiring Lydia for that. As I say though, I will have to talk to Zebulun if Lydia is interested in that part of it."

"We'd be quite appreciative," Mrs. Hawthorne said as they stepped out of the door. "It would be mighty handy living so close, because Lydia could walk and getting there wouldn't be a problem. I know she would be interested in the housecleaning alone."

As Sarah and Zeb were riding home in the buggy that evening, Sarah brought up the subject of their new neighbors and where they lived. She pointed to the house as they went by it. She mentioned that the girl he had cared for was looking for household work.

He was quiet a minute, and Sarah quietly waited for him to digest what she had said and reply. She was not surprised when he said he thought it would be a good idea if the girl worked out, for he knew there was a lot to be done after being at the office with him during the day. He suggested she talk to the Hawthorne's about it.

She said she would at the first chance she got. In the back of her mind she thought it might be a good way to see if she was to be trusted with tending Clyde. She could watch their relationship as she was working in their home and judge Lydia's maturity. Actually, she would prefer that they find someone to assist Zeb at the office and she be able to be home with Clyde. Either way, heaven knew the household help was definitely needed. She did not mention anything about the offer of child-care. She was quite sure he would not be open to that.

The offer was made shortly thereafter and in a short time Lydia was doing a wonderful job at the house and they wondered how they had ever gotten along without her. They were both amazed at how the relationship between their little boy and this girl developed. If Sarah had not been so grateful for the extra help, and what a difference it made for her, she would have been jealous of Clyde's accepting her almost as a mother figure. Sarah's life became much easier and it was almost as if little Clyde had a playmate with the ability to apply the maturity needed to their relationship. Soon Zeb himself suggested that she also stay at the house and take care of Clyde which would allow Sarah to remain at the office as his nurse.

As they learned to accept this girl as a part of the household, she was a help on those days that Clyde might be ill and Sarah herself could stay home with him. On those days as Sarah could stay home and nurse her little boy, Lydia proved capable of going to the office and meeting patients, doing paperwork and giving slight assistance to patients in minor ways. Of course, it was only a stop next door on the way for Zeb to pick her up and then drop her off after work. It worked out as a wonderful arrangement all the way around.

All was not well, with the doctor's practice though. Business was not a consistent thing. Sometimes it seemed there was no need for him even to be at the office. People knew he was on call at times and they would know a quick trip out to his house was sometimes as quick as a trip to the office. It was not a large community and he did have other medical competition that had been in town a long time.

He did manage to make money in his hobby of wood-working. He built furniture for those that understood that his practice would come first. He and Sarah talked often of other ways to possibly start a new life. He had admitted to her that the war's atrocities had affected his enthusiasm for the physician's life that he had earlier in his life. She fully understood.

He had a strange employment offer that was repugnant to Sarah. A friend had told him of the money that was paid to Wells Fargo Overland Trail drivers. Work of this kind was not easy to obtain because of the security risks of transporting large amounts of gold and money and only the very trusted were hired. Zebulun's war history and his reputation as a physician had brought the offer to him through this friend connected with Wells Fargo. He was intrigued with the large salary offered. He mentioned it to Sarah and she quickly rejected it. This was not the plan she had for her husband nor for herself. She could not imagine him in that kind of a job to begin with. She was not open to the traveling it would involve for him and being left alone certainly did not appeal to her. She most certainly did not like the idea of the risk of robbers, Indians, and all the tales she had heard. She was adamant in her "no" when he brought it up.

The family had a problem around this time as Lydia told them she was moving away. It was the greatest loss of all for little Clyde. Lydia had been such a help to Sarah and Zebulun that it would really affect the failing business at this time. They knew Clyde could not be kept at the office and it added to their confusion of what the future held. Of course, at this announcement of her leaving, they sadly wished her well as she was going to Georgia with family.

Lydia walked over to their house early the morning of the departure to tell them all goodbye. Clyde did not understand the finality of it, but Sarah knew that with the passing of the days the reality that she was gone would be revealed to the small boy. Lydia tearfully told the little fellow she would probably not see him again, and as she did tears filled her eyes. As Sarah watched the scene, she was surprised to see tears in Zeb's eyes. Sarah emotionally wished the young woman goodbye with a long hug. Walking to Zebulun, Lydia shook his hand saying, "Goodbye, Doctor Ingrahm." He wished her luck and then said, "Let me take you to your house in the buggy and tell your mother goodbye." She accepted.

Later when Zebulun returned, the evening took on a more somber tone as they talked about how Lydia being gone complicated the trouble with the office. Again Zebulun brought up the offer he had been made from Wells Fargo. Of course, the offer had been made for a full time driver, but the amount he would make on this first trip would be enough to set them up in a business he had long desired which was a furniture building business he told her. He said that he could quit after that one time of separation.

He told her of how he hated the role of physician and how it brought back terrible memories of war injuries, and lives he could have saved possibly if he had made other decisions. Some of those lives were those of people he had known in his own town. He said he saw their pleading, pained eyes haunting him as he helped new patients here and now. He told her his nights were tormented. He wanted out of this physician's nightmare he lived. "Just the one stage run," he said, would be enough for them to start a new life, and then he would quit. They could start over. He reminded her of the beautiful woodworking he did and how people loved what he did. He stated he was at peace when he worked with the wood. Even now he was being asked to make furniture and he had to refuse because of spending time in an occupation he now hated as he completed his plea.

After much discussion, and feeling sadness over the agony he had been suffering in his role as a physician, and feeling somewhat guilty she had not recognized these inner feelings, Sarah agreed. She wanted his promise though, that this one long trip would be the only one he would make. He assured her it would be so. He hugged her gently, and so they began to make their plans of accepting this offer of a new job. He would follow through tomorrow to see if the job was still available. Sarah, kissed him, shaking her head in agreement, but her heart was crying no to this separation.

That night as they lay in bed and as Zeb peacefully slept, Sarah lay awake through the night thinking of this new unexpected plan that lay upon her horizon. She thought of the little boy, sleeping in the next room, and how he would miss his Daddy he so adored for those weeks he would be gone. Finally, right before daylight she drifted off to sleep. Zebulun arose early and went into town to accept the offer he had been made for he knew there had not been much time to accept it. He wasn't sure if it was still available. Telegraphs were sent and he found out he was not too late and joyfully he brought the news home to Sarah. She smiled, half-heartedly.

She reacted with surprise when he told her he had already put a "Closed Permanently" sign on the office door. "So soon!" She exclaimed. "How can you do that without notice to our patients?" She looked at him with surprise waiting for his answer. This quick move, without concern for their patients was not like the Zebulun she knew.

Plans had to be put in motion that day as Zebulun was now an employee of Wells Fargo and arrangements were already started by the company for his "first" transport trip to be made, he said. He further explained that the time and place of his arrival at the stage company would be taken care of by someone who would pick him up here in town and take him there for his first day's start, but starting immediately here in town his training would begin on this new occupation. Horses, buggies, and the covered wagon was the nearest thing he had ever managed but he had been assured there was little difference in learning about a stage. His friend that had managed to get him this job would spend the next few days in his training. Maps of the route, care of the horses, stations for stops were to be learned with no time to spare. All this Zebulun explained to the astonished Sarah who was not prepared for the quickness of it all. Trying to excite her on the great opportunity to fall into this job on such short notice was to no avail.

"You're leaving after two days!" she exclaimed in a high pitched voice, "And you'll be busy training those few days?" Her eyes filled with tears at the shock of it all.

Zebulun, on seeing her pain stepped forward and put his arms around her. "I'm sorry, Darlin'," he softly said, "I know this is all such a shock to you." A look of remorse came over his face. He had no other words. She seemed so tiny and helpless to him at that moment. After a moment of quiet he said, "I did ask Dr. Sullivan if I could direct my patients to him. He seemed very grateful."

At that moment, his little child ran into the room and grabbed him around the legs. "Hi Daddy," he said. All outward signs of distress changed and were directed toward the little playful boy. Zebulun carried his small boy all evening long.

The remaining time that they had together, they spent mostly in each other's arms. It was bittersweet to Sarah. She tried to reason with herself. It wouldn't be that long actually. Time would pass soon, she reassured herself. It's not like he's going to be gone forever. She, having spent a sleepless night, finally went to sleep with these thoughts in her mind right before the morning he was to leave and so she overslept.

THE DEPARTURE

The morning he was to leave, Zebulun awoke early with a strange feeling. He felt that everything was magnified and as if everything was so beautiful. He felt as if he was seeing what a wonderful life his had been and everything was pulling at him not to go.

The early morning sunlight was coming through the bedroom window. As he turned in bed, his eyes fell on Sarah softly breathing beside him. How extra sweet she seemed to him. How lovely he thought, with her soft brown hair falling over her face as she lay on her side with one arm under her pillow. How lovely everything seemed with the whiteness of her pillow and the sheet and her cotton gown.

He tried to softly get up, so as not to disturb her. He went to the wardrobe and pulled out the clothes and his bag and carried them with him out the door of the bedroom. As he walked into the living room, he draped the clothes over one of the chairs in front of the stone fireplace. He stoked the low flames and threw a couple of logs on the dying fire. Walking to the kitchen, he got the coffee pot and taking the dipper from the pail he poured water from the pail into it. Adding coffee from the jar that Sarah stored it in, he took the pot and put it over the fire. Going back to the chair that was his, he put his clothes on quickly because there was a nip in the air. As he waited for the coffee to finish he went to the window. Looking out at the bright sunny day, he realized how beautiful the Cedars around the house were. The bright red of the cardinals seemed especially red against their vibrant green. Again, it seemed it was magnified how he was seeing things in an appreciation of how beautiful and bright all things were. It was an extraordinary feeling of how good all was around him even though it was the same scenery they had seen since they had made their home in these last few years. He realized how blessed a man he had been.

As his mind went to the goodness around him, he naturally thought of his little son so he walked over to the bedroom door where the small boy slept. He tried to walk quietly on the wood plank floors into the room, and went to his crib that he had so excitedly built for him before he was born. I should have already built him a "big boy bed" because he's outgrowing this pine baby bed. He'll probably sleep with Sarah when I'm gone, he thought.

Quietly, without touching the bed for fear of waking the toddler, he stood transfixed, looking down at the little wonder that looked so much like him. With such a cute little baby face and body, the hair the color of his mother's softly curled around his chubby face, he thought how beautiful. He quietly stood, just admiring his child.

Suddenly, there was the smell of coffee and sizzling sounds and he knew the pot was boiling over into the fire and it required his quick attention. Half running he went through the door and to the fireplace where he knew he had created a minor mess and ruined his morning coffee with his daydreaming. Rescuing the pot with the poker he took it off the fire and set it aside.

Going into their bedroom to tell Sarah he was leaving now, he looked at the bed he had made for them before they were married. It was a thing of beauty although it was a simple design that he had lovingly painted. Again, as he looked at his wife he thought how beautiful and precious she is. He decided against waking her, which had been his intention, thinking "It will be easier to go with her asleep this way. I couldn't stand to see her cry and I know she will."

He went hurriedly through the living room and took his woolen plaid coat off the hook beside the door and put it on. He picked up his fur lined cap and his medicine bag that he always kept by the door. Then he realized he wouldn't need it. Putting it down, he picked up the small bag he had packed the night before and walked out the door.

Leaving the house, he went to the barn where the horses were. Actually, as he looked around he realized this had become more his work shop than barn when he saw all his tools. As a matter of fact, it smelled more like sawdust, than it did hay and feed.

This had become a place of contentment to him. He loved to work with his hands. He had even built a small wooden bench for Sarah to come and be with him when she could. Little Clyde would play there pretending he was working like his daddy. Sarah would be mending or sewing if he left the door open to let the light in so she could see well. If it was cold, they lit the lanterns and used the little iron stove.

That same feeling came over him as he stood looking around and he let sweet memories overwhelm him. He looked at the old sawhorse and the workbench. He saw the hammer, the saw, the chisel, all in his little carpentry area neatly hung or stored. Doctors had to have a certain order because fumbling around in his business could cause a mistake and be a disaster.

People on seeing his work commented on how strange that the soft hands of a surgeon would work with these rough objects. On that workbench he had just completed something special for Sarah that he knew she would find when he was gone. The shavings had been neatly put in the old metal can he used for trash.

He went to the stalls and decided he would take old Blackie and the buggy, but leave Maggie. He'd find someone to bring it back to Sarah from town. He realized for some reason he was spending his morning away daydreaming and he wanted to leave before Sarah awoke.

Giving Blackie a loving slap on his rump, he led him out of the stall outside to the buggy that was parked under the lean-to. Getting the buggy hitched up to his horse, he got in the surrey. He slapped the reigns for Blackie to go. They quickly trotted through the yard and under the home made sign on the gate that said "The Ingrahms" and out onto the road.

Sarah, just sitting up on the side of the bed, wondered why Zeb hadn't awakened her when he got up. She was giving a big stretch, and her mind was already on fixing the sausage and eggs for a special "goodbye" breakfast. As she stretched her arms, she knocked his pillow over and she saw the goodbye note under it that was signed "With All My Love, Zeb."

THE WATCHER

The slightly heavy-set man got off the horse and tied it to the hitching post. He walked across the porch and walked into the Wells Fargo office. He took off his hat and nodded hello at the four men sitting in the office. The agent sitting at the desk nodded back and said, "Have a seat," pointing to an empty chair. "Gentlemen, I think you all know Roy here, except you Glen." The men nodded at each other in recognition.

"Since Glen's new here let me fill him in on what this is all about. That way everyone will know what's being talked about. I won't take long to tell the back-up story, fellows." The men nodded in agreement.

"A while back we had a new Wells Fargo driver disappear on his first trip. We found the stage abandoned. We found no driver, no horses, and most importantly to Wells Fargo, no cash box. Believe me it was a big shipment. The driver disappeared and we have no idea what happened or where he went.

"Roy, here is a special detective that's been assigned to look into the whole matter. You've probably seen the posters out on this guy who took off with the cash. That is if someone didn't take off with him and the money and hide his body somewhere. The guy we're looking for is Zebulun Wheeler Ingrahm." At that, Glen acknowledged he had seen the poster.

"Of course the first thing we did," the agent continued, "Was to send some boys to this guy's house outside of Davenport, hoping if it was stolen by the driver maybe he wasn't too bright and he had high-tailed it home. They made entry into the house wanting to surprise them quickly but all that was in the house or on the property was his wife and a little kid. They searched the whole grounds and he wasn't there."

"Well, the next thing done was the usual thing which was to question the wife to see where he was. She really got upset and acted like she didn't know a thing about him being missing. She acted like she had thought he was still taking the stage to its destination. They reported she was a pretty good actress, if she didn't know where he was, and was acting like she was really upset about the whole thing. Of course, you know how they try to break someone down when they think they are in on the crime, and by the time they got through with her interrogation they were pretty sure she didn't know anything about it. If not, she sure was pretending to be hysterical like no one they'd ever seen. Just so you will know they weren't entirely heartless, one of the fellows took the little shaver out to look at his "pretty pony" and for a little ride.

"That's when we called Roy here in to stake out the place to watch to see if he came back to his house. So he's here to tell us what he found. Likely, since he ain't got nobody with him he didn't find much." All eyes shifted to Roy.

"Well," said the large man, "I ain't got the news you want. Sure wish I did. If that feller was robbed, kidnapped, or his body left somewhere that ain't been discovered yet that's one thing. However, if that mangy coyote really made off with that cash and disappeared he deserves to be caught and hung and I'd sure like to be the one that did it. If he had showed up I can't guarantee I would have brought him in alive after all I seen. That dirty, stinking...."

"Then if he didn't show, how do you know so much about him? You didn't talk to the wife did you? You were supposed to remain hid and see if he came back and then bring him in. What was it you saw?" asked the agent.

"I hid alright," Roy said, "I found a good place to hide. Right before you get to the house where he lives, there was a deserted house. Ingrahm had to go right by it since its right on the same road and there's no other way to get to his house. Its right next door you might say but not quite in shoutin' distance, right up a hill. There was a barn in the back where I hid my horse, and I just stayed in that house day and night watching. I can assure you that man didn't come back. One other thing I can assure you of. That lady didn't know he was leaving. I don't think she has any idea where he is." He paused, and leaned back in his chair as if he was through.

The Wells Fargo man leaned forward on his desk. "Why do you say that? What do you know that would make you think that, if you didn't talk to her?"

"I think that because of the way she screams," Roy said. "It's the screaming that makes me think she don't know where he is. She wouldn't be carrying on so if she was looking for him to come back. She's out of her mind with grief."

The Wells Fargo Man wrinkled his forehead when he said, "Are you telling me she screamed so loud you could hear her at the next farmhouse? She sure must have a set of lungs."

"No," said Roy, "That ain't it. I guess she didn't want to scare or disturb the little guy, but in the night time, late enough he should have been asleep, she would come over to the hill where the house I was holed up in was. She didn't want him to hear her grief, I guess. There I sat, crouched down in that house, night after night, having to listen to the most God-awful pitiful sounds from a human I ever heard. Out in that wilderness, in the middle of the night she would walk that hill and wail. It was downright scary! Weeping and wailing she was just callin' his name over and over. 'Zeb' she wailed. 'Zebulun' she shouted into that howlin' wind. 'Zeb' she cried in the pitch black darkness when it was so black you couldn't see your hand in front of your face. When the moon was full I could see her pacing back and forth like a little thing possessed. Then when you think she can't call his name anymore, she falls on the prairie grass and cries with her whole body shaking until a man has to look away. I had to crawl to the back end of the house where I couldn't see anymore. It's something no man wants to see no matter how strong he is. That tiny little thing's broken hearted crying cuts right into your being. No man has a right to spy on someone's misery. I had to hear it every night 'cause she didn't want her baby boy to hear it."

He paused, just sitting there for a few minutes shocked at himself at what he had heard coming out of his own mouth. Then in a low voice that didn't sound like the same voice he had been speaking in moments before he said, "That little lady don't need hounding! She needs help!"

He continued on, "She don't have no idea what's happened to that man, but she sure loves him. I don't think he's coming back. Whether or not, I ain't never been on a case that upset me like this one, and I came to tell you I want off this job. I'm doing something I ain't never done before, but I'm quitting. I guess you could say a woman that don't seem five feet tall done me in."

Again he raised his voice as he said, "I don't know where that sorry skunk is, but if he ain't dead, I'd like to be the one to kill him. Real slow like, just like he's doing to her."

Men never want to show emotion in front of each other, but they all sat silently for quite a few minutes. None wanted to say a word after the scene the detective had painted. They just looked down at the plank floor. The Wells Fargo officer looked at his desk with his lips pursed.

Finally he said, "The search won't be over for the Ingrahm guy until we find him dead or alive. Not the gold either." Then he looked up at Roy and said, "Leave the woman alone."

The detective put his hat on, stood, and started for the door. He stopped, turned, and said over his shoulder, "Send the money you owe me to that woman, anonymously." As he reached the door he said without looking at the men, "I don't know how you guys feel about God, but if you ever prayed a prayer before, pray for that woman and her little boy."

ALONE

Sarah sat alone looking into the fire. The silence around her was deafening. She got up from her rocker and threw two more logs on the fire. Pulling the heavy shawl closer around her shoulders, she sat back down in the old familiar chair. She remembered when Zebulun was weaving the bottom of straw in that chair. He was so proud of the work he had done to surprise her. She had wondered why he had spent so much time outside of the house. He had done it so it would be ready when the baby arrived so she could rock it. She smiled when she thought of how he took his fair share of rocking that wee one. Everything in this house shouted Zebulun. How she missed him. The whole house reminded her of Zebulun.

Now as she sat in the rocker alone, the silence seemed to produce a strange ringing in her ears. How desolate this house had been since he had been gone. It was frightening to be a woman alone in a house out in the middle of nowhere in the nighttime. She had never noticed all the wild animal sounds in the prairie before Zeb was gone or the many sounds of the house popping and creaking.

The child always went to sleep early, and so the nights seemed so lonely and quiet. As she rocked in her chair, she started to rock quickly, because this made a creaking sound and the sound drowned out the silence. She rocked just to have the deadly quiet go its cruel way.

How bleak this house that had been so cheerful when they first moved here. She wasn't going to allow her mind to go back to those days that used to be, for it always brought her to tears. She forced her mind to go on somewhere else, but only for a moment, and then her mind moved back to the same old thoughts that haunted her.

It was quieter than ever now that the house was practically empty. She had gotten rid of much of the houses contents as she was preparing to move away. Her mother, brothers, and sisters were on their way, even now, to take her and little Clyde with them to the new place they were homesteading in Nebraska. She had given or sold nearly all her belongings. How hard that had been for so many of the items were the work of Zeb's hands. What labors of love and beauty those things were. Yet, on this journey she was to take, she could not transport his beautiful handiwork in a covered wagon. It was some small comfort that she had been able to sell the house and most of its handmade furnishings to some-one who knew and admired Zeb and would care for them.

In the silent, empty house the rocker squeaked, as she thought about her family. How she loved her Irish mother. She longed to see her brothers and sisters. Her big family would surely be a comfort. It would be good not to be alone. They had telegrammed when they ex-pected to be here if all went well for them. Of course, one never knew.

As she sat in the infernal silence rocking, as usual, her mind went to her Zebulun. Her mind repeated that name that had become so dear to her. Strange, she thought, how time and circumstance change the mind on a subject. She remembered back to the day that she had first been introduced to him. She remembered thinking what a strange name the very name Zebulun was. As a matter of fact, she thought it downright ugly. Especially for a man she had immediately thought handsome. Now, her mind whispered that beautiful name over and over, bringing such pain to her, no matter how she would pur-posely try and think of something else.

As the day for their marriage had been approaching, while sitting under a tree in their little community square she remembered inquiring about his name. She had learned so much about his character and was not surprised to learn it was a Biblical name. He had spoken of his British mother with respect and he told Sarah she had been responsible for his name.

His mother, herself had a Biblical name. Her name was Leah, who was one of the Matriarchs of the Twelve Tribes of Israel and wife of the founder of that nation. Zebulun was a son of the great Patriarch Jacob who had his name changed by God to Israel. Zebulun was the 6th son of the Biblical Leah and also her last.

As the story goes, as it was told to Zeb by his British mother of why she gave him this Biblical name, it was a difficult pregnancy and when the boy child was born, the doctor told her it would be her last. Long story, short, since he was a sixth son that would be her last child and the Semitic name meant Dwelling of Honor, Zebulun was the name decided on. Sarah decided early on to call him Zeb.

Sarah, not knowing much about the Bible, was not much impressed with the whole story on that day. She had only heard heavy Bible passages read in church as a child. It was at that time an interesting story that had something to do with someone she was very enamored with.

As she sat in his chair and tried to rock the quiet away, she thought on the meaning of his name. This was something she found herself doing often in her day. Feeling she was driving herself mad, she stirred herself from her thoughts. She had learned when these tormenting thoughts came to get busy or change what she was doing.

She got up, opened the door where Clyde was, and saw the small boy sleeping quietly under all the quilts she had piled on him to ward off the chill of the northern bitter winter. She decided to join him, hoping she could go to sleep quickly and all the nighttime quiet would go away. She went back to the mantle and got the lamp and carried it with her to the bedroom.

Getting ready for bed quickly as the room was so cold; she hurriedly crawled under the heavy, layered quilts with her softly breathing boy. She put out the lamp on the table beside the bed and the room became dark. Oh so dark! As usual, it was a long time before she could go to sleep, for the loud quiet kept her awake.

THE REUNION

"A Single twig breaks, but the bundle of twigs is strong." - Tecumseh

What a joyful reunion it was when the family arrived at Sarah's little house in their packed wagons. There were tears and laughter at the arrival. Sarah cried out of relief and joy at the sight of her close knit family. Michael Jr. picked up little Sarah and twirled her around in his usual jovial manner. Jerome and Frank waited their turns to hug her with huge smiles on their faces. Their wives, Emily and Ann remained to the side while the greetings were individually given. Her sisters had to wait a long while for their greeting as Sarah, with tears flowing, embraced her mother Catharine. Catharine too, had known the loss of a husband tragically, and did not loosen herself from the embrace of her daughter until Sarah was ready to let go.

Waiting patiently, Ann, Mary, and Jane, while Jane's husband Sam stayed in the background, all ran and hugged her together, while the four did girlish, dancing circles. The greetings rang with laughter and awe filled remarks filled the air at how each person had changed. The family closeness had been formed out of necessity when their father Michael Sr. had been killed in the tragic wagon accident. With their mother, Catharine, being left alone, it fell on the shoulders of the boys, Michael Jr., Jerome, and Frank to become the men of the family. They had become very protective of their sisters, Anne, Jane, and Sarah. They had been in Knox County, Illinois and there it was that Sarah had spent her life from the time she was fifteen. When she moved to Davenport with Zebulun, it was the first time she had been separated from them.

Sarah's son, at first tried to hide behind Sarah's skirt, but in all the chaos of the greetings he was forgotten and he climbed back upon the porch in shyness and fear. He had never seen anyone pick up his mother before, nor had he seen such show of emotion. Laughter and crying at the same time were puzzling to him. As Mary introduced her husband, Oliver Anderson, to Sarah, Clyde was carefully watching with interest their little son, Victor. The boys had been born the same year.

Soon, the family all raced to her child to see this boy that they had not yet met. They did not know, but his emotions were going wild in the commotion of all these strange people. Sarah, reading her son's body language, went to him and picked him up. In turn, her sister Mary tried to introduce her smallest son Victor to his cousin, but the boy remained shy. Sarah began trying to explain that these were her brothers and sisters and made a special effort to explain that the older woman standing there was her mother; his Grandmother Catharine. The young boy didn't seem impressed at that fact and turned his head.

He was also overwhelmed with all the menagerie of animals and the covered wagons, plus other types of wagons that were now in his yard. This large extended family made up its own mini-wagon train. Oxen pulled the covered wagons, horses pulled the canvas covered buckboard wagons, and there were also assorted horses belonging to the brothers that were being used as pack horses and for riding on the journey they had made. As he looked at the small zoo he saw a crate of speckled chickens in one of the wagons. There was a lifetime of accumulation in animals and yet there had been so much of what they had in personal livestock and things that they had left home with close friends. They had to suffer through the same wrenching decisions that Sarah had in what to leave.

After a short time of refreshing themselves and re-filling their water barrels at Sarah's well, many hands helped load her belongings. Then the signal was given to go. They wanted to make a quick departure in order to take advantage of the daylight.

Sarah made one more trip through the house and barn to make sure she had secured everything for the new family. The people that had purchased her house would arrive soon and arrangements had been made as to where she would hide the keys. When she disappeared into the barn to hide the key, the family waited some time for her to come out.

Finally, getting impatient to leave, Michael went in to check on Sarah. He found her sitting on the bare barn floor with her face buried in her hands, sobbing. A small yellow stool she had found hidden behind a small haystack was sitting in front of her. Beside her was a crumpled note. He picked up the paper to see what it said. It read:

> *"Dear Sarah, May you always think of my love for you as you rest your little feet on this little token of my love. Now you can throw away that wooden box you use in the buggy to reach the floor.*
> *Love, Your Zebulun"*

Michael gently lifted her to her feet, and gave her his handkerchief. He led her out of the barn, as she held the beautiful flower decorated stool to her breast. Michael took the stool from her and helped her into a waiting wagon seat next to Frank. He put the little stool at her feet. Catharine, on seeing the emotional state that Sarah was in, took the surrey seat with Blackie that had been awaiting Sarah to drive. Little Clyde watched this all from the back of the familiar Maggie, where his new friend Uncle Jerome sat behind him.

Sarah began the journey from her prairie home, looking back as they started the trip up the road and bidding it farewell in her heart. Yes, it had been a lonesome place the last years for a woman alone, but the memories of her life there with Zeb were sweet. She savored them all, while looking back as the wagon moved forward and she saw the little house slowly fade into the distance and disappear over the horizon. When her visual past life, so to speak, disappeared from her view, she turned her face forward and stoically faced, at least mentally for the moment, her future as this whole little family moved on to a new life.

Clyde soon got over his shyness of these big men, when they allowed him to ride horses with them and played with him and little Victor. The other children in this group of Stanton's would be familiar playmates before they reached their Nebraska destination. These attentive strangers were providing him with the adventure of his life and they were forming bonds that would last a life time for this little boy. The men especially would be a rough and rugged plainsmen influence that a little boy being raised by a woman would need.

What had caused this move and the leaving behind of a lifetime's worth of accumulation for the Stanton family? Land was being given away to fill up frontier spaces by a law called the Homestead Act of 1862. It was a plan by the Government to get Americans to populate this land. In other words, free land was to be given away to fill up the empty spaces and stretches of land. This caused this family to venture out into the new land they had heard about. After the passage of the Homestead Act about half a million families took advantage of it and went out into the unknown for free land. For some it was the only chance for land of their own that they would ever have. It changed this land from an open, unsettled prairie to what would be a land of farms and villages.

The Stanton Family starting creaking across the plains on a tiresome journey in their covered wagons for this reason. The wagons were pulled by oxen to be able to plow when they got to their piece of earth. The cost would be only a very low registration cost. Their destination was Beatrice Nebraska to register. The land was open for all those taking the risk of starting over, so they had been told. The Stanton's were taking that risk.

While all this "settling of a new land" was happening and the wagons moved forward, someone was watching. An ancient people would stand on the horizon with their families and children watching the invasion of the land that had been their forefathers. It had been theirs freely with no boundaries or registration fees.

The year was 1870 that Sarah would move to a town called Tecumseh, Nebraska and the rest of her family would homestead south of there. The extended family would remain in small communities scattered in that area in the years to come. Names of Elk Creek and Mayberry are in early records. Family graves are scattered all over from Tecumseh to Lincoln.

As can be seen, the names of many of the early towns were named for heroes of their time. Lincoln, Nebraska being one well-known one, named for the great Civil War president known as "The Great Emancipator." All around Sarah Stanton Ingrahm the towns of the names of Indians would exist her whole life. Why? Because this was a nation of First Natives or Indians as some confused explorers would name this country's people. This descendent of Sarah, who writes this history, chooses to place in this chronicle of her people, the settlers, wise sayings of these people that have and still inhabit this land. Being Oklahoma raised, and having gone to school with these Native Americans, I choose to do this out of my respect of the first people of this land.

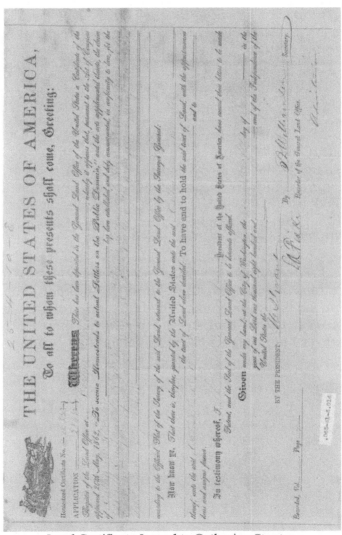

*Land Certificate Issued to Catharine Stanton
dated 1883, signed by President US Grant*

TECUMSEH

"No tribe has a right to sell land, even to each other;
much less strangers.....sell a country? Why not sell the
air, the great sea, as well as the earth? Didn't the Great
Spirit make them all for the use of his children?"
Tecumseh

Ironically, the town of Tecumseh rests within the county of Johnson, named after the army man that claimed to have killed Tecumseh in his last great battle. Richard Johnson was one of the men rumored to have killed Tecumseh in the Battle of Thames against Great Britain that was fought in Chatham, Ontario in Canada. With Tecumseh's death came the destruction of the Native Coalition which he led.

Just as much as a contradiction as the town of Tecumseh resting in the county of the man who killed him, so is the contradiction of my ancestors being one of those "settlers" that Tecumseh would have forbidden, and yet I must agree the Great Chief had a point.

A DAY IN THE LIFE OF A HOSTELRY

In the year of 1875, when Clyde was ten, Sarah bought a hotel that was located in the middle of downtown Tecumseh. This was quite an adventuresome thing to do by a lone woman in that day and age. Of course, judging from her past engaging in a war, it seemed Sarah seemed to like adventure. At first it was a different life for the boy, but being young he learned to adjust to guests coming in and he met some very interesting people. He would learn to move in and out among the strangers and some that became regulars; the ones that became boarders, would become special in his eyes. Some guests would take a liking to a child in the house. They would tease him and bring him gifts when they returned to Sarah's establishment. The boy was an outgoing child, and so he learned to be a personable "people person" which added to his role in his mother's business as a young man. The hostelry involved extreme amounts of work to manage and so it was that Sarah's son learned early what a day's work meant. Extra hands were required, including his.

Sarah had to hire help to do all that a boarding house required. From the start, she decided she would have a high caliber of commitment to her guests. It paid off. The first place she bought was a smaller business. The second one was a bigger scale. A guest would be welcomed in the moment she heard steps on the wooden boardwalk outside the hotel. The visitor would be taken through the parlor into the kitchen the minute he or she arrived. Then after being seated at the big oak table, the person would hear the clatter of cups and be given a steaming cup of coffee or tea accompanied by bowls of fresh cream and sugar. Next would be a large slice of pie or cake. This was a standard welcome. Visitors from the community were given above average service and the hostelry guests even more.

Her pantry was checked at all times to see that the finest of fare was available. List in hand, Clyde would be sent skipping down the street to the mercantile, where he was soon considered a standard daily fixture. It was a rare day when the boy didn't make an appearance.

"What's on your mama's menu today?" would be the daily inquiry of the store owner, or whatever customers were there doing their shopping. The smells of the flavorful food was already drifting down the street of the little city. Of course, when larger amounts were needed, Sarah would take care of it, by driving the horse and buggy for a large sack of flour, sugar, or a large bill of items when needed. Although it seemed a job to hitch up the horse for such a short journey down that main street for Sarah, it would be one thing that the horse loving boy would always volunteer for. As he grew, all the shopping would be part of his duties in maintaining the hotel. The grocer became used to the boy and his list. Down the street he came with the empty flour sack his mother had sent to bring groceries back in. Back he would come with the bag filled and a peppermint in his mouth, thanks to a generous grocer, who sometimes pried the unsuspecting boy for any gossip he could get about town-life that was talked about in the hotel. Clyde lived for the day he could drive the wagon to the store. Clyde was a fixture of the main street of Tecumseh.

They saw him grow from a small boy, to a teenager, to a young man. Finally, the day would come when Clyde would ride down the street with a pretty girl in the wagon or when he was lucky, in his mother's surrey. As it is in the passage of time, they did not even notice the growth, until the young lady appeared and then as humans do in their unobservant lives they said, "When did that happen?"

All day, wonderful smells wafted down the street from from the warm kitchen as there would always be something on the stove for breakfast, lunch, and supper meals. Continual preparation went on, keeping Sarah and her staff busy with peeling, chopping, slicing, frying and boiling. The smells drifting out into the main street were her biggest advertisement. The family hardly noticed the odor of the food. Sarah knew that the pungent smell of frying onions was her biggest friend.

The early morning started with rolling up her sleeves and mixing and kneading dough in the huge wooden bread bowls. Yeast bread and soda biscuits had to start the day. She would quickly shape the dough in a pan and set it aside to rise. The smell of the baking bread throughout the day conjured up thoughts of the thick rich butter that would go with the hot rolls or thick sliced bread. Honey and fresh fruit jelly always accompanied the warm bread on the table.

As the day progressed, her hair, which started the day in its neat bun, would fall in wisps around her face and her cheeks would be red from the heat of the kitchen. As her clientele grew, she added more help. There were pies to prepare and large fruit cobblers would be in the oven, according to what berries and fruits were in season. The huge pans she used had been acquired from the former owner. Sarah's kitchen was known for its chicken and dumplings and the noodles were said to be the best of any kitchen in town. Sarah never gave out the secrets to her food. You might as well not ask. She would smile and change the subject. Hot, bubbling tasty stews of beef, carrots and onions were her Nebraska winter favorites with the guests and home town clients as well. There is still in existence today in pristine shape, cards that were sold to the steady people that dined in her restaurant in the early 1900's. To those that purchased those cards, twenty one days would be punched.

The popularity of the hotel increased. Word spread. People traveling by on the nearby stage were staying over purposely. The town itself was benefiting from Sarah's hospitality, fine food, and soft beds. It was hard work. Nebraska summers could get very hot and the kitchen would be sweltering. Flies from the nearby livestock swarmed into the houses and Sarah's establishment. Screen doors were the rage but still, when the doors opened, they flew in. When the night fell and the flies would light on the ceiling, Sarah had assigned one of the tall men who helped her with the fire wood, to take a fire and singe their wings. Then they would be crushed and swept up with the straw broom and disposed of. The only way that Sarah seemed to be limited as a woman on her own was that she had a height handicap. All may sound grand and lovely but the truth is it could be steaming hot in the summer and teeth chattering cold in the winter. Sarah would see the need for a new place with windows to open for the guests, and a large parlor with a large fireplace to gather around in the winter. She felt the need for change and so was born another boarding house.

So a new venture and move was on the way.

A BOY ON THE PRAIRIE

Before moving to the town of Tecumseh, Sarah had stayed with her sister Mary's family on a farm. He and his cousin Victor played together being little horsemen, which was not unusual in that day. By the time they moved to the town Clyde was able to care for the horses used for the transportation of the day.

Clyde became attached to the horses that the family relied on for transportation. Houses in frontier towns were not as towns built in modern times. A frontier town would have storefronts and living quarters in the back. In Sarah's case, directly behind her boarding house, she had shelters for her cow, and a goat for milk for her guest's meals. Of course the family horses were sheltered there also.

In the shelter for the family horses, the boy was given jobs that included forking hay for the animals or seeing that the horses and livestock were fed and watered. It was then that his relationship with horses turned into something special. He would talk to them as if they were human. He combed their manes, and stroked them endlessly. He taught them to nuzzle his pockets for leftover carrots that came from the kitchen.

What started as a chore to help his mother became a passion for the young boy. As a very little boy, he had begun to try to climb on them, which had been a worry to his mother. Finally, she let him ride as she learned to trust his skills. He would beg to exercise the two horses, riding them bareback every day.

The townspeople got used to the young boy riding up and down the main street. He became a part of the daily scenery in the little town of Tecumseh. Soon, tricks started happening as they watched. He was teaching the horses to move to his commands. Clyde was quick to understand what the horses wanted to teach him, also. It seemed an extraordinary thing for a boy to be doing. He was not aware the town was watching. Main Street was just his playground and he went about his childish ways of playing, oblivious to the people who lived there that would be observing him. To this young boy without a playmate, play meant his horse and dog friends. He was completely absorbed in his pets. At times, children having no brothers, or sisters or friends develop deep affection for animals.

Sarah did not know that when he reached the end of the little town street where actual civilization ended, out on the big tufts of prairie grass and was out in the unseen world, he would run the horse as fast as the horse wanted to go. He was a small boy for his age, and it seemed as they ran with his hair flying back, that he and the horse were one, as both boy and horse were feeling the joy of the wind blowing against them. They both were feeling the freedom of being let loose with no restraints. Riding like the wind, took on a new meaning. You would have thought that this was some young Native American who was born to the back of a horse. It was a thing of beauty.

One particular spring day, as he was putting his pony through its paces, he was letting his own slender body take dangerous positions on the side of the horse while the horse galloped along. He had heard that the natives did that when in battle with men with guns. He was becoming a product of the popular *Dime Novels* which some of the boarders read to him out loud which spoke of such things. He had imaginary battles and other adventures as all children do. On a knoll in the prairie grass, hidden by a clump of trees some distance away, a small group of Pawnee Indians stood quietly out of sight watching. They had been there, as if transfixed, for some time watching this son of a white man ride very much as their braves had learned to do when they were much older. He never knew that they were there.

How extraordinarily different were his talents. It seemed it could not be coming from the same body. A young boy, riding like warrior across the prairie grass at one moment and "all boy," as some would say, and yet the next, his fine, slender hands playing a violin in his mother's parlor. He was, as he grew older, an entertainment on long winter evenings that the guests said not only made the violin cry, but made them cry also.

When he was young, Sarah discovered that special talent in the boy when a boarder moved in with a violin. He encouraged the boy to play with it, and was surprised to see that there was a natural ability to play. The child picked up little ditties quickly. To Sarah's surprise he became fascinated with the instrument and when his mother would not allow him out because of the cold, he would practice what the patient boarder had taught him. The boarder was pleased, and bought the boy an inexpensive violin. Before long, he was playing for the amusement of those "regulars" simple, lively Irish jigs that made their toes tap.

As the boy grew he, of course, had more chores to help with in the upkeep of the busy house he lived in. He was used to a lifestyle of people coming and going. Constant business was going on in the world he lived in. There was constant activity. Perhaps, that is why that during his days he would manage time to draw away to the quietness of the prairie, to do the things he loved to do with his horses, or to spend his spare time with the animals in the shelter that protected them from the brutal winters of Nebraska. Many days in the cold of winter he would huddle in their midst, drawing heat from their bodies and doing little boy things in the barn to pass the time.

There was always a dog. He obsessed with teaching the fortunate animal tricks. Fortunate, because learning tricks meant food scraps from the kitchen. Not just standard tricks but unusual things people did not expect a dog to do. The dog would be his closest companion. He was allowed to slip her into the back of the house to his room where no guests could see an animal in the hotel. She slept warmly in his bed. On a cold Nebraska night, the dog served as his heating pad also.

The ways of the people that were used to blinding blizzards and cold winters were varied to protect their valuable livestock. Even the poorest, with the smallest houses, relied on the horse or mule for their transportation and a cow for milk and butter, chicken pens for meat and eggs. Then there would be a mongrel dog or two of some kind to protect it all and give warning when predators stalked these valuable possessions. In the crippling snow storms, as the dark threatening clouds gathered, Nebraskans knew they must tie a rope from the house to the shelter that held their precious animals, so that when the driving snow was too thick to see, they could follow the rope to take care of their animals. Some had sod houses for their animals and some had very elaborate lean-tos.

Northern prairie living was hard due to the physical landscape. There was little shelter from the devastatingly hard winter winds, because of the flat, almost treeless land. What few trees there grew in small groves together. Generally they were near water, but not always. This is why history shows us pictures of sod houses in the early pioneer primitive pictures. Wood was scarce.

In the winters, Sarah's son would bundle up in layers of his warmest clothes, step out in the stinging ice, bend his well-covered head to the howling wind, and make his way through blowing snow, or sleet, following the tightly knotted rope to what Sarah considered her livelihood behind her hotel. She did not have to coerce her son of the plains to feed and care for these animals, for they were his pets, and he was driven by the inner need to take care of his friends. They were his animals, or so he thought they were.

His dog had a litter of puppies, and this meant more friends to train to do his fascinating tricks. Actually, more friends for Sarah, at some point, to find homes for, which was not the young man's fondest desire. She was quite lively in convincing some fellow Nebraskan that they needed another dog to warn them of coyotes, or wolves and to protect their farm animals. Maybe, they really needed two. Not totally heartless, the boy was able to keep one.

A BOY AND HIS DOG

Clyde would have a dog or two his whole life long. As every dog lover knows, there can be many dogs throughout one's life, but there will always be one, or maybe two, that were special. This is a story of a special one.

As a young boy there was Nippy. Nippy was so named because he was a young dog, named by a young boy. As a little pup, the dogs biting in play seemed more like little nips. Clyde would sit on the board walk in front of, or possibly behind, the boarding house in the large yard and play with this little nipping ball of fur, and so Clyde named it Nippy. Of course boys grow up, and so do pups, and the name Nippy didn't seem appropriate to the young man's thoughts, and so it became Nip. As usual, the one who feeds and cares for a dog becomes the master, and is the one who obtains the faithful love of a dog.

Clyde always worked hard at training his dogs. One day a wise old man named Ben, who spent much of his day on the front boardwalk of the town, had been watching him work with the pup until it had learned to sit and beg. Finally, the little pudgy pup learned that if he sat up, food was the reward.

"You know what that proves?" the old man said.

"What?" asked the clueless Clyde.

"That you're smarter than the dog," said the old-timer who had nothing better to do than watch a young boy and his dog on the Main Street of Tecumseh.

Clyde doted on this little spunky ball of fur, and in turn the loyalty was returned. So it was that this little companion was at Clyde's heels at all times. As this faithful little companion matured, no longer at his heels, he would walk happily in front, but always glancing back to assure itself that the one he thought he was protecting was behind him. Should he find that his master had stopped, he too would stop and go back to the place where the boy was distracted. Then he would sit on his little rump, looking up at his only sought after companion, as if to say, "What next?"

Nip was a constant playmate for a boy who had no brothers or sisters. The little dog was allowed a nice warm blanket beside Clyde's bed. But of course after the lights were out, Nip had been taught by a signal, and only at that signal after the lights were out, he could jump into the bed and hide under the covers. At the boy's first sign of waking, the dog was immediately on the floor, looking expectantly for his master to start their day together again. Clyde wouldn't know that before he woke, there were brown eyes watching him expectantly, waiting for the slightest move that the little creature's day could start. For his day revolved around his boy.

Nip was not a pretty dog. He was a brindled color of brown, common in mutt type dogs. As he grew, it was obvious that his legs weren't going to. Not much anyway. It was a wonder that this little short legged dog that shadowed Clyde could jump up on anything his boy jumped up on. The boy, at times, would sit on some of the cotton bales that sat in the town waiting for shipment, and so Nip would join him there. He might have to make a couple of tries, but wherever his boy sat for any length of time, Nip knew his place was at his side.

The days of teaching him tricks started with a game of fetch. Early on, you would see the boy, sitting hip to hip, on the boardwalk with his little shadow. At some point Clyde would start to throw an object and expect the excited little pup to retrieve it. It was paramount in the game, that whatever he retrieved would be brought back and be laid before the boy. His boy established the rules. Then the dog would sit on his rump and look expectantly at his boy. Done right and there was a pat on the head and Nip knew he had done well. Clyde was never unkind to his little dog, and yet he established rules.

A boy and his dog was this duo no matter where the day took them. Of course, the dog thought it was a dog and his boy. Nip loved to go exploring beyond the little town out into the big prairie that surrounded it. Nip never went alone, because then he would not be right at the side of the one he thought he was required to be beside of, or in front of, or behind. What fun Nip had though when the boy got on that horse of his and they headed out to where all the wild things were. He had to stretch those short legs sometimes to keep up with the pony the boy had at that time, but oh what tongue hanging out fun it was. They were never going to get away from him. The boy made sure the little dog was never left behind and then they would come to their favorite place where the boy got down from the pony and just sat on the ground.

While the boy seemed to be just leaning against a tree, maybe petting the pony, Nip would run around the ground nearby exploring. Maybe he would be distracted by a butterfly or some strange crawly things. Sometimes he would just frolic through the leaves in this wonderful out of town place. He would be alerted to a bushy tailed thing in a tree, and would try and bark it down. The thing would just sit in the high branches and make strange noises at him while twitching his bushy tail, but it would not come down. The strange looking, long eared things with puffy little tails on the ground were fast, and he could never catch them, because his legs were too short, but it was always his duty to try. Then in the distance he would hear his boy whistle, and he knew he had to go back to the boy's tree. On the way back he would pick up a little tree branch for the boy and the boy would always take it and say, "Thank You, Nip." Then the boy would throw it as hard as he could, and watch him run and fetch it. Then Nip ran as hard as he could, pick up the branch, make a big U-turn and bring it back to the boy. Then, if he laid it down for the boy, he always got a pat and a thank you. He knew this made his boy happy.

Sometimes there would be the smell of strange animals nearby, and he wasn't quite sure what they were and he felt danger. Whatever it was, it was in the bushes around them and he felt like he had to warn the boy. He felt his ears perk up, and his hair felt like it was standing up. He felt tense and alert. He growled, telling whatever it was it better go away. He growled also because he wanted the boy to know there was something bad around. The pony knew too and was pulling away from where he was tied to the tree, wanting to go. The boy would quit leaning on his tree, get up, and look around. When that happened, he didn't like what the boy would do then. He would take the pony's reigns, and then pick Nip up and get up in the saddle with him. Then they would go. He didn't feel comfortable on the pony's back but that's what the boy did when the dog felt the danger.

There was something in Clyde that required a dog in his life. He saw them as no other animal. He would always have a bond with a dog. It was something about a dog's faithful love and how it stayed lying contented by his side. How if he stood up, the dog would stand. How if they had to be separated, he would be standing at the door anxiously awaiting his arrival. He saw the joy of the wagging tail at his appearance. How he was always watching his face in anticipation of his next move. He loved how the dog would always bound in front of him as if it was so joyful because it was in his company. To him, a dog was pure dedication and devotion.

As they both grew older together, there were times in Clyde's life that he would feel sad. At that time, just as he was feeling as if no one knew his hurts or cares, a soft nose would nuzzle his downcast head and that hairy, faithful, head would lay on him as though saying he felt his sadness. At such times, Nip would put a paw upon his arm as if to say, "I'm here." The wonder in that happening was that a dog would know the unspoken feelings within a man. At the few times that happened in his life, he would think of a Bible verse. Certainly his mother would remind him, should he speak it to her in reference to his dog, that he was certainly taking a scripture out of context. He felt that the LORD, who is the Giver of all good things, would not mind him saying that in reference to a faithful dog, "There is a friend that sticketh closer than a brother."

In time, Clyde would be allowed to have another pup that he could train to be a clever companion to Nip. Because of some phrase of the time, pertaining to running fast or racing back and forth together, he named his new companion dog to his old friend Nip by the name of Tuck. So the little town would see running down its main street its familiar little boy with his dogs, Nip and Tuck.

Clyde as a young man in Tecumseh

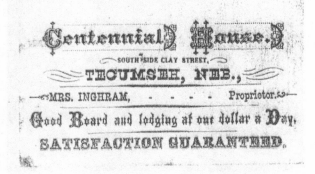

The company of Yourself
and Ladies is
respectfully requested at a

Reception,

by Mrs. S. E. Ingraham,
at the Centennial
House on

Thursday Evening, Nov. 8, 1885.

DANCING AND SUPPER.

Centennial House.

SOUTH SIDE CLAY STREET,

TECUMSEH, NEB.,

MRS. INGHRAM, - - - - - Proprietor.

Good Board and lodging at one dollar a Day,

SATISFACTION GUARANTEED.

Reception Invitation
Centennial House Hotel, Tecumseh Nebraska
Mrs. Sarah Ingrahm, Proprietor
November 8, 1885

THE CRACK-SHOT

Over the years, many people were required to operate the boarding house as the clientele grew and grow it certainly did! Sarah's great care to see that the above average care and stay was provided, caused the word to quickly spread. Out on the road, people who were accustomed to traveling in the area had spread the word to others. Some that were intending a brief overnight stay would add a length of time to their stay. Those in the town, who for one reason or another had moved in, were always amazed at the care they received. Everyone loved the feel of being pampered. Help came and went over the years. Some of the staff considered it the only place they would want to work, if that were their type of work. Others moved on from time to time for various reasons.

There was much work to do in keeping such an establishment going: the rooms had to be seen to, bedding laundry sent out, and the kitchen work with its food preparation was an all-day thing for the steady boarders. Food preparation in that day started from scratch, from the killing of chickens, or the butcher store, to the cooking. Vegetables had to be bought, cleaned and then cooked. Some local farmers, or the mercantile, sold them the vegetables. Sarah had a chicken yard and house which supplied meat and eggs. This was behind the boarding house.

Even with much hired help, Sarah would be the last to wearily crawl into her bed at night. It seemed she was obsessed with things being especially well done. Her lantern was the last to go out, always. This was something that had always been in Sarah's nature.

The latest help was Mary Edna Rainey, a young girl from the community who lived with her emigrant parents who had come from England. She adapted to the boarding house team very quickly, as she had come from a large family and had learned to help in the care of her own home. Her main duties were in the kitchen helping to prepare the meals and helping Sarah make the pastries in the morning. Sarah always rose early to prepare the yeast bread so it would have time to rise. Then she would prepare the baking soda biscuits that would be for the morning meal. Mary always helped to roll the cobbler crust out and help see that the fruit or the fillings for the pies were prepared. This took cutting and slicing. She had adapted quickly and was very helpful as a new employee. Mary Edna was one of those people that liked to be busy, so she was considered to be very helpful.

The work in the cold Nebraska winters was easier in the kitchen, which was kept fairly warm with the constant heat from the stove and the ovens. Of course, sweltering Nebraska summers could be another story. Help would have to step outside to do what preparations could be done, to escape the heat of the kitchen. Behind the building was prepared a shady seating place for the kitchen help for those summer days.

Of course, Mary Edna was noticed by Clyde, being a new young woman around the house. She was quite a bit younger than he was and he showed no particular outward interest in her, for he was very absorbed in his own activities. At this point in his life he was considered the man of the boarding house, and was definitely co-equal in the business. The community thought of him as owner of the establishment, just as they did Sarah. He and Mary Edna barely spoke to one another. She was of a character that would never speak to a man and he just had no interest in her. She was also a little intimidated because he was her employer's son.

One day while on a household mission, Mary entered the room where he was cleaning his hunting rifle.

Always seeming oblivious to his presence, she let her eyes wander to the rifle. The gun, being cleaned and loaded, caught her immediate attention. Clyde was getting ready to go out to the prairie to look for meat which was both a job and a delight to him. He loved the adventure of tracking, being on the back of a horse, and looking for game wherever he could find it - be it deer, or elk, or scattering a covey of quail or the abundant pheasant of these plains. It was a part of the life he lived and loved. Being a horseman and a hunter was one occupation of the household he took pleasure in. It seemed he was born to be these things.

He and his cousin Victor spent their early child hood in horsemanship and he loved the open prairie where he seldom saw a human. He had even learned from a Native American friend how to use a bow and arrow. He and Vic had spent hours practicing with targets as a pastime. The westward migration of the white man had taken its toll on the animal population. Once the prairies had swarmed with herds of grazing buffalo and massive herds covering the Nebraska plains. There were herds of elk by the thousands covering the grass lands of Kansas and Nebraska in the early 1800's. They grazed along the Platte River and it had been the great hunting ground for the Indians, his friend had told him. As man migrated west, they too migrated to the higher territories where the white man had not gone. His uncle lived at Elk Creek, so named for the herds of elk that were once so plentiful.

Had Clyde been given a choice, he would have lived beyond civilization. He was never truly at home indoors, although his mother had tried to make it a pleasant thing for him. He had always been a little outdoors boy, and now as a young man he stalked these prairies like the young warriors that had been so plentiful in days past. However, in his day, hunting was as common as the supermarket.

He would have loved to have been one of the early explorers of this great untamed land. Yet, he would never leave his beloved mother. He felt as she had chosen to remain alone, it was his job to care for her, as she had so faithfully cared for him single handedly. He knew there had been men that had sought her attention, but she had avoided any attachment of that kind for some reason. He so respected what she had done so bravely in a man's frontier land, alone and without help. She had built a life and a home for them by sheer work alone. She would forever, to his dying day, have his utmost respect.

As he sat there, tending his gun, his mind went to something he needed to get from another room, and not ever noticing Mary standing there, he left. He would be gone for just a short time, so he left the gun on the table beside his chair. When he returned to the room, Mary was holding the gun in firing position, looking very much as if she knew what she was doing. Unnoticed, he stood quietly inside the door, watching her, and was quite surprised as she drew a bead on a chicken outside the back window.

"Going to shoot supper?" he asked jokingly.

Mary jumped, not knowing she was being watched. She quickly laid the gun back on the table. Feeling embarrassed at being caught at her "imaginary target practice", and also feeling she was being made fun of, with red cheeks, she retorted in her very British accent, "I most certainly could, had I a desire to."

Laughing, the belligerent Clyde said, "You'd sure have to prove that to me." Hhe stood there with a slightly impish grin on his face, as if he was seeing her for the first time.

Mary, standing with her hands on her hips, said, "I'll wager you I can. Here's a wager for you, since you think I can't. If I shoot three chickens for tonight's supper, instead of wringing their necks, you will have to pick their feathers. Are you brave enough to make that bet?"

For the first time he realized she was serious. Pausing a moment, and then with a gleam in his eye, he took the challenge and said, "It's a bet."

"Just a minute," he said, "I've got to warn Mother there's going to be gunfire." He quickly ran into the parlor, where Sarah was helping some ladies set up a quilting rack for their day's entertainment. "I'm going to shoot at that pesky rat that's been hanging around the back yard. You'll probably hear a bunch of shots." Then out of the room he ran.

Sarah heard exactly three shots. In less than five minutes Clyde ran back into the parlor saying excitedly, "Mom, you won't believe it! Mary Edna just shot the heads off of three chickens - first shot. She's a sharpshooter!"

Then he turned quickly on his heels, saying excitedly, "I've got a job I gotta do in the kitchen."

Sarah's forehead wrinkled in a question. The kitchen, she thought, He hates kitchen work! Wondering for a second what had possessed her son, she returned her attention to the assembling of the quilt rack.

Strangely enough, Clyde started hanging around the kitchen a lot, volunteering for all kind of work to help Miss Mary Edna. Strangely enough, it was not long until Sarah sensed than this was more than one of the girls Clyde had seemed interested in for a short courtship, as had been in his usual experience. Their common interest in marksmanship and her unusual leanings in that area made it an activity they spent their spare time in while providing for the kitchen meat. It was easy to see that this was far more than just a casual thing that was calling her son to this young woman. Of the girls that had been in his small town acquaintances, this girl definitely produced a joy in his step and a sparkle in his eye. She had his attention in a large way. She was a strange combination of seeming very dignified from her British accent, and yet this was no dainty little flower that had to be carried on a delicate pillow, as many young ladies that lived in town were. Mary Edna was to the outward eye, a reserved and ladylike woman, with a warrior's heart for the prairie life he loved. To Clyde she was the best of both worlds.

Since Clyde had grown up in this little settler town as Tecumseh's boy, before the view of Main Street, and before all the farming community, all knew that Tecumseh's boy had found the girl of his dreams and all Tecumseh knew there would be a wedding soon. They were not wrong. The ladies of the town just knew, as women know, that this was the one. As the couple rode by on horseback out to the prairie with their guns, and not in the surrey as had been so with the previous town girls, the gentlemen smiled at each other and winked and said, "The wild-boys days on the prairie are about over."

The Caledonia never looked more beautiful as she prepared for this large event in her son's life and what a wedding attendance it was. A formal dance was held after the wedding. The groom was even persuaded to pull himself away from his especially beautiful bride to play several violin favorites for the celebrating wedding guests. Most of Tecumseh turned out for the event.

The largest room in the Caledonia House was turned into their suite and it was not long before two little toddlers became the delight of guests who were the permanent residents.

Mary Edna Rainey Ingrahm in her later years

THE STRANGER WITH NO NAME

It was dark in Tecumseh; darker than a modern day man can imagine. In the year of 1894 lights in their infant forms were invading only sophisticated parts of America. There were certainly no outdoor lights. The frontier town in the middle of the dark prairie where only nocturnal, wild things prowled was "darker than pitch", as a country man would say. It was past the time for all to put out their lamps and go to bed. Nothing disturbed the night except the distant howl of a prairie wolf.

Suddenly in the distance a noise arose on the road leading into the sleeping town. At first it was faint. If anyone had been awake, they would have heard the growing sound of the rattle of wooden wheels down the rutted road. Out of the prairie silence, came the sound of horse's running feet. The prairie things that did their night time scavenging when humans were asleep scattered into their hiding places. The wagon was traveling at a great speed for that time of night. The lanterns that were hanging from the front of the wagon were swinging wildly giving light over the rough much traveled road. A man in the back of the wagon was holding a lantern over the cargo being carried.

Sarah Elizabeth was sleeping soundly, and did not hear as someone stopped the horses outside the house and hitched them to the hitching post. Nor did she hear the heavy footsteps run across the wooden planked porch in front of the boarding house. She awoke with a start as someone was pounding heavily on the wooden door. She reached for the lantern and put on a wrapper that was hanging in the closet. She yelled out Clyde's name, as she did not want to answer the door alone at this time of night, but yet knew it was some kind of emergency from the rapid knocking and the repeated sound of the pounding on the door.

Her sleepy son, who had slipped out of bed without waking his wife, was already coming down the stairs, lantern in one hand, and his hunting rifle in the other. He had been startled awake when the sound of the team approached the house, even before the weary Sarah had.

Sarah turned up the dim light from the lamp in the parlor, and then looking at her son first to see if he was standing ready, opened the door only a crack. Recognizing the man as a man she knew well from the town, she swung the door open.

"Hello, Red," she said, as she looked past him to a man standing at the back of a wagon, holding a lantern over something in the wagon bed as he bent over it. Sarah looked back at Red and asked, "What is it?" She recognized the other man as another townsman who worked for the railroad nearby Tecumseh. Sarah, due to her medical skills, was not unused to people calling on her in emergencies. By this time, Clyde was at the back of the wagon holding his lantern over the wagon bed.

"A man's been hurt bad, Miss Sarah. Someone found him in one of the railroad cars. He heard some moaning and went to check. Then he came and got me. He's bad, Miss Sarah. He might even be dead by now. I cain't tell if he's breathin' or not. I don't think the ride did him any good."

Sarah walked quickly out, and lifted her lantern over the man who was crumpled in the rear of the bloodstained wagon. Hanging her lantern on the wagon, she pulled herself up into the wagon bed and put her hand on him to see if there was a pulse. Clyde held his light over her so she could see. She sat still, listening for a moment and then said, "He's got life in him. He's got a head wound and they can look worse than they are because they bleed a lot."

She turned to Mary, who by this time had come downstairs, and was looking over Clyde's shoulder at the stranger with her lantern. "Mary, would you go around back to the lean-to and bring those canvases we put there last week? Bring them out here for the men to put the man on one. Then you take the other one and put it in the spare bed room in the back of the house. You'll need to strip the bed mattress of its sheets and put the canvas on it. Then put the sheet back on the top of the canvas and make sure the beds ready to put him on, while we clean him up out back."

Looking at Red and Wade she said, "Will you need Clyde to help you carry him or can you manage alone? He needs to be taken to the back pump and cleaned up before we take him in the house. He doesn't look very heavy."

"No Ma'am," replied Red, "He weren't no trouble when we lifted him out of that train car. He's as light as a feather. We'll manage him just fine."

"Clyde," she said, "Run out to the pump and by the kitchen door you'll find the two buckets. We'll take him back there first to wash off the blood before we take him into the back room off the kitchen. Go get the buckets filled."

Sarah quickly jumped down from the wagon bed, and ran into the parlor. The now aroused guests were standing at the door, looking out curiously to see what was happening. Sarah told them that a man had been hurt but there was nothing to worry about. She assured them it was no one that they knew. He was not a local. It was a stranger. She requested they go back to their rooms and not to worry. They unwillingly complied, looking back over their shoulders to see what was happening, but started walking back toward their bedrooms.

Sarah went back to the door, just as the two men had lifted the wounded man from the wagon onto the canvas tarp Mary had laid at the foot of the wagon bed. He had quietly groaned when they picked him up, and again as they laid him down on the canvas. He lifted his trembling hand to his head wound. Wade gently lifted his hand away from the gash and laid it on his chest. Although he did not open his eyes, Sarah thought, He's conscious. That's a good sign.

She carried her lantern before the men and their smelly burden. Wade said, "I told Red you wuz the nearest doctor I knew, Miss Sarah, and I wuz sure you would help him."

"Wade, I keep telling people I'm only a nurse," she replied, "My husband was the doctor." Despite her outward protest, she knew that actually she had earned an invisible degree when she was allowed to work with Zebulun in the war. Her doctorate had been earned on the field of battle. Her nursing skills had been proven far above any teaching skills she might have acquired, by working at his side. Her doctorate had been earned in the war between the Blue and the Gray. She had seen it all. Her prejudiced heart said that she had learned at the side of the best.

After the man was gently washed, dried thoroughly, and carried into the small back room and put into the comfortable bed that Mary had prepared, the two tired men were ready to leave and get home to their own beds. Wearily, they started for the door as Sarah accompanied them. They both thanked Sarah for her kindness, shaking her hand gratefully. As they were going out the door, Sarah called them by name and they both turned around.

"Gentlemen," she said, "I am very much a believer in The Good Book. I read it daily. The one whom the book is about, and whose words we should live by, says that those who are merciful, and he mentions strangers, will one day obtain the same mercy. I believe you will be repaid someday."

Being very touched by those words, Red said, "God Bless You Ma'am." He would long remember those ancient words. In a future time those words would come to his remembrance when a little child of his was at the point of death and he would pray to the One whom Sarah had talked about, and against doctor's dire predictions, his little beloved girl recovered. He knew he had received the mercy spoken of that night. Going out the door, he repeated the words again, "God Bless you, Miss Sarah."

None of the three involved that night ever realized they had acted out a scene described centuries ago by a gentle Galilean. The story He told, was of a merciful man who took pity on a man he did not know; a stranger and one of a different religion and culture. In that story the man took him to be helped. The most outstanding likeness of all, the stranger had been taken and left with an innkeeper to be cared for. None of the three involved that night ever saw that the Parable of the Good Samaritan was lived out in their actions. Yet, an invisible stranger, that Sarah had encountered years ago, unbeknownst to her, stood watch that night in the room as Sarah kept her vigil over this strange man.

When daylight came that morning, as Sarah kept her weary watch beside the stranger, and light finally revealed the swollen face of the helpless man, Sarah exclaimed out loud, "Dear Lord, it's a China Man!"

INTRODUCTION TO A STRANGER

Clyde had spent the night, or what was left of it, sleeping fitfully. He arose early, having seen that Mary had already risen and had left the room. He quickly dressed and went downstairs. He went into the kitchen where Mary was kneading the bread that his mother generally made first thing in the morning. He kissed her on the cheek, saying, "Thanks Mary," and went to the cabinet where he took out two cups. Going to the stove, he poured the cups full of coffee from the simmering pot. Leaving the kitchen, going down the back hall, he went to the room where he knew his mother would still be watching her patient. She was sitting beside the bed in an old straw seated rocker. Her head was bent over, as she slept. In her hand was a rag. The water basin was full of water on the bedside table. His father's old stethoscope and medical bag were lying on the side of the bed.

Clyde looked to the bed to see the stranger. His surprise was the same as his mother's had been. Neither mother nor son had ever seen an Asian man before. It was a total shock. It was as if he was something you had heard of all your life in stories, yet you had never expected to see. It was as unexpected as seeing a giraffe in the Nebraska prairie grass. It was a sight he had not seen before in his 29 years.

Of course, they had both seen pictures in books with Chinese people in their odd clothes and funny hats. There had been newspapers that reached their part of the country with pictures of Asian men working on the railroad tracks or in Chinese camps, as was called their places they lived.

Clyde had learned the love of reading from his mother. From a small boy she had read to him almost daily until he started reading on his own. She had enjoyed that time together as much as he had. There were stories of strange and exotic lands. Some stories were real and some just made for a little boys imagination, especially for an imaginative little boy like Clyde. Although, in that day and time, there was not an overabundance of books in the remote land they lived in however, she always managed to have books with interesting pictures in the house. Some kind guests had left books and newspapers when they saw the boy's interest. Some he never tired of. He looked at the pictures over and over. He was especially drawn to people of different lands and animals not found in America.

There had been the strangers coming through the boarding house that would love to tell an interested boy of the stories and tales they had heard and seen. That would draw him to their feet. At times, his mother seemed pleased with that, and then there were times she would take him away from certain ones, to do something else, as though she did not want him to listen to their stories.

It was the stories of a man called Marco Polo that he was remembering now, as he looked at the sleeping man. His mother had told him of wonderful tales of a man of great adventure and courage who went to the land of an exotic and imaginative people of China. He saw and tasted new food and saw new inventions not known to the rest of the world. He loved the true stories of a man who dared to go where others hadn't gone and lived with a people that were not his own and saw sights foreign to his eyes, and unknown by his people. When he was a little boy he decided that when he was big, that's what he would do. He would be an explorer.

As a boy on his prairie he had been drawn to what was to him the romance of the natives of this land, for it seemed to him that they lived their lives in pure freedom. He saw them as a simple people, wanting to live off the land and not requiring all the things his people did. He was fascinated with their way with horses. It was not as his people, who seemed more inclined to use them as beasts of burden. As he watched them, they seemed almost as one with these beautiful animals in their plain lives together. His mother would have been alarmed if she had known that when he and his dogs took his prairie rides he was observing these people beyond the outskirts of the town. He had actually made some friends with the Indians. Even some of the older men of the tribe seemed fascinated with this young boy who was so at home with his horse and dogs on the prairie. He wisely, so he thought, had never spoke of these encounters to his mother.

Naturally, now as a young man, his curiosity was heightened by this phenomenon that was laid at his doorstep. Since he was grown, he was aware that these immigrants were coming here, as his Grandma Catherine had come to this land from Ireland. He knew that the Chinese had settled the west coast and followed the building of the railroad, just as his grandparents had come to the opposite coast and had traveled from New York State to Illinois.

Now that their town was opened through the railroad and people from other places were coming to their house, he was able to read in the newspapers of what was happening in this vast land. He had heard the tales of the emigration to the Pacific coast of these people in 1848 when gold had been discovered. They had come for the same reason his people had come to the other coast. They were driven by poverty and famine. They were seeking a better life. He knew that large numbers came. He was not aware that desperation had driven more than

300,000 to enter the United States. Although a few were artisans, and merchants, as he was to find out this man was, most were unskilled country folk. In some cases, families pooled their money to send out a son, but most travelers, desperately poor, obtained their passage through Chinese middlemen, who advanced them ship fare in return for the emigrant's promise to work off their debts after they landed. So these adventurers came.

Although many returned to their homeland, disappointed, many Chinese stayed, he had read. "Chinatowns" sprang up where opportunities presented themselves in railroad towns, villages, and cities. They stayed in their own areas of towns, spoke their own language, and enjoyed their own fellowship among themselves. His Irish folk would call them "clannish."

In the first generations in America these new immigrants had to make a living doing the jobs that many didn't want, just as his ancestors had done. He heard stories of his own people people working on the Erie Canal at hard jobs, and yet one had become an assistant surveyor for the Canal. Many hard working Chinese did manage to open their own restaurants, laundries, and other small businesses. These were the things Clyde had read and learned on those cold, blizzard times in Nebraska when no one would venture outside and when reading and sharing stories were the only pastimes. To his knowledge no Asians had been near Tecumseh or at least he had never seen one.

Clyde looked from the stranger to his sleeping mother. His thoughts changed to her. He suddenly felt a surge of gratefulness for her open mind and kindness, and that he had been taught not to think himself better than others different from himself. He knew these thoughts came from that book she read every day.

As he watched her sleep, he thought how young she looked for her 46 years. Looking at her hands, though, the work they had done gave away her age. He gently touched her shoulder and she aroused, quickly looking toward the sleeping patient. Then her eyes moved toward her son's face.

"Surprised?" she asked, nodding her head toward the bed smiling.

"Yeah," he grinned back, "It was so dark last night and also the swollen face....," Looking down at the man again, he asked, "How is he?"

"Well, his lips were really parched so I don't think he had had any water for a long time. I gave him a drink and he is seeming a little better. He drank so fast, I had to make him slow down. Hopefully he'll gain some strength from the broth I gave him. I wonder how long he had been on that train?" Pausing, as if trying to fathom his situation, she said, "That's a pretty deep gash on his head. The blood was so dried I know he had been in that railroad car a long time."

"What do you think made the gash?" Clyde asked. "You've sure got it wrapped up good."

"I hate to think, son. I haven't seen that kind of a head wound since the war. It's deep and needs some stitching. Do you think Mary Edna is up to helping us do that? We'll have to shave the front of his hairline since that's where most of the wound is."

"She won't mind, I'm sure," Clyde responded, "You know her background. She had to kill animals since she was small. Blood doesn't bother her at all." Then laughingly he said, "That's what drew me to her in the first place. She didn't seem to be one those squeamish "city girls." I'm not sure what happened in that English background of hers, but she's sure a trooper."

Changing the subject he said, "Why don't you first go get some breakfast and relax just a little from sitting here all night? He doesn't look like he's going anywhere. Maybe stretch a little. Eat a little biscuit and jelly or something. I'll sit here while you do and you can bring me back another cup of coffee, when you come back."

He turned his eyes back to the deeply sleeping man. "Don't worry about making the bread. Mary came down before I did and said she'd make sure the kitchen work got started."

She smiled feeling relieved, and was thinking how happy she was to have such a hard-working and considerate daughter–in-law, as she quietly slipped out the door. Tired she definitely was, but she was quite sure the kitchen couldn't get along without her. She had to take a look, before she thought about any breakfast. A good breakfast for her guests had always been her motto. She stifled a yawn as she went down the hall to the kitchen.

Clyde leaned back in his chair, thinking about the surgery they were going to do, and not really relishing the idea of it. He wasn't squeamish, but he did not inherit his parent's medical leanings. As he studied the man, he wondered what got him to this place in his life. "I wonder if he can do any of that 'fancy Chinese fighting' I've heard about?" he thought. "Hope we don't experience any of that while Mom sews him up", he laughed to himself. Then he laughed out loud as he thought of his feisty, little Mother. That's alright. Mom could probably whip him!

THE AWAKENING

A few days went by before the man seemed to be responsive to where he was. Sarah took heart at that. She knew that his vital signs seemed to be improving greatly.

Up until that point, he drifted in and out of sleep. He, at first sign of recognition, would open his eyes, squinting at his surroundings, as if trying to discern where he was at. This was just briefly, and then he would close them and drift off into sleep. Then a day came, as Sarah was arranging his bedding, when he looked at her fully and questioningly in the face for some time. Again, as if trying to put together a puzzle in his mind as to whom she was, or where he was, there was a question in his eyes. His eyes were studying every inch of her face, and though she smiled and spoke, there was no verbal response. There was no recognition that she had done so. There was just the studying of her face and then he would close his eyes again for hours. This became routine. He was sleeping less and less.

Finally, at the exasperation of no verbal response of any kind to her speaking to him, she decided he must not speak any English. So her communication with him became smiles alone so that he would be at ease with being in this strange place with an unknown stranger. She began a game of pointing to the pitcher or bowl to see what his needs were.

He rallied enough so that she could raise his head and pillow up so that he was somewhat inclined upward. On one day she brought him a cup of green tea which she had heard was an Asian drink. She had known it as a medicinal. As she sat by the bed, she raised the drink to his lips which to her surprise he drank the first sip, and then moved his head again towards the cup as if wanting more. She had that day, along with the chicken broth, brought some white rice because she decided it was time to try solid foods. Her reading to Clyde as a boy, and her studies of other things, had given her the knowledge that rice was a Chinese staple and food. That was about all she knew about the Chinese diet. She knew that broth would be strength for his body. As she spooned the mixture to his lips, he surprised her by chewing it quickly, spoon by spoon as soon as she could get another bit on the spoon and to his lips. That was briefly. Then he laid his head back on the pillow and to her surprise after shaking his head no, he smiled a brilliant smile at her, while looking deeply into her eyes. Ever so briefly it was and then he shut his eyes and seemed asleep. The smile was like music to Sarah's heart. She decided it was good to leave him upright for a while since he was asleep. So she quietly left the room and pulled the door slightly closed.

The others in the house had orders to look in on him to see if he seemed alright as they passed his door. So the door was left ajar at all times. The time came, when she brought him a brass bell and showing him how to use it, she put it on the table by the bed. She left the room and stood a short way down the hall, leaning against the wall. As if waiting.

As she thought and had hoped would happen, curiosity got the best of him and he picked it up and as he did it rang. When it did, she immediately went into his bedroom door. She said, "Yes?" looking expectantly.

She then picked up his water pitcher and pointed it toward him, looking expectantly, at which he shook his head no. She picked up the rice and broth bowl, again pointing it toward him, at which he again shook his head no. She pulled the chamber pot from under the bed with the same procedure, at which he did the same shake of the head. Sarah smiled hoping the message without words had gotten across, and left the room. It had.

At that point, as was a pattern he was forming, Clyde came to sit with the man for a time daily, partly to spell his mother and partly because he was intrigued with the man. As Clyde and Sarah sat together by the man's bed one day, a conversation started about the business.

"You and Mary are working yourselves to death and I am doing all I can. We definitely need some more help since the Swedish girl, Sondra, left to move west with her family. We've got to at least have one more person, before we all drop."

"I know," Sarah said, "But the blizzard this past winter hurt us badly. The help was snowed in with us and I felt beholden to pay their salaries although there was no income from ice bound travelers. It all hurt so much financially because of the business falling off. One more hand would help enough but we just don't have the money. As they talked they had not noticed something changed in the stranger's countenance that day.

Clyde left and Sarah went about her usual business of cleaning the man's wounds. As she reached the door, she froze. From behind her came the words, "Thank you very much."

She turned and the stranger's eyes were looking into hers seriously. Astounded, she said, "You are very welcome."

After pausing a moment, and finding herself speechlessly shocked, she left the room. She had convinced herself he could not speak or understand English. This was like a bolt out of the blue. Sarah went directly from the stranger's room to find Clyde. She could not wait to share with him her unexpected news.

She found him cleaning out the barn. He was just finishing forking the hay for their little group of livestock. Of course, he had taken care of his prized horses; wonder horses some called them. They were quite a rarity in this small town. As she approached the wooden building she stopped to listen to her son who was singing. He did not sing for people as he used to do when he was younger. No more did he lead the guests in the nightly sing-along. He still enjoyed reading to them but the singing and leading them in songs had fallen away.

In days gone by, guests would listen to the small boy sing, and then as he got older Sarah could get him to sing in his beautiful voice in entertainment for the guests on long winter evenings. Then he would get them to join in and sing their favorite songs. It was enjoyable to most and it passed a long winter's eve. Now he could not be persuaded to do that nor did he play publicly his violin. The sweet sounds only came when there was only family around or to his children.

How sweet it was to hear him sing in the company of his horses. She had kept alive some of the songs his father sang and they would be some of the lilting tunes that would touch her most. Also there were some her father had taught her that he had brought from the old country that she had taught him. Once when he was younger, he could literally captivate people with his voice.

There seemed to be special gifts in him. There was much talent that all could see. There was something from the old country, to where strangely enough, he had never been. Nor had she, for she was born here, but he seemed supernaturally filled with a certain thing that was unexplainably transferred through the ancestry genes. "Sure there 'tis Ireland in his blood," an old timer would say. One said, "He could entrance you with his darlin' sweet voice." These things seemed to war with the "wild west ways" he seemed to be so interested in now.

As she stood there quietly listening, with him unaware, she mourned those days when he was younger and was not shy about his talents. She thought of David in the Bible who was called the sweet psalmist of Israel. Surely he could not have sounded sweeter than this son of hers, when he thought no one was listening.

It seemed it all disappeared when he became obsessed with horses, saddles, bridles, and riding the prairie with his riffle. His literature of choice became those popular *Dime Novel*s of the time; books that were glorifying the heroes of the west and of the prairie. History, adventurers, and explorers seemed to interest him now. He had put away his musical talent.

She jerked herself back to reality. She had forgotten the joyful news she had come to share. "Clyde," she said as she was walking into the barn, "You won't believe it. Our man from China can speak English." Clyde looked up at her in surprise.

What they did not know, and would not know until later, when the stranger finally shared his past with them, the man from China as they called him, had come to America one year before Clyde was born. Clyde was now 29 years old. The stranger was thirty-nine years old. He had come to America when he was nine years old. This had been his country a long time. Yes, he knew English.

This Asian man, as they were later to find out, had been born in Canton, China, on April 22nd, 1855. He came to San Francisco, California with an uncle in 1864 as a small boy, after his mother had died in Canton. Even though they didn't know all these exact facts, Sarah and Clyde decided it was time to find out what this man's name was. They were tired of calling him the man from

China or as others would later call him, 'The Chinaman'. The next thing on their agenda was to find out his name.

Shortly after Sarah and Clyde had left his room that day, the stranger shakily raised himself up in the bed, turned himself, and sat on the edge of the bed. Sitting there for a time, to draw his strength, he then slowly raised himself off the edge of the bed. Standing awhile, and leaning back against the bed to balance himself, he then turned around. Clinging to the bed, he bent down, got the chamber pot from under the bed and then raised himself up. Placing the pot on the bed, he relieved himself. He then bent down again, placed the pot under the bed, raised himself up again, and got back into the bed. He turned upon his side, lying there with his eyes open, as if thinking for a short time. He smiled a big smile, pulled the covers up and went to sleep.

As he had laid there so sick and so helpless, he had wondered how he would repay this family their kindness to a perfect stranger. Those that had thrown him on the train had taken his money. He had nothing with which to repay. Now, he had his answer. He must get strong quickly. His strength was needed.

A STRANGER IN A FOREIGN LAND

It was a beautiful day. Fluffy white clouds floated over an azure, blue sky. Sarah Elizabeth was resting in her favorite place on the property. One of Clyde's dogs, Charlie, who seemed to think he might be half hers, was lying asleep at her feet. Her boarding house was situated right in the middle of the town that was Tecumseh, in a line of wooden buildings sitting side by side with an adjoining wooden plank walkway. It would with time, develop into a square. The town looked much as frontier towns looked in the late 1800's. However, the view from the back of the house could be spectacular at times.

Her unobstructed view stretched clear to the Nebraska horizon. It was the Nebraska scenery that she had learned to love. It was pure prairie; flat with grass land clear to that blue horizon. There was nothing to obstruct that view in the back of the house except the barn her son had built for his horses, and the assorted animals they required for the boarding house food. When the boarding house, or hostelry as it was called then, was originally built, the barn was a low sod building, as so many were in the beginning, because of the shortage of trees on the prairie. Over the years, Clyde had seen to the building of a wooden building for the protection of the animals. He had built it first of all for his horses, and then made it big enough to house all the other animals needed to supply the boarding house. No animal could live outside in a Nebraska winter at its most brutal. There was no finer or warmer barn in the area. It was built close enough to the house so he could reach the animal shelter easily in the winter snow storms.

The air was pleasant, as Sarah sat peacefully on the small back porch of the house. That is peacefully for Sarah, anyway. Her hands had to be always busy doing something. At first it was a necessity, she must be working just to keep up with what was required to run their establishment, but now being busy was a part of her being. She was cracking and shelling pecans from a metal pail into a large bowl. Pecan pies would be on the menu soon.

The leafless trees were now starting to bud out. It was a good sign. It had been such a brutal winter. Nebraska was not a kind place in the wintertime. Frigid blasts of wind whipped over the prairie in an average winter. This winter would be one they would talk about in the record books. These pioneering sons and daughters of the plains that settled these flat, vast prairie lands had to be a hardy bunch. The ice and snow that pummeled the prairie this year was a record breaker. Many lost most of their livestock and their livelihood had been destroyed in the bitter, icy snow that had swallowed the state.

For now, though, Sarah sat enjoying the warm weather that was making its annual appearance. It was good to be outside again. Today there was no anxiety of mind. She was serene, seemingly for no reason, as the economy was what it was. Over the years she had learned to put aside the fears of things that could be, and put her trust in the one she read about each day. His book brought her peace and even optimism in times it might seem foolish. There were dark periods, but she had learned that they always passed.

As she was in the back yard enjoying her day, she was unaware the stranger had left his bedroom. His name they had learned was Lum Seow. He had spelled it for them, telling them that the last name sounded like the American girl's name of Sue. He was walking through this strange house for the first time. He slowly walked through the wonderful smelling kitchen. He knew he was getting better as the scent of food was appealing to him. He could still catch the aroma of the ham that had been fried that morning. He had hoped that there might be some rice, but scanning the kitchen quickly saw there was none. He saw on the back of the stove a pot but it had coffee in it, not green tea. On a sideboard were jars of thick cream and sugar bowls along with cups, all ready to be set on the table. The table, covered with a white table cloth was exceptionally long. Longer than any table that he had ever seen. On either side of the table were long beautiful wooden benches.

Lum Seow was not yet aware he was in a boarding house. From his eavesdropping he knew they served food, and seeing all the cookware and dishes, and the fact that there were many water buckets, with dippers in them, it was obvious many people, but something seemed strange in this house arrangement.

On a cabinet there were biscuits ready for the oven. He saw also pies that looked to be fruit. His taste buds were obviously coming back to life. Since he had come out of his room for the first time to see this place in which he had been recuperating from his wounds, he was glad there was none of the people in the kitchen he had seen periodically pass his door while he was in bed. He felt free to take the whole place in with no one watching him.

As he was walking through the kitchen, meaning to explore the rest of the house, and find his two hosts, he glanced at the screen door going out into the back yard. He saw Sarah, sitting in the yard with her back to him, obviously busy with something. As her back was turned toward him, and gazing down at the task in her lap, she could not see him.

As Sarah sat preoccupied, on the old weathered bench that had seen too many winters, she suddenly was aware that someone was standing behind her. How startled she was when she looked up and saw Lum Seow standing there. She wasn't aware he had even been getting up.

As a matter of fact, he had been a man on a mission. He had been getting up for some time, pacing around the room trying to get his strength up. He had been doing exercises from his country to strengthen himself from that day he first heard her talk to her son about the need for help. They had revealed much about their lives during the time they did not know he understood English.

Lum Seow was more startled than Sarah was, for he was looking out at the landscape that surrounded them. This being his first view outside that small room, from the night he was taken from that pitch black railroad car into the dark of a dimly lit room to be cared for, he was amazed at this new outdoor scenery. As he looked out over the wide open prairie and to the blue horizon, he felt he had suddenly been transported to another world. A gust of brisk prairie wind blew across his face and he shivered. Was it the chilly feel of free blowing wind, that is loosed in wild areas where there are no buildings to block it, or the shock of being in what looks like another world? He did not know, for truly Lum Seow was in another strange world. Stranger than any he had ever seen. As he stood, as if transfixed, a jackrabbit, which he had never seen before, bounded across a path into the prairie grass.

On the distant horizon, a sight he could never see in the place he had come from, because of the buildings that had surrounded him, were a line of trees that seemed dwarfed for they were so far away. He stood in awe, while looking at the clear blue sky, untouched by smoke, beautiful white fleecy clouds and a view unlike anything he had ever seen in such a colorful, natural, scenic, and beautiful panorama.

Was this heaven? He thought to himself. Strange, he reasoned, but I thought I was getting better! Perhaps this strange woman that was looking at him now, with such a glow on her face, was one who had been sent to prepare him for a heavenly world that all men hoped to go to. Amazed as she cared for him over the past days, he had thought how angelic and gentle she was. Perhaps, she really was! Did angels wear aprons?

At that point, he turned his head from the breath-taking scenery he had been looking at, and turned his eyes, to the surprised, glowing face of Sarah. Unable to speak with her surprise and joy at seeing him not only up, but outside, she jumped from her chair and grabbed both his hands. Wordless, with outright joy still on her face, she withdrew one of her hands and pointed to the bentwood bench for him to sit down. The glow on her face confirmed what he had just started to suspect.

He did what she had bid him do, for he suddenly realized he wasn't as strong as he thought he was. His legs were getting shaky. As he seated himself, he wondered what the protocol in heaven was. Do you bid an angel to sit beside you on a lone bench that she had been sitting on? He smiled to himself, knowing his thoughts were foolishness.

Sitting down, slowly, he again gazed out to the landscape in amazement and in awe of this strange new, beautiful and spacious land he was seeing.

This was indeed a different view from the city he had been raised in since he was nine years old and had never been outside of. John, after the death of his mother, brought to the land of America, had not been outside of San Francisco China Town. While in Canton his memories as a young boy were few, outside of losing his mother, but he remembered a few fuzzy things. However, to him, the scenery and life in San Francisco China Town didn't look a lot different than China. He did remember how terribly sick he was on the 30 day journey from China and people trying to force him to eat on that long ship ride. His uncle raised him in the town of San Francisco and he had never been outside of that place that had become home to him. It was the only scenery he had seen for thirty years.

San Francisco China Town had only buildings crammed together. There was no land to see. Buildings, shops, little stands, and businesses side by side was the place Lum Seow knew his whole life. His uncle's mercantile was one of those places, and as he grew to manhood, he inherited his partnership in that business. His life had been a city crowded with people, and ever busy and noisy with the talking of many people. If he looked straight up, he could see the sky in the place he called home, but sometimes clotheslines overhead above the busy street hid the view of the sky. For the Chinese laundries flourished in China Town.

Now he was staring out over an expanse of land where the view of the land went to the skyline on a faraway horizon. He could not see it, but on the other side of the trees, on the edge of the horizon there was a creek that until recently had been iced over. It had been the place the earliest settlers had gotten water.

A strange looking bird flew overhead. A bird he had not seen one like before. It floated or soared in a big circle, not seeming to even move its wings. Not as one of the gulls he was used to flying over China Town. Where am I? His mind cried out. As he watched, the large floating bird was still circling as if looking for something. Then suddenly it swooped down, and picking up some small struggling thing, it flew quickly out of sight. What it had captured he did not know.

He turned his gaze back to Sarah as she had sat down by him on the bench. He surprised her by talking. "Is this your land?" He pointed to the horizon.

Sarah saw he was overwhelmed with the view, but thought only that he was enjoying the beauty of spring as she had been this morning. She did not connect with the fact that he had never seen a prairie.

She was pleasantly surprised as he engaged her in conversation and questions. She had picked up her bowl of pecans and again her work started as they talked. He certainly must be getting better she thought to herself. She wished Clyde would hurry home from the wheel-wrights so that he could see Lum Seow's remarkable recovery. She didn't know how weak he was suddenly feeling at the moment.

Lum Seow turned his full attention to Sarah. It was his first time to see her in sunlight. Only had he seen her in the little room with lamplight and in the day-time the curtains had kept bright light out. She had arranged the windows so he could rest. He took in every feature of her face and took note that her upswept brown hair was graying at the temples in an attractive way. She had pleasant facial features he decided. He thought maybe she was about fifteen years older than he was. He had already seen in his room that she was about the same build and stature of Asian women. Maybe she was a little taller than some. His brow wrinkled for a moment as the question came to his mind of why a strange woman, a perfect stranger, of another culture would take such tender care of him as she had.

To her surprise, he reached over and tried to take the half full bowl from her hands. She smiled, and shook her head no. Looking at her with pleading eyes, he simply said, "Please."

She relinquished her work to him. It would not be the last time. Sarah did not know Chinese ways, but Lum Seow had a debt he felt he must pay. In his weakened condition, this was at least something he could do.

A PUZZLEMENT

Sarah arose at the usual hour, much before daylight. She put on her robe and went down the stairs with her mind already in the kitchen. Actually, what she did, she did by rote, and she was on her way mechanically to get ready the breakfast meal for the guests and tenants. When she passed the table in the entrance she picked up the Bible on the small table.

In the hall way in the dancing shadows of the lantern, she was passed by Clyde who was bringing in the firewood for the day for the cook stove. She put down her oil lamp and the Bible on the kitchen sideboard, and said hello to Mary who was pouring the cream into the containers. She had already attended to the lamps in the kitchen. Clyde had done the milking that morning as the pails were sitting full on the cabinet.

Sarah turned to wash her hands in the basin beside the water pail, as Mary said, "Sarah, I see that you got up early to make the bread, this morning. Didn't you sleep well?"

Puzzled at her question, she turned and looked at the kneading bowls. They were full and covered with the cloths she used for that purpose. Obviously, the bread was in the process of rising. Sitting to the side of the dough for the bread for the day, were pans of floury baking powder biscuits waiting for the oven for the breakfast meal.

"Mary," she replied, with a surprised tone, "I didn't do this! Who did?"

"Well, I know it wasn't Clyde. You know he couldn't cook a lick, even if he was starving. He wouldn't know the first thing about putting together a recipe."

"Mary are you sure you didn't do this, and you are just trying to be funny? Who else could have done this? No one else arrives this early," said Sarah.

"I swear Sarah, I didn't do this," Mary replied. "Maybe the Swedish girl Sondra came back. Maybe she changed her mind."

"No Mary," Sarah said as she started to investigate the kitchen. "I saw their covered wagon leave town myself. I waved goodbye to her family." Looking at the cook stove, she asked, "Did you make this green tea?"

"No Ma'am, I would never do that! The only time I have ever taken a taste was once when you made it for Lum Seow and I felt some curiosity about the taste. I thought it was a terrible tasting concoction. No proper English person who knows her tea would ever swallow that foul, evil substitute for a tea. I would certainly never take another tiny taste of it, even were I to be horribly, pitifully sick."

The light came on in Sarah's mind about the mystery cook but plain sense said the man could not make flour dough yeast bread. Surely not! However, there could be no other answer. She turned, picked up a lamp, and left the kitchen going down the hall to the bedroom that had been made for their Chinese patient. Slowly and quietly she opened the door, lifting her lamp to peek inside. Lum Seow appeared to be sleeping soundly. She quietly shut the door, taking care not to awaken him. She turned and went back to the kitchen, wondering what had happened.

When the door closed behind her, Lum Seow's eyes opened, he raised his head a moment, smiled, turned over, and then laid his head down. The smile remained on his face a long time until he really drifted off to sleep.

As Sarah entered the kitchen, Clyde walked in with more wood for the parlor, so it would be warm when the guests began to rise. He looked surprised as Mary stopped him.

"Clyde," she said, "Did you make some bread dough this morning?"

Clyde looked at her with a funny look on his face. "Yeah, sure," he said sarcastically. Then he saw that she was serious. "As close as I ever came to raw bread dough was when I got that belly ache from snitching some of Mom's cinnamon rolls before they rose. I've had a hard time even looking at any raw dough since then. Why? Why would you ask me that?"

"Never mind," said the perplexed Mary. "Go put the wood in before the guests start to gather in the parlor. You know how fussy old Mr. Suggett can be early in the morning. We would never hear the end of it if there was not a nice fire for him to sit in front of. He always tries to beat everyone in there so he can get the best place. Then he spends the rest of the day fussing and fuming about not being able to sleep due to the other guest's snoring. It's quite ridiculous about him not getting any sleep when his snoring all night keeps everyone else awake. Then he sits in the best chair, sleeping all day, but refuses to get up and go to bed if we suggest it, because he's afraid someone might get what he thinks is 'His chair'."

"Yeah, I know," said Clyde, "If it was up to me, I would ask him to leave, but you know how tenderhearted Mom is."

"Mary, if you don't have as much work to do this morning, do you want to help me get the fire started? Since we've been short-handed we haven't got to talk much lately. I've been thinking on an exciting plan, I want to share with you."

"Clyde, it seems as if you always have an exciting new plan going. Sometimes you just amaze me. What outlandish thing have you been thinking on of late?"

"Mary, now don't be a talkin' to me in your snooty English ways." He pulled her close and said with a grin, "Ya know you used to always like my outlandish ways, as you call them."

"Well, that phrase came to mind because my parents accused you of being outlandish and too impetuous when I said I wanted to marry you. Of course, I would defend you to them, but I have to tell you, I never know what to expect from you. I was hoping having children would settle you some, but instead you use them as an excuse to play their silly little games just as if you were one of them."

"Are you saying I'm childish?" he said, as he stiffened up and pulled away from her.

"Oh no, Clyde! I wouldn't change you for the world. The children love you for the way you can play imaginary games with them. I'm the only disciplinarian in the house and so they like you better. You're childlike with them in a good way. They adore you."

Clyde now softening, said, "I know you've been upset with me over putting little Jack with me on the horse, as small as he is, but you know I would never let anything happen to that sweet little baby boy. Just look at our Ruby, she's just a wee bit 'o lassie and yet can ride the paint just like her dad could at that age when Cousin Vic taught me."

"I have just given it all up. I've had to or go crazy with worry. Between you and your wild-west ways and your mom spoiling them to death, I wonder what on earth they will be when they grow up. Ruby is sure not going to be a proper lady, as I would wish she would be."

"Have ya forgotten our early days when we first met? Remember how after you got off work you would ride with me out on the prairie? You know you loved to watch me do my trick riding, when we were out there alone. Remember how we would have contests on who could shoot the most pheasants. It took me a while to get used to you being the best shot. Yet all that was what made me want you for my own. That was the thing that drew me to you. You seemed to like excitement. You did things that most girls were too prissy to do. Well, I want Ruby to be just like you were. That's why I take her ridin'. Don't ya be a worryin' now, my little Mary," he said pulling her close again, "She'll be as fine and beautiful a little lassie as her mother is. And don't ya be a worryin' about Jackie me boy. There canna be a finer lad in this prairie land."

He knew she loved it when he used his Irish accent. He had picked it up from spending time with his uncles and could fall back into it easily. He used it many times to relieve tension between them. She laid her head against his chest for a moment.

"Come on into the parlor, Mary. I want to talk to you about this plan I've got." And as she always ended up doing, the ever so proper and serious and conventional Mary walked with his arm around her into the private parlor, as a lamb to the slaughter. As they would say in the land of his parentage, which he had never visited, "Surely he had kissed the Blarney Stone." He was full of it and his Mary loved it.

A short time later, as Sarah was rolling out pie dough in the kitchen, she heard a loud cry from the parlor. "No! Absolutely not! No, No, NO!" Sarah, alarmed at the usually calm Mary yelling in such a way, wiped her floury hands on her apron as she ran into the parlor.

"What on earth is wrong, Mary?" she asked. Mary, with a reddened face, pointed to Clyde who had his head down looking at the parlor carpet, exclaimed in a distressed tone, "He wants to start a Wild West Show!"

Resorting to an old expression passed down from her father's people, with her hand to her mouth, Sarah exclaimed aloud, "The Saints Preserve Us! So it's come to this!"

A BARGAIN STRUCK

The man was now spending more and more time out of his room and more time trying to help with the chores that were being done. He was continually taking things out of Sarah's hands and trying to complete her task, whatever it was. Finally, Sarah would allow him to do so, not wanting to offend him. Not so with the not very appreciative Mary. Somehow she took offense, and would grasp tightly whatever he would try to relieve her of. She would give him a discouraging look that only the very British Mary could give, and so he finally gave up his attention to her. In her mind he was "that interfering Chinaman". Observing Sarah, though, he would relieve her of her chore and she would move on to her next task. She realized that he was trying to not only be of help, but many times he was observing, so he could learn what the daily routine was. Many seemed to be the things he was not familiar with, but he caught on quickly and was really being a great help. As he went about these things, he was usually quiet, unless he was asked a question.

Surprisingly one day he started a conversation as he and Sarah were working together preparing some vegetables. She was startled as he spoke to her. "I would like to work for you as an employee," Lum Seow said. Sarah's heart dropped, because she had learned to like Lum Seow, but she knew what circumstances said the answer must be. "Oh Lum Seow, you work so well and you are so much help, but I do not have the money to pay another person, now. It is such a bad time for us. We are not financially able to hire anyone now because we have had a really bad season."

"Miss Sarah," he spoke slowly, as if gathering the words he wanted to say. "It is I who owe you money."

She was startled, as he had not called her by name before.

"I have a need to give money to you. You have taken care of me and I think was it not for your kind care to me I would have died. The time you gave to care for me took you away from work you needed to be doing in the kitchen or with your guests. I have taken up a room you could have used for a customer. You have fed me food, and given me medicine. It is I who owe you," he stated firmly. He seldom looked directly into her eyes, but he was looking pleadingly so now. He continued, "Surely you would not think I would need pay. This would be a way you could allow me to repay you what I owe you."

She looked at his face, feeling a strange compassion that he would feel any need to repay her for what she would do for anyone as seriously hurt as he was when he arrived. She was prepared to say that she would have done that for anyone in such a situation, when he continued on. She listened, quietly amazed, as this was the most words he had spoken since he arrived.

He went on. "As for the room I have been taking, if you would allow me to stay and help, I could pay for what rent you lost on that room. I would be happy to stay in the barn. It's better than many people's houses."

That did it. Sarah had to interrupt. "You don't understand Lum Seow. That room, because of its location behind the kitchen, and because it is near the back of the house, we don't use for our guests. We generally keep it empty, unless we have some kind of emergency, or there is an overflow or staff stays overnight because of weather. We took you there because it was an easy way to get you in the house and it would be a private place where you would not be disturbed and it would be quiet there. There we could care for you out of the traffic of what goes on here. I have actually felt badly we have had you there as it is so small. We have never felt you owed us anything. That was just our way to help someone who had a need, as you did. It's our way. You would have done the same for anyone of us, I am sure."

"Would you please do this kindness for me and allow me to stay here and work?" he again pleaded. "It would bring me great pleasure to help you, since you need someone to help you. You and your family work too hard, and Mary has two small children that need her. It is the Chinese way to help someone who helps them. Miss Sarah, you saved my life. In my culture, I owe you mine. I could be of help. I would leave when you decide it's time for me to go. Anytime, you could tell me to go."

Sarah's heart was greatly touched at this man's offer but her mind went to Mary's exasperation at his continually trying to take things out of her hand. She knew she couldn't make this decision without Clyde and Mary's agreement. Clyde seemed to already have developed a great liking for this man, but she wanted this to cause no repercussions to the family.

"Lum Seow," she said, gently touching his arm, "Let me think about this please. We will talk later. I really can't say now. I will think about it."

As Sarah and Lum Seow were having their discussion, Mary walked into the barn where Clyde was doing chores. "Clyde," she said in a questioning tone, "You haven't picked flowers for me since before we were married. What a nice surprise!"

Clyde looked up with a surprised look on his face, his pitchfork in midair. "What flowers?" Clyde asked, "I haven't been picking any flowers."

Mary at once knew he had no idea of what she was talking about. She stood with her hands on her hips, thinking for a moment. Her blue eyes squinted as she tried to fathom the mystery. "Who else would do that?" she queried.

Clyde, still perplexed said, "What flowers are you talking about?"

"Someone put a glass jar of flowers on the table in our room. They are on the little round table in front of the settee. Who would have done that?"

Clyde, continuing his hay work said, "Did you ask Mom about it? Maybe she did it. She's never done that before though, has she?" Mary, shaking her head no, stood with a questioning look on her brow. She paused for a brief time watching Clyde. Then she went back to the house to see about the children. With two that small she couldn't leave them unsupervised very long without expecting them to get into mischief. She was right. They had pulled up a chair and were enjoying the fresh cherry pie, leaving much evidence on their faces and had wiped their hands on the tablecloth.

In the meantime, Sarah sat in her favorite chair, furiously shelling Green Peas, having a wordless conversation with herself. There had never been help that had been allowed to stay in the house overnight before. Least of all, this man they knew nothing about. On the other hand, he had proved himself when he surprised them with the light bread and biscuits, which is rare for a man. However, what would it do to her daughter- in-law's disposition to have this "overly helpful" man under her feet? Would it cause family problems? Mary also seemed to resent all the time Clyde was reading to Lum Seow while he worked, as he was so interested in the daily news in Clyde's newspapers.

On the other hand he had been in the house a long time and there had been no thievery, murder, or mayhem. He was a very likeable, sweet, attentive man to the guests. As to them thinking it was strange, she understood some of the high class restaurants in Omaha had Chinese men in special costumes to cook for the guests. Plus, the work load he had taken on was phenomenal. They really needed someone desperately and he was someone that didn't have to be continually told what to do, as some help had required.

Also, as to being on the premises, that would solve the problem of the staff getting here on snowy, icy days. He would be here ready to work. That really was a problem in the winter.

She really liked the idea of having Lum Seow as an employee, but she would leave the final decision to Clyde. After all, he had a wife and two children to think about. It would be his decision. She knew that if he liked the idea, he had ways of getting Mary to see it his way with a little sweet talk and coaxing.

As she got up from her seat, and placed the bowl of peas on the straw seat and went to look for Clyde, she saw him carrying a heavy bag of feed across the barnyard. She thought, it surely would be nice to have some dependable help around the place. At least until they got their feet on the ground again. If he proved himself, he might be the dependable one that might stay on for a while.

As she paused and watched her over-worked son continue on with the back breaking work that was his daily to do, she knew that the offer that was made was certainly a Godsend. If Clyde agreed, though, Lum Seow certainly wasn't going to sleep in any barn. If things worked out and all went well, he would also get more than room and board.

She approached Clyde to tell him of Lum Seow's request. She could tell by the look on his face, as he was wiping the sweat from his face with his handkerchief, that the timing was right. He was just quietly nodding his head.

A NEW EMPLOYEE
Just John

The family council met and all agreed. The meeting was called to order and the decision was unanimous. Lum Seow was now a permanent part of the boarding house staff. Even Mary found herself agreeing, being won over by the flowers.

Lum Seow was called into the meeting and was told the decision. The little family happily, on seeing his smile at being accepted, gathered around him extending a hand to shake. With a huge smile from ear to ear, he went around the little welcoming circle. As he shook each of their hands, he then gave a deep Chinese bow. Even the very proper Mary smiled and found to her embarrassment herself bowing back. Lum Seow asked, "May I ask a favor?"

Clyde becoming tentative and wondering what the request might be said, "What's that?"

With a now serious look on his face, the Asian man said "Would you call me an American name I would like to take?"

"Of course," Sarah answered, "What name would that be?"

"John," he replied.

"That's a good name," Clyde said, "John what?"

"Just John," he replied.

"No last name?" Mary inquired.

"Just John," he said firmly.

All looking at one another in the little circle, and smiling, Clyde said, "John it is." So it was that a Chinese man started his life in a prairie town among all the other immigrants that had moved to the frontier town of Tecumseh, Nebraska. Somehow, in the midst of the other immigrants, he stood out more, being the only Chinese person in town, and so acquired the name "Chinaman John" for identification when they discussed him. However, they called him John to his face. Of course, there were a few of those that called him "the Chinaman."

To those that learned to love him he became just plain "John."

Lum Seow (John)
as a young man in Tecumseh

JOHN FINDS HIS PLACE

The day was half over. The new cook in residence was well past the chores he had assigned himself. As Sarah and Clyde were sitting in the back porch chairs doing some work that would lead to the supper meal, he came and sat beside them. He picked up the peas that they were shelling and started to speak as he worked with his hands.

"I have something I would like to do with your permission. I have in the past planted gardens. I have found it is helpful to do this because it is cheaper than buying vegetables from others for my own meals, but also it is something I have liked to do in my spare time. With this big space of land behind the hotel, you could have a good size garden and not pay the farmers for the vegetables you are using. I think it would save you much money.

"It would seem as no trouble to me, as it has been something I have liked to do. In my past, I have always had a garden and it would provide me joy. This would be big enough to supply your guests and save much money," he repeated. "I have seemed to have good fortune with plants. I like very much to work in the soil. It is as rest to me when I do it. I could do it when I am through with the other work that needs to be done in your employ."

Clyde and Sarah both looked at him in amazement. This was to them a new idea. Sarah, who had started her business as a young woman, had never gardened and was just overwhelmed with the work of the business itself and never even considered the extra work of a garden. Clyde was small when she started the business and certainly he had never any knowledge of gardening. They sat there stunned for a minute, mainly for the man who worked so hard, they couldn't imagine him crowding this into his day. They were shocked at him offering to do this.

Clyde said, "John, I see how this could save money, and it's a wonderful idea of you to volunteer more time than you already work, but there would be an expense of going into it to begin with. Money, as you well know, has been a problem."

Sarah interrupted Clyde, for she was interested in this new idea. "John," she said, "Are you sure you could handle the gardening? It sounds like an awfully big job? You already do so much for the hotel."

"But Miss Sarah, some men read in their spare time. Some men play cards. I see many people here in the parlor, not only playing cards but checkers. Other men hunt, like Clyde. Some men like to fish. Some men play games with horse shoes near here in your back yard behind the barn. They pass their time every day doing a thing they enjoy. I have always liked to work with the soil. I like seeing things come out of the ground. I have missed it so much since I have been in Nebraska. You have so much land here that could be useful. Could you please consider this?"

"Clyde," said Sarah, turning to her son, "Mr. Swenson at the mercantile told me that if I ever needed to charge for a little while, he would be glad to let me do that. Maybe we could charge some seed. I actually think this is a most wonderful idea John has."

Clyde was getting excited now. "We could borrow the plow and oxen from your brother, Mom. I'm sure Uncle Jerome would be glad to loan them if he's not using them now. I could get Victor to go with me and help me bring them here. I haven't been to their homestead in a while now. I'd like to visit with the family."

John sat there quietly as everything was unfolding between his two employers with a smile in his heart.

It was his plan to dig the garden on his own. He never dreamed there could be help from a plow and oxen. The Nebraska ground was packed hard. He was not sure if he could use the oxen or not but he would try, he thought. To be able to help this family that had been so kind to him was his fondest dream and this seemed to be a way. He did know there had always been a gift in his hands to bring forth from the earth. If he could get the hard ground broken, there was no limit on how much garden he could make for Clyde and Miss Sarah. Maybe even enough to sell.

Clyde, always ready for a new project, jumped up and said, "John, come with me. We'll go up to the General Mercantile and we'll get started on the seed buying. I'll hitch up the buckboard."

While Clyde was getting the wagon ready, John went in the house to get his flour sack. It was his special sack that people had learned to see him with when he went on an errand for the kitchen. Of course, that sack always held candy, and Ruby and Jack got excited when they saw the sack. Coming back from errands he would throw it over his shoulder and start his short journey home. Clyde had taught him to drive the team not long after he became a part of the hotel. However, on foot, he was always seen by the town, walking with that familiar sack over his shoulder. That was the way it had been done in China Town.

At first, "The Chinaman" had caused a stir in Tecumseh. There were no Chinese residents there and he was used to being stared at. Any Asians that had come to America, the west coast had been their point of entry. As the railroads crossed the continents they began to be seen with the building of the rails. He was stared at, this Asian man. He was probably suspect at first. Whispers and gossip where prevalent at first. People talked about the mysterious ways that they had heard about when they discussed "those kind of people." Outright lies in years to come would be told about his role at the boarding house and in the life of the family there. Heads turned as he walked down the boardwalk to the Mercantile or took the wagon to the feed and seed store. Who knows what was in his heart when he was stared at?

Whether John was just kind, or whether he was trying to make people trust him, the citizens saw this man do kindnesses to them, as he gradually was seen among them on a regular basis. So it was he was slowly accepted by the population, but he would forever remain "Chinaman John."

Whether he assumed it was a way for a new people to recognize him, for there were many Johns in America or there was some other reason, John never expressed what he thought about his new name. He knew, more than anyone, he was a rarity in "this neck of the woods", if you can use that expression on a treeless prairie. He must have noticed that no one ever called Clyde by the name of Irishman Clyde, or for that matter, Clyde's wife Mary Edna by the name of Englishwoman Mary Edna. He was "the one and only" in this little town. He would be forever Chinaman John. None meant any disrespect. It was his name.

The word "Chinese" would be there, as if to point out his birthplace, the rest of his life. When he was made a member of the Tecumseh Presbyterian Church, in 1899, it seemed strange that a Pastor J. A. Pollock, declared on a certificate that "To Whom it May Concern, that Mr. Lum Seow, a Chinaman, is a member in good standing of The First Presbyterian Church of Tecumseh". Many years later when mentioned in a newspaper obituary of a friend, he was called "Lum Seow, a Chinese".

One thing he never discussed was how he came to be on a train and found by the family that adopted him. He chose not to tell. They chose not to ask. He told of his background. He had been a mercantile owner in China Town. Was he accosted by a Chinese-type Mafia, who charged merchants money for "protection", and to add further injury to a refusal to pay threw the severely wounded man on a boxcar, bound for wherever? These are questions that have been speculated about, but have never been answered for certain.

Railroads brought masses of Asian men across this continent as the wonder that opened this continent to settlement was laboriously built by the last, bottom of the work force immigrants to come. Whatever it was that put that man in a Nebraska Hotel in his thirty-ninth year would impact another family's life forever.

Together, he and Clyde took the wagon down the dusty street, and seeds were carefully selected. A good supply was loaded on the wagon and was brought back to the shed in the back. John then went back in the house to see to the things that needed doing in the kitchen. His chores called him.

In the meantime, Clyde had bid a hasty farewell to Sarah and Mary and went quickly off to his next big adventure to pick up his Cousin Victor and go to his Uncle Jerome's farmhouse which was a distance from Tecumseh at Elk Creek. Those left at the boarding house had to take up the slack. He knew the three could get along, they always had, even before John came along. .

Now the idea of planting was not Clyde's idea of an adventure nor did it appeal to him, although he could see the advantage of it. Men of his time and his bent, so Clyde thought, were made for another life on the prairie. They had to subdue beasts for food. The frontier prairie was their kingdom. They must shoot game from the sky.

Even battle the cold and hot elements to do it. He might spend days looking for his prey. The prey being used for food was just a special perk, so to speak. It was all in "The Hunt". For Clyde, on for something new would always be his hearts wish. He was not made to cultivate the earth. Now he could whack his way through the tall, thick prairie grass to look for elk or deer, but to take care of a field, that was another man's kingdom.

Now some men, such as John, are made to subdue the hard earth. The earth is their adventure. The soil is the thing they love and wrestle with to bring forth their sustenance. These two men would make a good match in the life they were choosing – one a hunter and one a man of the soil. Each to answer his own call to take care of that thing they were born for.

Clyde would always hear the call for adventure. It seems he and his Cousin Vic Anderson were made of the same adventuresome blood. Adventure calls and they must go.

In the meantime, the guests were to be taken care of. Boarders were now at the table as they had been missing during the winter storm. The travelers were back to pay their room and board. Heat from the oven brought forth the aroma of baking bread. There was the smell of the fresh, sweet cinnamon rolls. John was dishing up bowls of hot, bubbling soup and roasts. Ham and potatoes were the main meals. There was sweet cream butter being set on the table along with frosty milk, jellies and pies. Life continued as usual.

Mary was quickly and efficiently attending to the guest's needs along with Sarah. Sarah's grandchildren were taking the place in the boarding house that Clyde had in his youth. The center of attention and taking for granted that they just had a big family of people around them of both familiar and strange people. The children were quietly having their meal in the corner of the kitchen at the little table and chairs that Clyde had built for them. The baby was tied to his little chair and little Ruby was carefully minding him as they ate. The puppy that their Dad made sure they had, was lying beside them hoping they would drop a crumb. John continued his work and all the while thinking joyfully of his garden for the family. Sarah must have been thinking the same, for when she caught his eye, her eyes crinkled and creased with a smile.

The guests were summoned in by Sarah, and all set in their places if they were the usual roomers. Those that were new were escorted to a place at the inviting looking table. All smelled the kitchen aromas, appreciatively. The taste of the food would not disappoint them. Tried and true favorites were always on the menu. To the guests, even a Chinese man wearing a white apron and white kitchen cap serving up steaming soup to each individual, seemed a nice addition to a well set table.

Sarah took a moment to look at the ever working, flush faced Mary. She was never still a moment and always doing what needed to be done. Yet, she seemingly effortlessly took care of two very small children. Clyde definitely had picked out a hardworking wife for himself.

Sarah turned her head in time to see John carrying out the coal bucket and knew he would see about the kindling to make sure that all would stay warm tonight. The spring air got cool at night on the prairie. She knew that all would all be taken care of, even with Clyde being gone for a short spell. What an asset John was.

She suddenly realized how blessed she was to have those in the kitchen that were there. As if to add a large amen to her thoughts, the babies started giggling together, as the puppy licked their toes.

THE HOUSE OF ZEBULUN

Oh that I had in the wilderness a lodging place for wayfaring men. - Jeremiah 9:2

As long as Clyde could remember he would see his mother doing one thing very early in the morning for it was her routine daily. She would get up, pour a cup of tea, and get her Bible. Sitting down by the lantern, she began to read in the old rocker. That Bible had always rested on the table by that chair as long as he could remember. If they moved, the table and Bible took up the same place of prominence. He remembered from his childhood it had rested on an old trunk. He did remember because he had asked to see what was in the trunk. She had said no and he had secretly tried to open it, as a naughty child would do, and found it locked.

He knew from what she had told him that the Bible was very important to her. She made sure as a child that he knew all the famous Bible stories. More than anything, she made sure her little boy knew about the God Man named Jesus and that he needed to believe in Him and make Him important in his life. He didn't learn just by her telling him to talk to Him every day, but seeing her do it and hearing her prayers. He had seen miraculous things happen in answer to her believing prayers.

When Clyde was a much older man, Sarah revealed to him why this Son of God was so important in her life. One day just before leaving Tecumseh, while sitting in the kitchen, Clyde asked her when God had become such a part of her life. It was then that she started talking freely about her relationship with Jesus and the Book and how it came about.

Sarah revealed a story he had not known existed. She explained that when he was small, and his father had died, she was so brokenhearted without him that she was terribly depressed. She didn't even want to live. She was in sheer misery every day. Her mind was totally upon his father, Zebulun, and the mystery of what had happened to him. Her misery and grief consumed her and she thought of ending her life to shut her mind off and kill the day and nightlong overwhelming pain she felt. Nurses know ways to do that medically, she had said. However, she said, the thought of her young precious son would come to her, and with the knowing that she could not abandon him, she would dismiss the thought. She could not leave him alone or in someone else's care even though she knew her family loved him very much. Sheer love for him kept her from doing the unforgivable thing of ending her life. The sunshine of a small beloved boy would break through the menacing thoughts she would have when he would come and hug her or do something cute or sweet. Her mother's heart had prevented her from taking her life.

One day, as she was alone, the pain was overwhelming. She felt as though she was literally being driven crazy with painful thoughts of Zebulun and his memory, and her loss and the crying started again. She was so tormented and she felt as if she could face her loss no longer. How, she asked herself, could she raise this son of hers if this insanity gripped her mind?

As she told her story to her son it seemed she drifted off, and was no longer talking to him, but reminiscing to herself on something she had not thought upon for many years. He had never seen this side of his mother and he could not imagine it existed. He had always thought she was one of the strongest women he had ever seen and took a certain pride in that.

As she continued her story, she told him of a day when a dramatic change came. In the midst of her agony and in the darkness of one of these moods that almost drowned her, she cried out, "God if you're real, help me!"

"To my surprise," she said, "Right there where I was sitting, words that my mother Catherine had spoken flashed into my mind out of nowhere. I had not thought of those words since the day they had been spoken. Almost like a phantom, I could see mother sitting and facing me. I saw her lovely face as it was then, when that forgotten conversation came back to me".

She had asked her mother why she read that worn Bible of hers every day. She inquired of what value the old archaic words were to her. She told her that she tried to read it, because it seemed important to her, and yet she understood nothing it said.

"Oh my Sarah," she had said, "It's not the book. It's the person who is behind the book. It's the LORD Himself. Once you ask Him to come into your life, He comes to you in a life-changing way.

"I remember too, having the feelings and pains you are feeling once Sarah," she had continued as she looked at her compassionately. "When your father was killed, I wanted to die myself. I too, as you have, became overwhelmed with the pain of my loss. I had questionings about the Bible up until that time about its very truth, in one way, and yet knowing down deep, that those that had gone before me didn't doubt it or the One of which it spoke. I remembered the faith your father had and something began to pull at me in my mind. Of course, at first I had no idea it was God Himself that was pulling me closer to Him. He was calling me to seek Him. It was Him who was drawing me to come to Him. Even, the wounds of our terrible, painful experiences can be Him calling you, Sarah. He's calling you to search Him out for He is the only one that can take away life shattering pain. I've heard others who said they came to Him through great pain, trial, or mourning. He calls us to Him in different ways, and with me it was the sudden death of your father in the horse runaway."

She had continued, "In the midst of that terrible pain and loss, I picked up Michael's tattered Bible. My eyes fell upon a passage of scripture spoken by Jesus that said, "If you seek Me with your whole heart, you will find Me."

"Then something else was magnified as I flipped the pages," Catherine had said, "I saw the words that said, "God is not a man that He should lie." So it was then, Sarah'" she said, "That I made a determination to test Him finally to see if I could find Him. If he would take this terrible pain away and cause me to want to live again. I set my mind that I was going to seek Him in the only way I knew how. I was going to give Him some of my time to see if He would come to me and prove He was real."

"He supernaturally came to me one day in a way I could never have expected," she said. "I got away alone with myself and that old Bible and just kept calling out loud the name of Jesus. The day I did that, He came to me and took my pain and gave me absolute peace from then on, and a love for God I had never had before."

"These are the words my mother had told me and I heard them supernaturally that day as though she were saying them again that day," Sarah said to Clyde. Then she said, "My beloved daughter, I give you the same advice. It was so real. No, I didn't see a ghost figure. I don't believe God talks to us that way. She was still alive when this happened. That day, just when I needed it most, God did give me total recall that day of a conversation my mother had with me when she was trying to share a truth with me in the past and I hadn't listened.

"Clyde, it was during a time your Uncle Jerome had asked if you could come and spend some time at his home," she continued. "You remember that week you and your cousin Victor spent time out at Elk Creek at his farm. You weren't there for me to care for and so I decided I was really going to seek God with all my heart as much as I could. I would see if He could really be found and at least take the pain away and give me a desire to live. I determined I would get alone with my Bible, for I had heard the preacher say that was the way He talked to you. I was going to spend the day with that Bible, and pray until He proved Himself to me.

"I realize now, He was drawing me to do that. The only way I know to describe what caused my decision to do that thing was that I knew some other people in my life that talked about Him as though He was real. As if God was in their lives every day. As if he heard them and answered them. They didn't just call Him God, but they called Him Jesus. I wanted to know Him like that. At that point the word Jesus made me slightly uncomfortable. God seemed ok, but not Jesus.

"So," Sarah continued, "With that longing to know Him as they did, or feel him, or discover Him, I got the Bible, put it in that old leather saddlebag, climbed on old Star and went down to a favorite place I knew on the creek. It was a place few people knew about. A secluded, leafy place where I knew I could be alone. I had gone there and cried many times, as it was away from my sister's family. I tied the old horse to a tree and walked down into the brush to a small clearing out of sight under the overhanging trees. I had made up my mind that He was going to show Himself to me in a real way. I would find Him if He was findable.

"Before the day was out Clyde, I had told God, whether He revealed Himself to me or not, I was giving myself to Him regardless. That I would do whatever He had for me to do or be. After all the reading, and all the praying I could work up and all the pleading for I wasn't sure what, Clyde, He came to me. Not in a way I thought it would be, but He literally came *into* me. He came *into* me like light, and sunshine, and love for Him, and love for His word. Love for His Bible. Love for other people. It seemed that God had come inside me *big* and there was no question that something had happened. I had some kind of encounter.

"I can look back to that day that I went after Him wholeheartedly and know that something dynamic happened to me that started to change my way of thinking. You ask me why I read that Book? It's because from that day, Jesus started talking to me from that Book. After that when I read His words my heart would pound. As I read his words, they started changing my thinking. My thoughts started sometimes being His thoughts. His words excited me and they made me want to do them. They made me feel bad when I didn't do them. Now they give me peace. They direct me many times. They give me joy. It was as if I had never lived before.

"The only way I can explain it to you, is that after that day that I gave Him my life, that very book that was old, dusty, dry words, and an old outdated book, became alive to me and made the author of that book alive and real and the most altogether lovely person I had ever known. After that day, I started to read the New Testament and it was like Jesus Himself got up off of those once dry pages and came alive. His beautiful, loving life appeared before me. He showed me how He loved me and mankind so much He gave His life for us. He showed me that I am but a sinner that He saved by His wonderful grace. The most wonderful thing is that even with all my sin and failing, He says 'I love you. Come follow Me.'"

Gripping his hands in hers she said, "Clyde, He calls you to that too. He loves you so."

After pausing and looking deep into his eyes she said, "That day I held my breath lest that love of him and his words would leave. I bowed my head that day, as I was kneeling under a tree, and to the God I had never known, I cried out and said Thank you! Thank you!

"With my eyes closed, I felt someone touch my face softly."

Clyde listened raptly to the story she told, knowing that there was a feeling like electricity in the room as she unfolded the next happening. It was something he had never felt before.

Sarah had not understood that day that it happened, but later would know that her praise and thanks to God released a dynamic that only few earthly men and all the angels know. Praise to the Creator brings Him on the scene.

She continued telling the experience she shared with her mesmerized son that day. With her head and face bowed down, she was suddenly aware someone was standing so close to her she could feel Him. It caused her to draw in her breath and stop her thanks. As she bowed there, frozen in her position, she felt a soft hand stroke her face as softly and as gently as one would stroke a sleeping baby you did not want to wake. The feel of someone standing next to her could be felt by her body. He was that close. She did not lift her head to look at this visitor, for she was afraid any movement on her part might cause this mighty, yet gentle, heavenly visitation to leave. She just breathlessly waited.

That soft gentle touch released something in her that had never been there before. Without being able to control her mouth, the thanks to God started over and over. The emotion stemmed from the thought that God Almighty would stoop from His great place to come to her! To her! Just little Sarah! He had heard her! He loved her that much! He had come! It was real!

Then she listened carefully. She heard a voice. Not a voice as one hears one on the sound waves of the air, but she heard a voice within that ripped through her mind as loudly as a voice one would hear in the natural. It reverberated through her being. It was the sweetest voice she was ever to hear. It was even sweeter to her than had been the voice of her beloved husband.

She waited, still not lifting her head in the leafy hallowed place she knelt. She knew more was coming somehow. The voice continued in its sweetness. "You allow Me to be your dwelling place and you will be Mine. I will prepare you a House of Honor. It will be a Dwelling of Honor." As those words were spoken, she suddenly remembered something she had learned long ago. The Semitic name for Zebulun had meant "Dwelling of Honor."

She continued to share what had happened in a moment that day with her son. She had felt such peace fill her. She had felt it the moment of that supernatural touch. She just stayed without lifting her head, relishing the peace that had replaced all the depression that had consumed her when her husband had disappeared. The depression was gone! Only peace! Unexplainable peace! Only joy! Unexplainable joy!

With an astounding revelation it struck her suddenly! She knew she had felt this Giver of Peace in the very midst of a living hell years ago on the battle field. It was He who had touched her and given her peace. How had she forgotten Him? How had she forgotten to keep being thankful to Him? How had she forgotten how real He was? She raised her head, wanting to see Him again.

He was not there and somehow, before she lifted her eyes, she knew he would be gone. He had left His touch, His healing of her soul, and a message. She bowed her head and continued her sweet revelry of peace. She just knelt there, enjoying the absence of all that emotion that had been like a terrible, black, consuming storm in her very being all those years. She was just enjoying the emotion of being truly thankful to the stranger that she had met on the battlefield so many years ago. He no longer was a stranger. She knew his name. It was the name others spoke so easily. Unexplainably she felt she had known Him before she was born. Even though she could not see him now, she knew his presence was still there. This Jesus!

"Clyde," she told him, "When I finally opened my eyes, He was gone. I knew who it was though and I was left with such peace, and even joy that I knew I had had a visitation from that heavenly visitor. For days and weeks and months I could think of no one but Him. From that day on, the longing and mourning for Zebulun was gone. I could not get enough of reading about Jesus in the New Testament just as my mother had said had happened to her. The peace remained. When I read his words it was like Jesus was no longer in a book but that He got up off those pages and walked across those pages. My heart would pound with their message, just as my mother had said. To this day, when I read that word, I feel He speaks to me. He guides me. He directs me. Most of all I know He sees me when I read it and He knows I am looking to Him to guide me daily and so He does." Putting her hand on the Bible on the table beside her chair she said, "That's why, my Son, I read this book."

Clyde was transfixed with this story that she had not told him before. To him, this was the adventure story of all adventure stories. He couldn't believe he had not heard it before. He couldn't imagine the mother he knew as ever having been such an anguished person. He sat for a minute, silent, taking it all in. Then he asked a question.

"Mom, what about the message? What did the House of Honor mean? I understand the dwelling place because you said you felt like he lived in you every day since the encounter or at least His word did. What did a dwelling of honor mean?"

"Son, I don't think I ever told you about your father's name."

"Yes, you did. You said it was some Bible name. It came from a tribe of the original people of the Israeli people. It was the tribe of Zebulun. You told me he was a son of the Patriarch Jacob, who was later called Israel. You told me that my father's mother, who knew her Bible, named my father that because number one, her name was Leah and dad was her sixth son so she named him Zebulun. In other words he was a sixth and last son of a woman named Leah like she read about in the Bible.

"Of course, the main thing I know is something you have always reminded me of. That I was to live up to the original meaning of my father's name, Zebulun, which meant "A Dwelling of Honor." You reminded me my whole life in every little thing I was to do, to do the honorable thing. Later, as a man as I have had decisions to make you have said no more to me than to 'Remember you are from the House of Zebulun.' Of course, it would be kind of aggravating to me at times when you said that, because sometimes I would be leaning toward doing something else which would seem beneficial to me and not always being the honorable thing. That's what The

House of Zebulun means to me. It meant a standard to live up to in an honorable way."

Clyde shifted forward in his chair. Taking her hands he said, "I wish I could have known him, Mom." There were tears in his eyes.

"I have wished that many times son, when you do things I'm proud of you for. I see him in you in so many little ways. Especially in the bent to want new adventure that possesses you. I have wished it for his sake too, that he could have seen you as the man you've grown to be. As the man I am proud of."

At that sentence, Clyde leaned forward and laid his forehead on her hands for a minute. It was an emotional moment for the two of them. After a moment, Clyde raised his head and slid back in his chair while taking a wrinkled handkerchief from his pocket. For a moment neither spoke, not knowing what to say to one another. As men are, Clyde was embarrassed by showing emotion.

Sarah interrupted the awkward situation with a continuing explanation of the name of Clyde's father. "There is one thing I've not shared with you about this name influencing me in my decisions," she said. "It concerns the word spoken to me by the Lord when he said, 'Honor your husband's name in all you do.' It was a long time before I knew what that meant. It concerns some of the things you have seen me do in business and relationships. I know you know I'm very careful in my honesty with all things. 'Down to the last degree and in excess' you've called it.

"I know what I am telling you seems possibly foolish, but I want to share with you what has directed my life," Sarah continued, "But now I feel it's time to share with you the motivations of things you haven't understood. You thought I made a bad decision once and I've always wanted to explain it to you.

"As you became older, you had to be aware there were men that crossed my path, either here in Tecumseh, or travelers who spent their time here as guests as they traveled through, that seemed interested in me with romantic intentions, which I didn't return. Some intentions were good, some were not. A few were just traveling men who had wives and families at home and I quickly discouraged those. Actually, I have never seen anyone that I ever felt a drawing to in the way of a romantic entanglement or as to marriage. That never was a consideration. My mother never felt allegiance to anyone but my father, and I guess some women are just that way.

"I really felt your disapproval when Mr. Carlyle became one of our regular guests and he was making it plain he had an interest in me and I was rejecting him. I knew you liked him and thought he was a great fellow. He seemed to be, and you also knew, he was a man of wealth, and that had been much spread around. I remember you outright told me you didn't know why I was so rude to him and you thought he would be a great man to think about spending my life with and that I would never have to worry about working for a living again. I never told you the truth about Matthew and why he quit coming here.

"He did actually make his intentions toward me plain, and asked me to marry him on several occasions. At first, I said no, for there was no love in my heart toward him, although I do have to admit he was an attractive man. Here's my confession: after the second proposal I started to consider it in my mind. The draw was that he was wealthy and as you had said, I would never have to worry about either of us again and also you would not have to work so hard in this joint effort the boarding house has become as you've gotten older. You would be free to go about whatever you decided that you wanted to do. Also, I had decided by that time I was never going to love anyone but your father. What would it hurt? So in actuality, I was thinking of marrying this wealthy man for his money alone. It was all financial in my mind. I had made up my mind on the next trip he made through Tecumseh I would agree to be his wife. I was on the point of telling you my intention. Then something happened that I do not feel was an accident.

"The day that I had decided I would tell you of my intention, that early afternoon the traveling peddler Mr. Goodman stopped in for an evening meal and a stay for that night. As I had just served him the welcoming piece of pie and cup of coffee, he told me that our boarding house was known all over his traveling territory for its generous hospitality and delicious food. He continued that he was about the country quite a lot and he heard our name spoken of favorably and he in turn recommended us to people should they be traveling by stage or a train near our town. Of course I was pleased and said thank you.

"Then he added a sentence that seemed a strange thing for any prospective boarders to use as a recommendation he had heard. 'Someone just told me,' he said, 'In the last town I went to do business that when he heard I was coming to this town and would be staying here, it seemed to him your establishment was an honorable house. Somehow Miss Sarah, I just kept thinking about that phrase of an honorable house. I guess maybe that's the way he had of saying you are a God Fearing folk here.'

"All, I was hearing at that point, was the word 'House of Honor.' I don't even know what the peddler was saying after that, but I knew that at that moment my heart had been set on marrying some poor man for his money alone, when I didn't love him. How was that honoring your husband's name in all you do? Could I ever call this house honorable again? Or myself, for that matter.

"I knew you didn't understand later when I told you Mr. Carlyle wouldn't be coming back. I knew that you were upset with me, but I knew I had to be honest with the poor man and tell him I had no feelings for him and could not marry him. It was a matter of honor.

"There's more to this story, Clyde. When I turned Mr. Carlyle down he quit coming here when he passed through town on his business. Word got back to me from the hotel he was staying at that he was a heavy drinker who spent much of his time at the saloon and was often drunk. Then the mercantile man said that he had a wife in Omaha. The last rumor I heard was that he was the one spreading the word he was wealthy and he died a penniless drunk, whose wife had left him because he was living with someone else here in town.

"Shortly after that, when the next wonderful boarding house fell into our lap as it did, I saw it as a miracle and gift of God. How awesome it was and how the clientele increased and I knew the Lord had taken note and he had said, 'If you allow me to be your dwelling place and you will be mine, I will prepare you a house of honor.' It is the reason I have strived so hard to make each hotel we have had an exceptional place.

"Haven't you ever wondered, Clyde, how strange that a woman alone has done so well on her own with a child to support? How many 'dwelling places' for people we have had successfully? Just think how many houses of honor he has prepared for us. What else is a boarding house than a dwelling place? I give God credit for all these dwelling houses we have been given. He knew what he had planned with the word 'Dwelling of Honor' when your father was even named. He knew, regardless of all that happened, you and I would have in our lives, 'Dwelling Houses.'"

Clyde just sat back in his chair and shook his head. He never forgot what his father's name meant from that day. When he got up that day after listening to his mother he said, "Guess it was good you didn't take my advice as a marriage counselor, Mom. I never dreamed all that happened with that man." Sarah just smiled.

Then as he was going through the screen door, out to the woodpile, he paused with a big grin and said, "If you had taken my advice as a marriage counselor, I would have probably had to shoot that guy and just think where I'd be now! I'd either been hung or living in some dwelling house with bars on the window." That's how her son would deal with the seriousness of such a talk. Sarah had to smile. Between the axe blows, she heard him still laughing about "his dwelling house with bars on it." She just shook her head and arose to see about business, as there was a boarding house to be run. She never knew how deeply that talk had affected her son.

JOHN GOES TO BIBLE SCHOOL

It seemed to Clyde that it was a day that went from the divine and heavenly to the ridiculous. It all involved that sweet old cook they were learning to love as family. In the afternoon, of the same day as Clyde and Sarah's talk, something happened that would set in motion a new thing in the household of this family.

Everyone in Sarah's house knew what The Book meant to her. John started to see that The Big Book was important to her. He really didn't know much about it, but would ask Clyde. Clyde in his homespun way would try to tell him.

He was curious. The China Town he had lived in until he literally fell on their doorstep, talked about Buddha's, Confucius, and great stone gods, but he knew nothing about the God of the Big Book. Just as he was curious about the things in the American newspaper that Clyde would read to him each day about what was going on in American life outside their little town, so he was interested in the thing that was so important in Sarah's life that she read it every day. However it was just curiosity and nothing more. When Clyde read his paper, John would ask him to read aloud to him while he was doing his chores, for he wanted to learn what was going on in this big country he was learning about. He had been educated in Chinese, but this was the only American schooling he had ever had. It also made the kitchen chores go faster.

Something changed that day, though. John started another school in that boarding house. A school conducted by Sarah Elizabeth. It all started with a happening that Clyde still would laugh about until he was an old man. Clyde would think back on that day as the day his mother had shared her heavenly story with him, as a day most profound in his life and at the same time a day he heard the funniest thing he had ever heard the ever learning Chinese man say. This was a story that Clyde would tell his whole life, much to the embarrassment of the man that was then called in their town Chinaman John.

Anne and Jane, Sarah's sisters, had surprised Sarah with a present. It was a lovely picture to go on her wall. She found just the place for it and put it on the wall that afternoon where the guests dined. It was the famous picture of The Last Supper painted by the great Italian artist, Davinci. Sarah loved the picture and was very proud of it. Sarah had recently hung it when John entered the room and noticed it. He was standing with his face turned up to the picture with his back to Sarah as she walked by. Now John had only one curse phrase. As Sarah was walking by, she stopped to watch John's reaction to her new picture. She watched him standing there intently, hands clasped behind his back, studying the picture and its contents. Seeing Sarah out of the corner of his eye John said without turning, "Golly Damn, big card game."

At that point, Clyde had just walked into the room, and literally doubled over with laughter. Sarah stood there with her hand over her mouth and her eyes as big as saucers. Clyde knew that would be her reaction and tried to smother his laughter, but the more he thought of it, he was snorting and sniffing and the more he tried to hold it in, the more laughter came out. Clyde knew his best plan for the moment was to exit out the kitchen door before his laughter got him in serious trouble and so he did. As the screen door slammed behind his back he heard his mother saying, because she really couldn't blame the one that didn't know better, "Clyde, that's sacrilegious!"

Sarah heard her son out in the cow lot laughing for at least ten minutes. Intermittently during the evening she would hear him through the screen door as she worked in the kitchen.

The next morning Sarah asked John if she could read from the Bible to him every day. Of course, what would John say but yes. After all, she was the boss lady. Sarah decided they would start with the book of John. John kind of liked that. He wanted to learn about this man he was named after. He liked the idea that John thought Jesus loved him best. Over the years, the book of John would be his favorite.

John would become an attendee and then later a member of the Presbyterian Church of Tecumseh on the date of February 1st in the year of 1899.

He may have been converted, but he never lost his two swear words, "Golly Damn."

John became one of the most well-read men in Tecumseh. Well, one of the most read *to.*

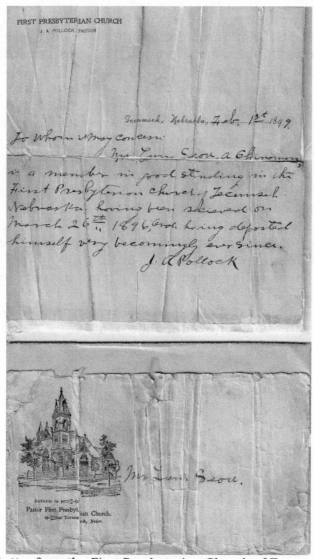

Letter from the First Presbyterian Church of Tecumseh indicating that Lum Seow was a member in good standing. February 1899

JOHN'S DAILY NEWSPAPER LESSON

Oklahoma, the Territory of the Red People

John was near the potbelly stove, his place of choice for such chores, peeling potatoes for the next meal. Clyde walked in through the kitchen door and pulled up a chair with the newspaper under his arm. He put his hands over the stove to warm them.

"What's in the news today?" asked John.

"Doesn't seem to be any big happenings in the headlines so far," answered Clyde. "Of course, I always save the small print to read out loud with you. There is one headline that caught my eye, though."

"Now let me see," said John with a twinkle in his eye, "Could it be about the Wild West, or some explorer or some outlaw gang, or maybe the Indian Territory?"

"John, you spook me sometimes," said Clyde with a grin. "You know me better than I know myself."

John just smiled, and kept on with his peeling.

"This article is kind of interesting. It's about how Indian Territory got its name." Clyde went on. It was 1886 to be exact when they named it. It says that the Five Civilized Tribes sent some delegates to Washington to make new treaties. While they were drawing up plans and rules for the new territorial government, the commissioner of Indian affairs asked the delegates, 'What would you want to call your territory?' Immediately, Allen Wright, one of the Choctaw delegates, replied, 'Oklahoma.'

"The name was accepted and the Choctaw-Chickasaw treaty provided that the new territory should be known as the 'Territory of Oklahoma.' The name is from two Choctaw words, 'Okla,' meaning people and 'homma' or 'humma,' meaning red. So the meaning of 'Territory of Oklahoma' is 'Territory of Red People.'"

"So the Indians gave it that name themselves?" asked John.

When Clyde nodded, John interjected, "It's funny to me that people in this country call themselves by colors. You call my people yellow and your people white, and these Indians called themselves red. Who is brown?"

"I think the strangest thing of all," said Clyde forgetting John's question, "Is that my people are called white, and we actually are all becoming mixed mongrels since we come from everywhere to this land, but I guess the guys that were here first have the right to call themselves anything they want.

"Actually," continued the opinionated Clyde, "This was their land in the first place, and instead of all this assigning territories which is a bunch of....................Oh well," he said stopping midsentence, "You've heard me too many times on this subject."

"Yes," said the relieved John, "Spare me your preaching. I've heard it a thousand times. Get back to the newspaper."

"OK," said Clyde with a grin, knowing his Chinese friend was right, continued, "I'll read this paper word for word without any of my thoughts."

"In 1890, when a bill was passed by congress known as the "Organic Act" it provided that the western part of the Indian Territory should be organized as 'Oklahoma Territory.'

'After the outbreak of the Civil War, many of the Indians had gone to Kansas, seeking protection beyond the Federal lines. They remained in this region as refugees until 1867, when the Government sent them back to their former location in the Leased District, near Ft.

Cobb. These bands included Delaware, Wichitas, Tawakonies, Wacoes, Kichais, Shawnees, and Caddoes."

As Clyde read these words, he had no idea that the very land, down to the very location mentioned in this article, would be the place that this family and their adopted friend would live out their very lives. They themselves would be residents of Caddo County. That very Fort named Fort Cobb that was abandoned, and yet a town would arise there, and would be just a short distance from a town which he and his family would pioneer.

In this time they lived, to them this was the land of the Red Men. Not land of the Ingrahm's.

INDIAN STORIES AROUND THE FIREPLACE

Learning About the Peace Pipe

"Let us put our minds together and see what life we
can make for our children.
Warriors are not what you think of as warriors.
The warrior is not someone who fights,
because one has the right to take another life.
The warrior, for us, is one who sacrifices himself for
the good of others.
His task is to take care of the elderly,
the defenseless, and those who cannot provide for
themselves, and above all,
the children, the future of humanity."
Sitting Bull

One long evening, when the snow lay deep, and
the Nebraska north wind blew, the family and guests sat
as close to the roaring fire in the parlor fireplace as they
could get. The potbelly stove in the far end of the room
had its little circle of people around it. As usual, to pass
a long evening Clyde read from the things that interested
him. As they huddled closely together with their chairs
pulled to the fire, the women pulled their woolen shawls
tightly around their shoulders. All wore their warmest
clothes and most had a wool blanket over their knees,
even the men. Clyde's interest at the moment in Indians
involved those who were from around their area in the
north, the Pawnee. Time would cause that interest to
expand.

The subject for the evening was the religious ceremony known among all Indian tribes and that most
white men had heard about. Clyde, after throwing another log on the fire, returned to his seat near the glowing

lamp and picked up his old book he had kept from his teen years. Little Ruby drew near to his knees on her little stool so she could hear of the stories that she had learned to love from her father. She laid her head on his knees, and tightened her shawl around her to ward off the chill in the room.

Mary was seated in a rocker in a far corner of the room with the baby on her lap rocking. He was wrapped tightly in the warm woolen blanket that Sarah had knitted for him. His eyes were heavy and Mary knew he would soon be asleep for it was his bedtime. After clearing his throat, Clyde started to read in his animated voice, which was raised so all could hear in the big room. Sarah never ceased to be amazed at his theatrical reading skills. He could make even a history book interesting. So it went:

Singing the Calumet

"Singing the Calumet is a religious ceremony known among all Indian tribes. The Calumet is a sacred pipe. There are two kinds, a war pipe and a peace pipe. The war pipe is smoked by members of the Indian council when their tribe is starting to war against its enemies. Members of the council thus pledge their honor in defense of their people and their country. The peace pipe is smoked in council when establishing peace and friendship between tribes. The Indians sing and dance during the smoking of the peace Calumet. This ceremony is often called 'Singing the Calumet.'"

John arose from the place where he was sitting, and walked over to Mary to take the sleeping boy from her lap. It was a nightly routine, and she knew he would place Jack in her and Clyde's room in the children's homemade pine bed and then be back down to hear the rest of the reading.

Clyde continued, "The making of the Calumet is a great art. It takes many days to make the pipe bowl from hard red or black stone. The pipe stem is made from cane or reed carefully gathered near a river bank. Sometimes the stem is made from a young sapling of the ash tree since an ash sapling can be hollowed out for smoke to pass through. The stem of the Calumet is painted and decorated with beautiful feathers of many colors. Calumets of different Indian tribes are not decorated alike because many kinds of birds are found in different parts of the country.

"Birds and animals in the far North have white feathers or white fur to match the pure white of the snow. An Indian tribe of the North often decorates its Calumets with the feathers of white birds. The Calumet decorated mostly with white feathers is the peace pipe. The Calumet decorated mostly with red feathers is the war pipe." Clyde paused while Mr. O'Reily had one of his coughing spasms. All waited patiently and sympathetically.

Continuing on, Clyde read, "When the Pawnee artists or medicine men make a Calumet, they choose the straightest ash sapling found in the forest. After cutting down the sapling, the bark is peeled off and the center hallowed out for a pipe stem. Since everything has to be kept clean and neat when making a Calumet, every bit of bark and wood trash is carefully swept up. While the medicine man slowly gathers the little pile of trash and places it upon the fire, he sings a song. This song means that the Pawnees wish to please the spirit of the trees.

"A small groove is cut along one side of the shining ash stem. It is then painted and feather decorations are added. The stem of this Pawnee Calumet is painted bright blue to represent the sky, the home of the Great

Spirit. The groove on the stem is painted red to represent a pathway to the sky. Wing feathers of an eagle are attached to the pipe stem because the eagle soared high above the land and carried messages from the day from the Calumet. Next, the bright red crest of a woodpecker is fastened to the pipe stem because this bird carried messages to the trees. Near the middle of the pipe stem, owl feathers are attached for the owl carried messages into the night. Brilliant duck feathers are carried to the stem of the calumet, for the duck carried messages to the water. On the pipe stem was hung a white eagle feather fan which waved to and fro when the Calumet was passed from one person to another. When completed, the Pawnee Calumet with its many colored feathers and white eagle feather fan reminds one of a beautiful bird. The Indians believe the Calumet sends messages from their council to good spirits in the world."

Suddenly Ruby got up and ran out of the room and up the stairs to the bedroom. Mary is watching her, thinking "I hope she doesn't wake Little Jack."

Not seeming to notice, Clyde reads on, "The medicine man begins to sing, keeping time with the rhythmic beat of a small drum. Dancers begin their dance in a cleared space near at hand. In the meanwhile, the beautiful Calumet, with the white feather fan waving to and fro, is passed among the council members. Each draws a puff or two of smoke, thus pledging his loyalty to peace and friendship. Singing the Calumet is a ceremony greatly enjoyed by the Indian people." Clyde finished and closed the book ceremoniously.

Suddenly everyone looked toward Ruby, standing in the parlor door proudly holding a beautiful multicolor pipe. The guests all gave the appropriate words and awes of approval.

"Look what my Daddy let me help him make out in the prairie trees," the little girl said. She was beaming with pride. So were Mary and Sarah, in appreciation that Clyde must have worked so hard and long with his little daughter to fashion this work of art. That is until Ruby continued, "He let me smoke it with him, too."

As all eyes were now moving from Sarah and Mary to Clyde, he cleared his throat, stood up, laid the book down, and quickly left the room saying he needed a drink after all that reading. He walked past innocent little Ruby, holding up the pipe for all to see, still beaming. Mary immediately arose from her chair, following him. As the guests strained their ear toward the kitchen to hear what the voices were saying, they quickly decided that Mary was not interested in smoking any peace pipe at the moment.

After a moment of embarrassment, Sarah loudly said, "Let's sing some of our favorite songs," hoping to drown out the kitchen noise. "Let's start with *Sweet Betsy From Pike.*" After pausing for a second, she said, "Only the nice verses, gentlemen."

THE SPANISH-AMERICAN WAR

The Ultimate Call to Adventure

It was the year of 1898. Again, as happened periodically, Mary Edna and Clyde were having one of their "discussions". These discussions were always to persuade the practical Mary into agreement with what seemed to her radical, outlandish thoughts that surfaced at times with her adventuresome husband. These discussions always ended with Mary putting her foot down with a definite "no." It always seemed negotiable. However, not this time.

A new spirit was thrilling America. A spirit of national pride and it was a spirit that frightened Mary. Mary didn't like this spirit. She was born after the Civil War, and she was nine years younger than Clyde yet it was not that far back in America's history that she knew full well what men having a desire to liberate a people could do. She had seen what "patriotism" could produce and its heavy cost. She knew how far it had set America back. How gallant and wonderful it is when men are willing to march off to war in a noble cause they are sure will be won swiftly, for they think it's the right cause and yet how bloody and costly a price had America already paid, be it right or wrong. Yet, she knew the cause had been right.

She wasn't so sure this latest "cause" was right. How much was this intervention in another country's business, anything that America had any right to do. Was interfering with this Cuba thing the right thing to do?

As was her husband's custom, she watched him devour every line of news in the newspapers he could get his hands on. She heard him read it heatedly to his captive audience, John. She saw that old familiar thing rise in him and she recognized that agitation in him surface when a new "adventure" was on the horizon. Because that thing arose in him as he read the unfolding of this new battle that America was about to get itself involved in, Mary was troubled, but hoped it would pass, as many of his ideas had. In retrospect, in the past it had all worked out. Yet, her heart cried out to have a normal husband, satisfied with family life and content with where he was.

Her mind went back to "The Great Adventures" of their married life. The first thing to surface, after the adventure of their marriage, was his delight in her shooting skills, and him helping her develop that, along with teaching her his riding skills, to a small degree anyway. She had innocently enjoyed the excitement of that, being young and newly married. Then, the next thing she is hearing is "Cousin Vic and I want to produce one of the Wild West Shows that are so popular now." If that weren't enough, he said, "We want you to be in it, too, as a sharpshooter. Every Wild West Show has one, and a female gun expert is a showstopper." Yes that was an adventure, alright. More than any British born girl had ever expected.

Then, when the family was settling down, and the boarding house business became something beyond their wildest dreams, what was the next wild adventure? Lately, he was talking about some wild land give-away he's heard about down in Indian Territory and he was talking about leaving this land that they had worked so hard to make a good life in, and take part in a wild give away scheme that guaranteed you nothing. Yeah, leave this settled, modern, secure town we've helped establish, travel, in of all things, a wagon train for endless miles of uninhabited prairie land, to a place of absolutely nothing but harsh ground, no wells, no gardens, critters they'd never seen before, not to mention rattlers and scorpions. The most frightening thing of all, it was called Indian Territory. Just that word was enough to scare her to death. Not only did she have to leave everything behind they had worked so hard to get, and take only what they could get in a wagon, she had to worry about getting scalped when she got there.

She had heard about those early days that Sarah had talked about when there were no buildings or houses and there was no water well on that piece of "homestead land." She remembered what Sarah had said about homesteading and how "woman's work" consumed those settlers from before daylight until long after dark, because there was nothing to work with. Besides all the "woman's work," they were short on men so guess what? Men's work became woman's work also. That was this last "Great Adventure" Clyde was talking about. There wouldn't even be a mercantile, she finished up her thoughts. However, though, this volunteering to go away to war thing was worse than anything he had thought up before!

Now, here she stood face to face with her passionate man who had a desire for her to see how important it was for this country to go liberate a country fighting for its freedom. A country that she didn't even know where it was; this place that needed help to fight against Spanish aggression. How he painted them as the underdog. "Have you not been listening?" he inquired, as he read to John from the paper of the terrible things that were being done to this people that wanted no more than to be free? They were herding this poor country's civilians into refugee camps where these innocent people were dying of deadly diseases because of all the filth.

Surely she had been seeing the headlines in the New York Journal he bought when the peddler's wagon came by or the other papers that were circulating, crying for vengeance against the horrible carnage done in the sinking of the innocent people on the American ship named the Maine, by those dastardly Spanish People. The innocent people on that ship were just making a visit to that Havana harbor to protect and evacuate Americans if a dangerous flare up should happen. That cowardly, despicable country of Spain had killed 260 officers, Clyde animatedly said. Had she not been hearing the cry that was everywhere? "Remember the Maine. To Hell with Spain?"

"Yes, I've heard it all," Mary protested. "I also hear people say if we go to war there, we would only be invaders because we have such interests in the sugar cane there and also we have some commercial interest in a canal that affects American trade. Also, there are many that say it would be American imperialism poking our noses in somewhere we don't belong. That we would end up taking all that land for ourselves and would be no better than the Spanish or my family's country Great Britain, which invaded this land to put it under their empire.

"Some are saying we are no better because of what we have done to the poor Indians that were the original natives of this land. That we herded them up and put them in camps too. That we would be the opposite of what America was established for. I've heard that America's motives are impure and it's not about them, but it's really about our good."

Clyde was becoming red-faced with anger, but Mary was going to have her say, before she was stopped by him, for she knew she was fighting for something that could affect her and the children future's forever. She was desperate to persuade him because of the rumors she was hearing. A deadly fear was gripping her now, as though she was fighting for her life. Neither one knew that John had come in the house for a moment to get a hammer, and was quietly listening out of sight.

"Let me tell you something else I think. I think that the press in this country is getting too powerful. I think it can stir up a Devil's Hell in causing the minds of this country to believe things that aren't so. Their headlines are telling people how to think. What to do. It has the power to make people think black is white, and white is black. It seems to me those big publishers like Randolph Hurst and that man named Pulitzer control the mind of the people of our country. The New York Journal and the New York World put in the headlines what they want to make the people believe. They like to feed emotional fires. Someone said that they heard that's what the man named Hurst said concerning this very subject, 'Watch him start a war,' or something like that. That's frightening, Clyde. I heard Grannie say the other day that if people read the Bible every day, as much as they read the newspapers, this would be a whole different world."

Mary seldom spoke with the force she was speaking now, but she wouldn't take a breath until she said what was on her mind and so she continued. "This country just doesn't think right, sometimes, as wonderful as it is. I heard the other day that this government is talking about *allowing* the Indians to become citizens! Can you imagine? The people that this land originally belonged to and we are going to *allow them* to become citizens? Talk about a bunch of nonsense!

"Getting back to Cuba, everyone knows about the rumors of the call of 25,000 volunteers that's gone out to assemble some kind of Cavalry, mainly from the southwest. What's that all about, anyway? I heard the president wants only volunteers because after the Civil

War slaughter he wants only people who want to fight in this thing that seems to be brewing. That I understand, but why do they need a horse Cavalry?"

Clyde jumped in quickly, "Yes, that's one thing you heard right on, and they picked the areas where they knew men drove cattle on horses and knew how to handle guns and were good at being horsemen so they wouldn't have to do much training for a mounted Cavalry that will be needed in that little scuffle we're going to have in Cuba," answered Clyde.

"Well," he continued, "I may not be an original cowboy horseman, but this is one Nebraskan that can ride just as good as or even better than any cowboy and I guess you know my shootings top notch. They are going to have to teach me what to do with that sword though."

"Clyde," Mary screeched, "You're not going to volunteer? For my sake and the children's, say you're not!"

Clyde dropped his head, looking at the scuffed plank floor. Saying nothing, he shifted his feet.

"Clyde," Mary said, her voice trembling, "Answer me. Please say you're not."

Not lifting his head, he quietly said, "I enlisted yesterday." Taking courage to look into her tear-filled eyes, he reached into his back pocket and put a folded paper into her hand. A very official paper stating the date, bearing his name and sayings that Clyde F. Ingrahm was a member of the Co. 1, Second Regiment.

John, not wanting to hear anymore, went back outside, deeply worried about his friend. He had been talking to him about his plan, and John had counseled him against it. Pleading for his safety, and for Mary's and the children's sake, he had beseeched him not to do this foolish thing. When he could not persuade him from what his mind was already set on, he could only agree he would take care of the family, no matter how long it was needed.

Once when he was working on his English fluency, John had learned a word from an English dictionary. Clyde had even looked the word up for him. The word had been stubborn. The book said, "Stubborn: one who will not change." John had learned a long time ago something about his friend. The minute he heard about the upcoming war, his mind was set. He would go. He would not change his mind. To him it would be the adventure of a life-time. The thing he had awaited.

He would never forget the devastated look on Mary's face. Not wanting to see the tears that were coming, John quietly left the house and no one knew that he had overheard.

When Clyde came home from his great adventure as a Sergeant Quartermaster, his Mary was not impressed. Their marriage was never the same. She felt as if she had been abandoned with two small children for a cause that was not theirs.

Photo from Clyde's possessions. On the back is handwritten: "SV Firing Squad"

THE SPANISH AMERICAN WAR FIASCO

The war itself was a short 113 days. On April 11th, 1898, President McKinley sent a war message to congress urging armed intervention to free the oppressed Cubans. The legislature responded with what was a declaration of war. They adopted The Teller Amendment. This proviso proclaimed to the world that when the United States had overthrown Spanish misrule, it would give the Cubans their freedom.

The American people jumped into the war in a spirit of glee. Songs of the day and time were *There'll Be a Hot Time in the Old Town Tonight* and *Hail, Hail the Gang's All Here*. These songs were so prevalent among people and troops that foreigners believed that those were American National Anthems.

There was such a confused invasion of Cuba it was laughable in retrospect. The troops had been pre-pared for war with heavy woolen underwear and uniforms designed for subzero operations against the Indians; a disaster for the tropical temperatures they would endure in Cuba.

The "Rough Riders," a part of the invading army, was a well-remembered part of history, mainly because of Theodore Roosevelt's exploiting them as part of his gaining recognition for himself. Some accounts of the time said you would think from his reports that he had fought the whole war himself. The Rough Riders were a colorful regiment of volunteers, who were not very disci-plined according to some stories. However, it was said they had a lot of dash and press. They were largely west-ern cowboys, and other charismatic characters that were known for their hardiness. Since they needed men who could ride there was a sprinkling of ex-polo players and it was said some ex-convicts. Commanded by Colonel

Leonard Wood, the group was organized principally by the glory-hungry Roosevelt, who resigned from the Navy Department to serve as a lieutenant colonel. He had no military experience but used pull to get his commission.

Around the middle of June a bewildered American army of seventeen thousand men finally arrived at congested Tampa, Florida. There was absolute confusion. The Rough Riders went to the place of embarkation. About half of them finally got to Cuba without most of their horses. Those ended up on foot.

> In my regiment nine-tenths of the men were better horsemen than I was, and two-thirds of them better shots than I was, while on the average they were certainly hardier and more enduring. Yet, after I had had them a very short while they all knew, and I knew too, that nobody could command them as I could."
>
> – Theodore Roosevelt 1903

All that is known of Clyde's war experiences was that he returned to his family safely. His rank at his return was Sergeant Quartermaster. A Quartermaster Sergeant of that time was in charge of providing for the quarters, equipment, and other supplies for the troops. Certainly sounds like a far cry from the Cavalry that was the grand plan for this invasion. According to current history reports, most of the horses didn't make it out of the states and most of the actual warfare was on foot.

Clyde prized his Spanish American War uniform, keeping it, and there are black and white pictures made of himself and John showing Clyde wearing that historic hat in several places, both at the Oklahoma homestead, and in later years in his Carnegie home.

A sad footnote to the Spanish-American War is that the high death rate was from sickness, especially typhoid fever. The disease was rampant in the unsanitary training camps located in the United States. Nearly four hundred men lost their lives to bullets; over five thousand to bacteria and other causes.

The Spanish American War was not what Clyde thought it would be. Whatever history has recorded, much of its purpose was to bring about important land acquirements to America.

Just as the planning of that War was a comedy of errors by men, so Clyde's enlistment in that war was a disappointment and a part of his life that did not turn out to be the adventure he thought it would be. However, new adventures would be ahead.

A LIFE CHANGING DECISION

*"Love your life and beautify all things
in your life. Seek to make your life long and in
the service of your people."* - Tecumseh

Sarah, viciously scrubbing carrots under the pump in the large pail, ran an appreciative look over the transformed area behind the boarding house. As she looked at the blue sky, powdery white clouds were drifting along the horizon. How beautiful the stretch of property behind the hotel was. Suddenly, as she kneeled there, her mind went back to a time in the past before John had entered the family's life. The back yard had gone from a barren stretch of land into lush green rows of a beautiful garden. John was indeed a master of the soil. How that one thing had changed the life of this establishment.

She and Clyde had been amazed at what money had been saved by producing their own vegetables instead of buying them. Having never been around farming, John had so increased her knowledge of the wisdom of farmers. She also was awed at the hard work and sweat that went into farming. They had watched John labor over this piece of land in wonder. He had not misled them. How he loved to garden! It was his passion in the same way riding and hunting was Clyde's. It was as if he was born for this.

When the plowing was finished, the careful nourishing of the soil began. He would come back from the feed and seed store with his old familiar flour sack over his shoulder; things unrecognizable to them such as nitrate of soda. He used manure and dried blood to enrich the prairie soil. Constant attention to the earth was given in any of his spare time he had. It was as though he were driven. She even saw him working when it was night when there was bright moonlight.

In the backyard when doing other chores his eyes would be looking to the garden as if he was thinking of things to do later. How patiently he had sowed and gathered. His daily posture, when not working inside, was bent double. He carefully saved leftover vegetables to make a decayed fertilizer to enrich the soil. Of course Clyde still claimed first choice on carrot leftovers for his horses and meat scraps for his dogs.

John could not walk anywhere near the garden on another errand in the back of the house without stopping one time, at least briefly, and pulling some errant weed, or piece of grass he considered an interloper. On occasion, a pretty wild flower might be allowed to remain, which would later be picked to give to someone he might want to honor on his trip through town.

When the sun was burning hot, and sweat was on his brow, ignoring himself, he would take his pail of water to give a drink to his plants lest they be overcome by the blistering heat. One by one, as if they were his little thirsty children, he used the dipper to quench their thirst. When the heat was bad, and the need was great, he would put a pail on each side of a pole, and carry his life giving water balanced on his shoulders.

Clyde had seen pictures of that being done in China. When he first saw John do this, he laughed out loud. Saying nothing in reply to Clyde, he wondered why these Americans had never thought of it, for he felt he was getting twice as much done at once. Plus there was no hard steel handle cutting into each of his hands. This work had made his shoulders strong.

Now, as Sarah was looking at the beautiful tomato vines that were ready for picking, she thought of all the things that had come to their table in the spring and even in the fall of the years. The large patch of huge, round tomatoes were scarlet red in the sunlight now waiting to be picked, among those greening up for later. The small size tomatoes were wonderful for the salads and wonderful to pop in your mouth, if no one was looking.

From this land had come, thanks to Clyde's plowing, and John's planting, all manner of foods to feed guests and family in the past years John had been with them. The early planting of sweet potatoes were for vegetables, soups, and deserts. For the same purpose the orange pumpkins and the yellow and green squashes. How the green and yellow peppers had livened up the dishes that John had added to the meals. She had not once, when she looked at the land behind this house, thought of the treasure this soil held until John had arrived. There had been cabbages, carrots, turnips, and peas of several different varieties. Even little red, nippy radishes garnished their table. Huge crock jars would be filled with the green, bumpy cucumbers with the pickles her guests loved, both sweet and sour. Green beans on the vine had thrived. How delicious they were when cooked with the little round new potatoes. There were onions, small and large to flavor it all, not to mentions John's special kind of garlic with which he flavored so many dishes with.

He had planted something new to them called soybeans, which he said was invaluable for Chinese to cook with. He seemed to like them either cooked or raw after they sprouted. With them he made some kind of strange brew which he liked on his food. It was a special sauce. It was too salty for her taste but he seemed to prefer it on meats and rice. He allowed their cows to be staked out on the soybean patch as a feed when he was through with them. The sweet corn from the patch was relished by the guests when it was swimming in their freshly churned butter. It was so sweet it needed nothing, however.

Meat was not always easily available when Clyde's gun skills found slim pickings. Wildlife couldn't always be guaranteed. At those times they would make an especially hearty vegetable dish with noodles, dumplings, and hot bread with lots of butter and just to make sure all were satisfied, a special desert. Sweet cream, butter, cinnamon and sugar could always work miracles and having churned cream on hand always added a special treat to a meal. If a prairie chicken or pheasant couldn't be scared up, there were always the domestic chickens to fry or to make a huge pot of gravy. In the early days, flour in the larder to make some kind of gravy, could always keep the poorest homes stomachs full, even if the palates weren't satisfied. She and John, putting their culinary expertise together, always worked out even from meager pickings so that the palates were always satisfied at Sarah's table. Even in the worst of weather, Clyde would bring in buckets of fresh clean snow and they would make an icy sugared treat that all would enjoy.

The secret weapons since John's arrival were his special donuts. They remained to be a favorite until they day he died. Anytime Sarah had town guests drop in for a visit, or possibly a surprise visit by a relative, almost before Miss Sarah had them seated, John without being told, would have the sugar donuts on the stove cooking in his special deep cooker. That was always John's special way of saying "welcome." Although he always remained behind the scenes, the donuts would appear on special trays with glasses filled with frothy
milk. Clyde's favorite breakfast treat was donuts dipped in coffee.

When the family relatives came to visit, their visiting was always done in privacy, upstairs in Clyde and

Mary's special room that had been made into a suite for their family. The settee and chairs hosted brothers and wives, sisters and husbands, sitting on the bed was an option. Since Mama Catherine had died in 1892 at 84, her presence had been greatly missed.

Just as the garden grew in the yard behind the house, so did John's appreciation by the homefolks in Tecumseh. Over the past five years, there was much learned about the man who was considered different than they were at first in the clannish little town. At first tongues were wagging, at the appearance of "the China-man." There was plenty of gossip and suspicion when people weren't sure what his role was in town. Myths about people from China were started. Old fear of the unknown and the different raised its ugly head. There are always people with inbred dislike of those they deemed different. It didn't come to Sarah's ears and more thankfully not Clyde's, who had very different ways of dealing with anger than she and especially in defending a friend, and it was just as well for the gossiper.

He had become a welcome fixture in their lives now. Even those that in the natural had an inclination to judge by color, or race, or station tended to have a gradual heart change toward the little man they called John Chinaman. In any time or place or situation, John would rule the day with kindness. That simple virtue can change the hardest of cold hearts. Words may not impress. Words are easy to come by, but kind deeds were the thing that came to mind when people thought about this man. At times he had taken the wagon out to visit people out on the farms that he had met when they came into the town on business. Candy always made the trip for the children.

He did not speak a lot. Overall, he was generally quiet, unless someone would go beyond the ready smile, and make an effort to engage him in conversation. However, many would remember long after he was gone from their midst, the beautiful wild flowers he would bring to their door should someone be sick. Even more so, when his red roses, which Clyde formed a liking to, were in bloom in the summer, a beautiful, deep red bouquet of the most fragrant from his own vines.

If a little child was sick, a strange little handmade Chinese toy would appear that would keep a child occupied in bed. From the beautiful Nebraska Goldenrods, to the carefully tended red roses from John's own flower bed, or his freshly hot donuts as a special "get well or I'm sorry gift," John was known for his surprises that said "someone cares." The gifts were always quietly given, with no fanfare. The less pomp and circumstance, the better it seemed to John. Yet, they would suddenly appear at just the right time and all would know where they came from. The name Chinaman John was spoken with respect, and maybe a wish that there were more people in their town like him.

These were the things Sarah thought upon as she knelt at the pump, mindlessly washing the already clean carrots. She had taken so long that Daisy, the big old wooly blonde dog, had decided to take a nap at her side. This dog of Clyde's that looked so much like a sheepdog, had won Sarah's heart with its gentle spirit. It seemed to be a mutual feeling.

As Sarah thought of all the things that this man meant to her family, it made a decision she had to make even harder. John's future, along with the family's, was uncertain. The family would have each other, no matter what, but what about John? He would have no one. Sarah had not spoken to him yet.

There had been changes several times in their years of the boarding house. Sarah, had over the years, enlarged and moved to newer and larger property. Life, in their business, as well as the whole state's welfare, had changed because of the horrendous blizzards of the past winter. Transportation was a vital part of their existence. If people were prevented from traveling by snow and ice, the effects were devastating, not only to the livestock of the farmers of this land, but to them personally. Their livelihood was dependent upon travelers. They were not far from the Oregon Trail which in the past had helped birth the town itself. The railroad that had been built was the boon to Nebraska. The Burlington came right into Tecumseh. There were Wells Fargo Stages and Pony Express routes that changed the face of America, and helped this little beginning town to progress and grow. All these things were good for their trade, as travelers made their way across this early opening frontier country.

The weather, especially as far north as they were, where a blizzard shows no mercy on man or beast, and stops all before it, including those travelers who need shelter on their way, had played cruel tricks on their business these last years.

Sarah had started out in a small scale hotel, and because of increase in trade, she went to larger ones, already built. She had improved the service in each. Times had been very good. Her proprietorship, according to newspaper articles of the time, was considered upscale. When she outgrew each one she expanded to a larger building, according to surviving letters from that time. The last hotel she had built was larger than ever. However, things were looking dire now. A decision had to be made. There must be a family council. She and Clyde had made a good team, and it seemed they must make a decision together.

Finishing her chore and arising from her knees, she told herself that the past was the past. The present must be dealt with. The business was becoming a problem and the family could no longer maintain it. That was reality. The family had to have some serious talks about selling out. It was obvious they could no longer maintain the boarding house.

It was time for her to tell the family about the offer she had been given by a new businessman in town to buy the hotel. The offer had been made some time back. Circumstances told her that it would be foolish not to accept this offer now. As deep as the roots of her life went in this business, and this being their home, she saw this as an offer that needed to be accepted. She had hesitated when the offer came, because she had no plan for what to do in the future but it was time to hold a family council. They had all worked jointly in this and all futures were at stake. Also, two little children's lives were a concern.

She had no doubt that John could find work as a cook in any one of the eating places that had sprung up in Tecumseh. As his reputation had grown, others had tried to hire him away from their establishment, even at higher wages. He had not told her, but she knew. However, he seemed so much a part of the family now, that it seemed unimaginable that there would be a separation, even if she did have a plan. Not only was the bond so strong between him and Clyde, but the little ones called him Uncle John. There was no other choice now, though. The time to talk had come.

Taking the pail of shiny carrots, she walked through the back door into the fragrance filled kitchen, leaving Daisy standing behind her. As she did she heard a loud voice coming from the parlor. It was Mary, crying out at the top of her voice, "No, No, No!"

She quickly set the carrots down, and ran as fast as she could to the parlor door. At the door she stopped short, for she had seen this scene before, when Clyde had told Mary of a fantastic plan he had devised about a Wild West Show. This was the identical scene, with the exception that Mary had tears running down a red face.

Seeing Sarah standing at the door, she exclaimed in a high pitched voice, "Grannie Sarah, Clyde has decided he's going to Indian Territory. He's got some foolish notion about getting some free land down there among the Indians. He's determined he's going. He won't listen to me. He says he has made up his mind."

Sarah walked into the parlor, shocked with the news of her son leaving them now at this crucial time. None of them realized that on hearing the cry of Mary that John had rushed toward the parlor and was standing just out of sight in earshot of all that was being said.

"Clyde," Sarah animatedly protested, "You can't go off now on some wild scheme of yours! We've all heard the talk about that free land being opened in Indian Land, but do you realize, even if you got any land, which is doubtful, how hard it would be for you to start over?"

Getting more animated now, which was unusual for Sarah, she continued, "There will be multitudes of people with the same idea. I'm already hearing it in town. Besides, you would be giving up everything you have here!"

Clyde, who was looking very seriously into Sarah's eyes, very quietly said, "Giving up what, Mom?"

The room fell deadly silent. Sarah stood there stunned with the reality of what her son had said. She stood there absorbing his words, realizing that there was nothing for her family in this town of Tecumseh now. Nothing! Even if the businessman's offer for the boarding house still stood, they would have no place to live.

Out of nowhere, that old adventuresome spirit that she had passed on to her son since he was a boy, jumped on Miss Sarah Ingrahm, and to her own surprise, she found herself saying, "The whole family should go!"

"What", the agitated Mary screeched, "Are you *both* crazy?"

"The whole family should go," Sarah said quietly and firmly.

Unseen, just outside the parlor door, an old friend dropped his head at what he had just heard. The shock of a coming separation swept over him like a dark cloud. He knew very well that he was a good friend. He also knew he was not family. He lifted his head, and quickly went back to his kitchen chores, with the firm intention of not letting anyone know he had heard a private family conversation. A tear came to his eye, which he quickly brushed away, as he continued peeling potatoes. Chinese men must never lose face. They must always smile to cover. So as the family entered the kitchen, he did not mention the conversation he had just heard.

He steeled his resolution and responded, "Yes," when Clyde said to his dearest friend, "We need to have a serious talk today, when the work is done." All went about their day, as if nothing had happened. As usual, there was a hostelry to take care of.

ZEBULUN'S TRUNK

The time had come to leave. Sarah, knowing she was alone in the boarding house, went to the place no one had ever known was there. Underneath the stairs there was a compartment that could not be detected. It was a very small closet that was cut so well that no seams showed. She had this closet purposely built when she had the hotel built. She had put something of the past there that she wanted out of sight. It was her husband's trunk.

Now as she was leaving Nebraska for the Cherokee Strip, she had left this thing she attended to as the last thing she would do before she left the life she had built here. Here she was alone, sitting on the floor in front of Zebulun's trunk, about to face a big fear. She had opened it only once since he had died. Always before, she had carefully covered it with a small table cloth and had placed a coal oil lamp on it, beside her Bible. No one had questioned it to be more than a table. She had moved it from place to place and this last place had been the best of all to put the trunk out of sight. No one knew the trunk or the secret door under the stairs was there.

Only once since Zebulun was gone had she opened the trunk and then only quickly to slip something of great value in it for safe keeping. Then she had quickly slammed the lid down so she would not be accosted by painful memories of Zebulun. How she had loved him. She still did. It seemed the love had been so great that she never loved another.

Now at forty-nine she was moving to another place, far away from here where she would make a new life for herself. She knew she must open the trunk of memories and remove one treasure she had hidden there. The rest must remain because of room needed for the long journey before her. Besides, how fruitless to keep a thing that you cannot bring yourself to look into. However, one thing she must retrieve and take on her new journey.

She did not understand why her hands were shaking as she slowly opened the lid. Right on the top was the thing she had been afraid to see. There were his medals of honor from the war, lying on his old blue Union uniform. There was his medical insignia. Why she wondered was the wound still so raw?

She picked up the neatly folded coat and buried her face in it. To her surprise, it smelled not only of her beloved Zeb, but of the war in which they had spent so much of their life together.

After so many years, surely it was all in her mind. The memories all came back with a rush! She began to weep with the memory of Zeb and the sweet memories of young love and then the horrid memories of war they had served together in.

She remembered as if it were yesterday, brothers fighting against brothers in a divided nation. She always had felt that the trumpets blown by hordes of men to sound charge or retreat, had represented some heavenly trumpet sounded by heaven itself as a judgment on this nation: a mighty judgment against man's inhumanity to man.

Her personal wounding over her loss of Zebulun ran deep. Kneeling there with his coat in her hands, she saw him standing in his uniform. To her, of course, he was the most handsome of men; her warrior husband; a warrior with hands of healing; her lost companion.

He was the only love of her life and the only love that would ever be. Beyond her riveted gaze on that jacket, she was seeing their days on earth together and the sweetness of their life before the war, and the too short years after.

A noise from outside broke her trance. She knew she didn't have much time. The call of her son's voice came telling her that it was time to leave. The family was waiting.

She carefully laid down the jacket on the floor and picked up the thing she had so long ago placed under it. She reached into the trunk for what had been exposed after she had lifted the uniform; the thing that had caused her, after all these years, to open the trunk. She knew she must leave everything else behind, but not this one thing.

She picked it up and grasped it in her hands. It was the footstool. The very last thing he had made for her. She had placed the beautiful little yellow footstool in the trunk with his mementoes soon after she had journeyed with her family to the new land. Then she had covered it with the uniform.

She shut the lid, slid the trunk back into the closet, shut the secret door, picked up the stool and walked out of the room, knowing she was never to come back. She at last was parting with the past forever.

She turned and looked back into the parlor for a moment as she stood in the front door. It had been a time she had loved; a place that she had been meant to be. In her mind's eye she saw hundreds of people who she had housed in her parlors, setting in the warmth of the fireplace, sitting around potbellied stoves, talking, laughing, singing, quilting, doing handwork, men playing card games and checkers or getting ready to go play horseshoes in the backyard. There had been laughter and some arguing and fussing. She smiled as she thought of that.

Sitting in the midst of it all, learning and growing, she saw her small boy reading, studying and singing with the many people that had loved him and who he had called his friends. She saw the dear old boarder who had bought him his first violin. She saw the men that had left him books on science, and exploring and the wonders of the world he longed to see. Those that made sure to bring him newspapers from the east as he and his interests grew. Although he had gone to the little school house these people had been his greatest teachers on life. There had been many good teachers, and even some bad. All were human learning experiences. She saw that boy running down the familiar street with his dogs, close behind. She saw him later, riding his ponies with their guns with his cousin Victor out toward the prairie. She saw the boy meet the young woman he would marry. She saw him grow to manhood, become her business partner and biggest help, while also starting a family of his own.

She saw his dearest friend of all, John, entering the scene and bowing before each guest with his Chinese tray of doughnuts and coffee. He played his part so well, just as she had played her part as hostess, but the family knew him as a trusted friend and member, not a servant.

Her heart was filled with sudden thankfulness over the life she had lived in this town with its Indian name. It was here that God had allowed her to raise her son alone. It was here that their loyal friend and help, John, had come, without whose loyalty the business would not have prospered as it had, and who had been such a mentor to her son. How thankful she was that he had agreed to make this journey to a new land with them.

How long ago it had seemed since 1875 when she started that first little hostelry in the old Andrew Head residence and then because of success moved in to the old frame building owned by Mr. Myers on the west side of the square. Later she bought the already established hotel at the corner of Clay and Second Street which was her first really first class hotel. How exciting it was in 1882 because of the increased business she was enjoying, and also the growth of the town and the surrounding country, that it made it necessary for her to build a larger hotel. She had secured the site opposite of her old location and they would name the new house *The Caledonia*. She did not know now that the new owner would name it the Arcade Hotel and it would remain in operation many years, even into the 1930's as a historical place.

Over the past few days she had been saying her goodbyes to the people all around this little town that had been home. Of course, some very emotional goodbyes had been exchanged with her brothers and sisters who had lived in the area. Her brother, Jerome, would be the last they would see before they left. They would make a last stop in the wagon at his house on the way to meet the wagon train. Many of her relatives promised to visit them in their new land. Mary had said a sad goodbye to her parents last night who were weeping, thinking they might not see their daughter again.

She walked out for the last time into the street of the town of Tecumseh to her waiting family. It was time to go. It would be a long day. They were leaving early. The sun cast a glow of beautiful color as it was just rising with its morning light.

Clyde and Mary were in the first wagon that contained the personal things they were taking. There were two covered wagons; one borrowed from her brother Michael. The wagons were covered with waterproof canvas. The drawstrings were pulled closed at the ends because there was a touch of a chill in the air and inside one wagon little Jack slept. Inside that first wagon there were hooks on the wooden hoops. They held various things such as lanterns, milk cans, guns, and things they needed on the trip and when they arrived at their destination. Of course the old violin Clyde had cherished since a boy hung on one of those hooks. The axe was placed in the wagon near the entrance for the heavy work before it. Strangely in the last minute packing, not knowing where to put it, and yet not wanting to throw it away, was thrown haphazardly on one of those hooks old Nip's collar. All saw it, but none questioned it.

The bedding for the nighttime was piled up in a place where the children could get on them easily to take a nap during the long day. There was on the bottom of the quilts, a tent, to be taken out at night when they camped. On the side of each wagon there were large wooden kegs for water. There was a bucket of grease hanging down from the wagon behind it, to rub on the wheels to keep them turning smoothly.

They had packed as many needful things for setting up house as they could. Many things were left behind with friends, relatives and some needy people in the community. How little they could take. Heartrending decisions had been made on what had to be left behind. Some things dear as mementos were left with family with the hope they might retrieve them if they were ever given a chance to come back or should some of them come visit them in their new home. The dearest and saddest of all to leave was the family that had been together so long. Those goodbyes had already been tearfully said.

They had been doing some last minute visiting, to say their goodbyes. She knew they all would miss coming to their Hotel. She thought of her sister's Ann's family and how they enjoyed their get-togethers here at the hotel. The children, Edith, Floyd, Clifford, Rena, Kate, Lora, had always come along with Elsie, and gathered in the kitchen as usual, knowing as they stood there that John would make them all their own little round sugar crusts to eat.

Sarah and Clyde would now miss going to the Taylor house where Anne's kitchen was a delight for their family reunions. Her house was a three-story and the kitchen was built underground as a basement and Ann did wonderful cooking herself.

How she would miss her sister, Jane Freemole, and the children Mae, Winifred and Frank. Jane's husband, Sam, was such a tease and she would miss his laughing ways.

They had just made a trip out to Sleepy Lane a few days ago to say goodbye to her brother, Mike and his wife, Emily. She wept when she hugged Cora, Harry, Charles, Pearl, Florence, Irene and especially Lillie.

Goodbyes had been said to Frank and Ann and their two daughters Nettie Marie and Eva Merle. All had been left with a wishful invitation to come and visit them when they got established. Being such a close family, Sarah made her promises to come back when they were all settled. The word settle meant something different now.

The saddest farewell of all was to the one that could not be said. Sarah's sister Mary spent her late years in the Lincoln State Asylum. Her only daughter, Grace's head was blown off accidentally while one of the brothers was cleaning a shotgun. Clyde and Sarah said their goodbyes to her sons, Axel, Orson, Anson, Gordon, and most sadly to Victor - for he was Clyde's childhood friend and "wild west" riding companion. All were waiting. Clyde's wagon was pulled by oxen as was John's. Some were their own they had bought over the years to plow the big garden behind their house, plus they had borrowed all the brothers oxen they had for their plowing. The plan was to have a trip down to the new land by the brothers and their cousin Victor to bring them back when they were settled. The other horses they had acquired over the years and had used for their wagon team for errands, would help lead the oxen, once they got used to the travel. At first they would walk in front of them and lead them until they got used to the routine. Of course, Clyde's prize horses would go along.

They had packed flour in a large keg and yeast for baking bread. They had dried meat, crackers, cornmeal, bacon, eggs, potatoes, rice and beans, sugar, salt and lard. They would hunt for game on the way. John had packed many doughnuts just to keep the children happy and to go with Clyde's coffee.

Sarah's surrey was waiting for her, which was second in line hitched to Clyde's Hambletonian horses. Waiting for her, sat Ruby who wanted to ride with Granny in what she called "the funny buggy." She was beside herself with the excitement of the trip, which of course had been much touted as a great adventure by her father. He had already succeeded in making the little girl child into a cute little tomboy.

Whatever could be put at their feet was crowded in. It was a hard choice on what to take. Sentimental items had to be left for practical things like needles, threads, saws, hammers, axes, nails, knives and rags. These were just some of the practical that outweighed anything impractical. Under the seat was Zebulun's old doctor's bag with medical things that might be needed on the trip.

John was going to bring up the rear with a very utilitarian covered wagon. It was loaded to the last inch with things that would enable them to feed not only themselves, but if all worked well, things for another boarding house or at least a restaurant. The wagon contained kitchen utensils to feed others on reaching their destination. They had the dream to continue in the occupation that had supported them thus far.

On the back of the wagons John and Clyde had built heavy chests to carry the daily cooking gear that might be needed over a campfire. The chests provided things that would be needed daily such as metal plates, cups, knives, forks, pans, skillets, a coffee pot, soap and a huge kettle for heating water. All these things and more they would need easy access to on the trip at each stop.

All were loaded up and waiting for Sarah as she walked out of the boarding house. The gravity of what they were doing really dawned on her as she saw all that was left of their possessions in those two covered wagons. Clyde might tell little Ruby that it was a grand adventure, but to her suddenly it looked like insanity. Under her breath she said, "God Help Us." She realized they were homeless and getting ready to go out into the wilds of nature with no turning back.

John came to her side to help her into the surrey. With a questioning look on his face, he took the strange little stool from her hands and helped her into the surrey beside the excited little girl. He laid the stool beside Sarah's feet, pushing it back under the seat not knowing that it seemed to belong beside the old medical bag where he placed it. Saying nothing, he went back to his wagon and climbed up onto the old board seat. The two dogs, Daisy and Dinky, waited on the seat with tails wagging furiously. They, like Clyde and Ruby, were ready for the great adventure.

In the wagon that was for himself, Mary, and little Jack, Clyde, looked back to see if all were ready, and started with a lurch. Sarah, used to driving the surrey and the pacers, followed behind with no problem. Looking back, she saw John, after a slight problem getting the oxen to move, come behind their little procession.

All of a sudden, there was a catch in Sarah's throat as she looked up the length of the street. People were coming outside or were already lined up to say and wave goodbye. The word had gotten around this was the morning of their leaving and it seemed all the little families had come out to honor them and to say farewell. This little family that had helped them pioneer their own little town of Tecumseh, Nebraska, was off on a journey to another primitive land. They all knew firsthand what hardships they faced.

As their wagons ambled along to the end of the street where the prairie started, it seemed as if they were the center of a parade, as old friends and neighbors, many that knew Clyde from a small boy, waved and wished them farewell in unison.

Mary and Sarah had tears running down their cheeks, going down the dirt street, as they waved back to all. Clyde was trying his best to be strong. These were the people that saw him grow up. The people that had loved and scolded him as needed as a boy and who had been a part of his daily life. They had watched him place little dog friends in his own little prairie graveyard that he was leaving behind. They knew their names as they had run up and down the street with him. These were people that cheered a young widow on with her successes and had cried with her when her mother had died and at her sister's tragedy. These were people that had welcomed a man from another land into their midst and accepted him as one of them.

All of a sudden a team and horses came running up behind them. As Mary Edna looked back, she saw her Mother and Father stopping their buckboard and getting out to say goodbye again as they had the night before. They ran up to the side of the wagon to hug Mary one more time. As her Father walked around the wagon to shake hands with Clyde again, the Grandmother ran back to the surrey to kiss her little granddaughter. Mary, in tears, waved with her parents standing there watching, as they drove the wagon on. The father cried out after the wagon in his British accent, "Clyde, take good care of my daughter." Little Ruby was waving furiously back at her Grandparents and yelling to them in her excited little voice, "I'll see you tomorrow, Grammie Ann and Grampy Jack!"

As the lumbering little caravan came to the edge of what was Tecumseh's main street and pulled out onto the prairie, the last thing they heard was a small child's voice yelling, "Goodbye Mr. John."

No more "saving face." The man from China cried. After all, only the dogs would see. One did. Daisy licked the tears from the man's usually smiling face.

Ann Rainey, Mary's Mother

Jack Rainey, Mary's Father

ARCADE HOTEL

Arcade Hotel photo, courtesy of Tecumseh Historical Society

OFF TO THE CHEROKEE STRIP

*"Let us put our minds together and see what
life we can make for our children."*
SITTING BULL

The big decision to move to the newly opened
land was not one to venture into alone. After the
decision was made, Clyde had found the nearest
place to Tecumseh to meet up with a wagon train
that was heading for the land give away. Many people were making the attempt to go to the new land
in that way, for it was the safe way to go, rather than
making the perilous journey alone.

In this day of traveling through new fron-
tiers, there had arisen knowledgeable ways to travel
safely. The wagon trains that traveled across the
prairie would hire trail guides. These were profes-
sional men who had made the trip before and knew
the way. These men had gained special knowledge
that was helpful to the travelers. They would know
about creeks or rivers and of course the best paths
to follow.

The wagon train was made up of many peo-
ple wanting to start a new life or a better one. This
was an extraordinary time as the Indian Territory
was opening for homesteading. The price was unbelievable. The main cost was courage and a
willingness to give up everything that one had for "a
free great-unknown."

A proclamation had been issued by the new
President of the United States, Benjamin Harrison.
This proclamation made on March23, 1889 stated
that public lands in the Indian Territory, or The Unassigned Lands, would be open to settlers at noon
on April 22, 1889. Many people throughout the

United States rejoiced at the opportunity to own homes and farms in a young and growing community.

According to these rules so proclaimed by President Harrison, anyone could enter the Unassigned Lands from the borders of this region at exactly noon, April 22nd, 1889. Every person, even the "boomers" who had been active in their attempts to already settle the country and had been expelled, were given an equal chance to stake or claim either a farm of 160 acres or a lot in the places chosen for town sites. To this call the Ingrahm family turned their back on all they knew and all they had worked so hard to establish. They had done it before. They were determined to do it again. The cry for adventure in Clyde's spirit was going full speed. "On to Indian Territory," he cried out inside, as Sarah instead was weeping inwardly for all she was leaving behind.

After a couple of hours ride, the little family's caravan met with the wagon train heading for the Indian Territory. By this time, they had started to get used to the strange mode of travel. They were becoming adjusted to the feel of the wagon and the guiding of the animals.

At the junction, they were amazed at the number of wagons making the trip. There were families just as they that were wanting to start new lives. Many were the plans, should they find their own land. Of course there were farmers, planning to live off their own land. There were storekeepers, wanting to set up new shops. There were teachers, and carpenters. There were people who made and repaired wagons and their wheels, which were valuable to have along. There were blacksmiths and doctors and dentists. There were ministers and their families. There were many kinds of people, seeking new lives. Free land was the chance of a lifetime and had come at a time in their life that seemed to be their destiny calling to them. That was the way Clyde worded it.

The train would increase as it would journey through the land. There were children in abundance. Most amazing of all, there was a scattering of lone women or lone women with children. These were brave, hardy women who struck out alone, for whatever reason, to start a new life for them and their children. It was to be seen to that they received attention and care from the rest of the wagon train. Clyde's family was amazed at the size of the wagon train that would follow this winding trail.

They soon learned there were leaders who would decide when they would stop and where. They would wake everyone up in the morning to get them ready to leave by daylight. There were men who would ride up ahead of the wagon train line to make sure everything was alright. There would be plans made of who would stand guard at night to protect the animals from wolves, coyotes and wildcats and warn the people if anything was wrong. There would be a meeting to organize people to go hunting the next day. These councils kept everything running smoothly. Most importantly, were the hired trail guides. Usually they had been traders and trappers for many years. Some had been explorers and scouts of this relatively new land. Their knowledge was of great help.

It was an exciting experience at first, but very soon the newness wore off. It became obvious after the first day, before they had met the wagon train that they wouldn't ride for most of the day.

They felt every bump sitting on the board wagon
seat of the wagons. Even Sarah's surrey felt every
rut in the trail. Just a short ride and it was more
comfortable to walk. By the first night, their bodies
were aching and cramping. Despite throwing more
quilts on the seats, it was not long before the adults
were walking.

They would walk next to the wagon. On either side was tall, blue stem prairie grass, leaving
little room to walk. They were mindful of what
might be hiding in the grass that might be more
than waist high. Sometimes it was even over their
heads. They would stay close to wagon ruts made
by other wagons. By the end of the day their feet
were tired and sore. It was not going to be an easy
trip. Much of the time the oxen pulling wagons had
to be walked beside. Oxen did not adjust to reins
as horses did. At times Mary drove the surrey. Sarah would ride with Clyde or sometimes John. At
other times Mary let Ruby take the reins for the
horses were accustomed to the monotonous clip,
clop, of following the wagon before them. She felt
like she was really a "big girl" when she held the
reigns in her hands. Children needed to run and
play so she was given the reins to take her mind off
of being restless. Mary would sit back then and
hold little Jack, as she watched her little girl say
over and over, "Gidyup. Gidyup." Ruby was a pleasant child and thankfully so, but little children need
to move and she wanted out to do so. She was very
bored and would ask many times a day, "Are we
'bout there?" Mary didn't realize that to little Ruby
"there" meant back to the house she had always
lived in, for she had always returned there after a
ride.

Mary was thankful for the fact that Jack was a complacent little boy with a very good nature. He always had a smile for anyone who looked his way. Even the rugged men on horseback would talk to the little guy as they passed him, just to get one of his infectious smiles. A little conversation thrown his way would produce twinkling eyes, a head thrown back and a loud chuckle. Clyde and Mary were blessed with two pleasant natured children.

The sleeping arrangements varied according to weather. Some would sleep in the wagon. Some would sleep under it, and some in the tent. On special nights they would sleep under the stars. The children were usually put in the wagons.

It wasn't easy to keep completely dry when it rained but the canvas tarps on the wagons and on the tent were waterproofed and rubbed with oil for that purpose. The best place should a torrential rain come, which thankfully was not on this trip, was inside the wagon. The next best place would be in the tent. On the few nights it rained, it was a matter of everyone crowding together, and getting sleep the best you could in the wagon. A few nights "sleeping under the stars" was enjoyable, but most times it wasn't. It was spring and the nights were mostly cool.

Mary and Sarah learned very early that this journey had nothing to do with looking fashionable. At the start of the journey they were, as most women, wanting to look well in public. They were practical enough to know they would need a head covering and so had selected a reasonably attractive hat for the first days. Also, although not a church dress, one of their nicer ones had been picked because of women's vanity. It did not take them both very long into the journey before they dug out of the trunk their garden sunbonnets, and very practical dresses that weren't the more pretty Calico and Gingham they had preferred. Both wore their sunbonnets to protect them from being in the open all day and also to protect their eyes from sun and the dust. They wore plain colored dresses with high topped shoes. Jack fought wearing a bonnet at first, but finally he adjusted to it. Ruby didn't really care of course at her young age, but it was mandatory to wear cotton sunbonnets to protect her on the sunny, dusty trail. Sometimes her Daddy put his western style hat on her with the wide brim to protect her from the sun and she pretended she was a cowboy. She thought it went well with her "Gidyup".

For as cattlemen do, the men had been warned to wear the wide brimmed hat for protection and a handkerchief around their neck for the dust that was stirred up by the oxen and horses ahead of them. It might be pulled up over the face when it was needed due to plain old prairie wind. Oklahoma red dust and wind would be ahead, unlike anything they had experienced. They had all been warned before the trip that because of the walking, they needed to purchase sturdy shoes. Blessed was the shoemaker who happened to be on the trip.

At the very first day, it seemed as a joyful picnic to eat on the trail. Soon that was too a chore, as everything else was. In the daily schedule, most on the trail greatly enjoyed the break after a long morning of traveling. Eating during the day was kept very simple with non-cooked food such as jerky and dried fruits. Biscuits were brought from home along with things that had been baked before they left, but that would soon run out or spoil so all those prepared things were eaten first. The standard things that were essentials, such as the potatoes, bacon, dried meat, crackers, cornmeal, flour, and beans would be prepared later. Beans were the trail standard. Boiled eggs had been prepared and Sarah had prepared fried chicken for the first night.

At the night stop, the men and some of the children would gather small branches and firewood to cook their supper. Ruby was given a basket to gather small kindling wood. At the first this was an exciting thing for a little girl needing some activity.

The Ingrahms had brought a little portable oven for biscuits and for other things, as they had plans for it beyond the trip. On the days the guide would direct them to camp near a creek, the men or women would go bring water in buckets, to protect the water supplies for the stretches where they would have to use the water in the barrels that they had brought from home.

How the word home stung as they realized it was sitting empty and was no more their own. It was waiting for the arrival of strangers. At that thought, Sarah's mind flashed to Zeb's trunk, sitting there abandoned. She wished she had somehow had courage to go through it. At least she would always have the stool sitting under the surrey seat.

Late in the days as they journeyed on, they longed for the time to stop. They were tired and aching to rest. After the meal had been prepared, and their beds made, they learned to look forward to the time around the fire. It was a special time for the family when they were able to rest together with only the light of the lanterns hanging on the wagon and the light and the warm glow of the fire. If those in charge of the train could find a space that was relatively low in grass or better yet none, they would make the big circle they always made for safety at night in that place.

When all surrounded in the big circle the children were set free to play in that circle. What activity went on, when after their day of boring riding or walking was over! Clyde would get out his old violin, and as he had done so many times at home, play some of his and the children's favorite songs. Some were Irish and some were classical. Some were songs that were brought to this country by the pioneers from other lands that had passed through their hotels.

Since children never seem to tire as adults do, they would clap their hands and dance as he played. Their growing legs needed to dance and move because of the little running they did, having had to be close to the wagon. The prairie grass was higher than some of the children's heads. They lived in a prairie grass prison from which they were only released at the late evening time. It was good though that there was prairie grass for the animals they brought along. The people in the wagons nearby would peacefully listen, and enjoyed the music.

After they had been on the trail a short time, a family who also liked to sing, came and joined them, whose oldest son played a mouth organ. Before long, a lady brought her guitar and evening concerts were a nightly thing. After they started to get acquainted, all the people started singing.

Soon, the adults started to introduce dances from their countries and on the nights they weren't too tired they would dance and the instruments from other wagons were brought out. There were Irish dances and what we would now call square dances. Violin music produced lovely waltzes. It became a wonderful blend of joyful folk songs from far off lands.

Clyde fell back into what his old habits had been when he helped keep the people in the boarding houses occupied with song and stories in his younger days. He found that joy again and many joined him who had those talents. After long, hard, dreary days of plodding along behind oxen, horses, mules and wagons, or in them, this special time of rest and music was looked forward to.

To anyone looking on, in those pioneer days, in the middle of deep prairie darkness would be seen huge circles of wagons, glowing fires, lanterns, music, clapping, dancing and laughter. The gathering together of many people, and many cultures from many lands, that would bring about what would be one day just called Americans.

Long after that trail ride was over, many would remember those times under the stars, when they were homeless people, looking for a dream, and smile at the memory of the wagon train evenings. Even the wagon masters thought back with pleasure on that special trip to the Big Land Rush.

In the darkness, a native people listened and watched with wonder at this new music and dancing and also a foreboding of this people that were spreading over their land.

As they traveled on, and prepared their evening meals, new food was discovered. Wild berries they had not had up north. Fish from the creeks were a fried treat and new species of game or birds were on the menu. The best hunting game of all was deer. As long as the flour or corn meal barrel held out there was always fried bread, or fried corn cakes.

The next morning, before daylight, fires were started with wood and twigs that had been gathered the night before so the breakfast could be over before daylight and the tiresome journey of plodding along would start again. Eggs might be taken out of the flour barrels, where they rode for their safety and fried and maybe some boiled for the lunch stop. Daylight was important to get as much trail behind you as you could so you would be closer to the Promised Land called the Unassigned Lands, or as Clyde preferred to call it "Indian Territory." The wagons would start moving and travel until lunchtime. Then they would rest for an hour or two. After lunch you would travel again until there was only enough time to gather the wood and water before dark. Day after endless day it went on.

One day, on the distant horizon there appeared some Indians. The Indians were friendly ordinarily, but they were surprised to see this long wagon train moving slowly along their land. They were used to trading with strange, white people, but they were not used to seeing this long line of wagons with white sails, moving through the prairie grass like some big slow moving snake. Had they ever seen ships, when they saw the wagons with the grass over their wheels, with only the beds of the wagons showing, with big white canvases waving in the wind, slowly moving through an ocean of yellow prairie grass, they would have thought they were seeing ocean Schooners. That's where the name Prairie Schooners for covered wagons had come from. To their eyes now this was the strangest thing they had seen in this land. They had become used to the Iron Horses. They stood on the knolls and hills and watched this strange snake like thing until it was gone. Then they hurried back to tell their people what they had seen. Surely, they thought, it was an evil foreboding thing. It was.

On many days, good days, they could walk fifteen miles a day. If it was very muddy and raining very hard, they might make only one mile in a whole day. They would struggle on through the mud.

The opposite problem was when the ground was too dry. Then there would be dust. So much dust it got in all their eyes, if not sheltered in the wagon. It got in the horses and cattle's eyes. It was so thick you could not see your hand before your face at times.

The color of the land was starting to change. The black rich looking soil started to change to red. The wind seemed to be more intense. On the times that happened, they had no choice but to stop traveling because they couldn't see the trail. The gritty dirt and sand blew against their faces. Some of the time they kept going and hoped the animals could see the trail. They had to trust the animals knew where the trail was. That's when the handkerchiefs and rags were put over their faces. Thankfully there were not many days such as that.

Quite a way into the journey, Jack's little countenance changed. He would not smile. His little cheeks grew red. When Mary felt his head, she knew he was burning with a high fever. His mother got water from inside the wagon and tried to force him to drink as much as he would. The little dark haired boy, whose hair hung in wet ringlets, would shake his head no, and take no more. Mary at first thought maybe it was the last dust storm affecting him.

As the day wore on and his little hot body lay limply against his mother, his eyes began to look listless. Although she had told Clyde of her fears, and Clyde kept looking over at his little boy, he had to keep driving the team, as they had to keep moving with the wagon train. Suddenly, Mary felt the baby's small body become stiff and watched as his little eyes turned glassy and rolled back in his head. His small body started to convulse. "Stop the wagon, Clyde," Mary screamed. "Stop the wagon!" Clyde pulled the team to a stop. He jumped down from the wagon, and took the jerking baby boy from his mother's arms. He ran to the side of the wagon where the water barrel was attached.

Sarah, hearing Mary's scream, quickly jumped down from the surrey and was at Clyde's side now, and let the plug out of the barrel far enough that water gently poured over the little child's entire body. She cupped her hand over his nose so he would not choke.

John was standing at Mary's side, holding her closely, as she sobbed. She started screaming hysterically. "I'm not leaving my baby on this God-forsaken prairie in a grave", she screamed. "I'm not leaving my little Jackie here!"

A crowd had been gathering, and on up the train the news traveled that there was trouble in the rear. People from behind them were running up and watching the frantic action.

Suddenly, John loosened Mary and walked over to the baby, who was still quivering in his father's arms. He put his hand on the child's body and bowed his head in prayer. The still gathering crowd, quieted. Suddenly the crowd, one by one, bowed their heads. Weeping mothers prayed for the young mother in compassion. Fathers, seeing the quietly sobbing father, prayed in unison. Hardened, rough, cursing trail men removed their hats in reverence, and prayed to the name they generally used as a curse word, when they saw the plight of the little smiling boy child. The small boy stopped convulsing, lying limply in his father's arms. Sarah put the plug back in the water barrel and quickly ran to the surrey, where Zebulun's medical bag was. She hurriedly pulled out a small brown bottle of elixir and ran back to where the openly shaken father with the limp, still, boy stood. She put a tiny drop upon her forefinger, opened the little boy's mouth, and touched the liquid to his pink tongue.

Sarah took Jack from his father's arms as he watched helplessly. Clyde's entire body was shaking. Silent tears were running down his face. Sarah took the child and wiped him off, taking off all his clothes. She laid him on his blanket, naked, and said, "Let the air get to his body to help cool him."

She then said, "John, bring the medical bag." He hurriedly went to the wagon where the kit rested under the seat. Running quickly, he brought the bag to Sarah who was fanning the baby. Taking out the stethoscope, she put it to the little gently breathing chest. Listening for a few moments, as the crowd increased that gathered around the scene she lifted her head and said, "He's ok. He's just resting now."

Sarah put her hand on her sons face, wiping the tears, and said again, "He's just resting now. His little body is just exhausted from the convulsion. He'll be o.k. He's just resting."

Mary, having now gained her composure, and looking at the people gathered around, climbed up into the wagon, thinking Sarah would hand the baby to her. Sarah said, "I'll take him in the surrey with me. Ruby has learned how to keep the reins. I'll watch him. He's going to be fine. He's just resting now." Mary, trusting Sarah's nursing skills, let her mind relinquish her baby to Sarah.

Clyde climbed up in the wagon and slapped the reins over the horses. His mom had said little

Jack would be fine, so he believed it. "He's just rest-ing," he reassured himself. "He's just resting."

The confident looking Sarah wasn't so sure.

As Sarah with the baby in her arms, got Ruby seated and was preparing to hand the reigns to the little girl, Ruby asked Sarah a startling ques-tion.

"Who was that strange man, Grannie?"

Preoccupied with the baby, Sarah asked, "What strange man, Ruby?"

"That man with the shiny white dress," said Ruby.

"I didn't see any man in a dress, Ruby," Sa-rah said, still preoccupied.

"It was shiny, shiny white. I never see'd such white."

Sarah, now feeling a multitude of goose bumps said, to the child, "Tell me exactly everything you saw."

"When all the people were standing praying, and John was praying, I saw the man, just like he came out of nowhere, Grannie, and he was standing by Jackie. He put both his hands on Jackie. Then Jackie quit jerking around. He just laid still, like he was asleep. Then the man, he smiled at me. He had such purdy eyes. When he smiled at me I wasn't scared anymore. Then he said something to Jackie. Then he was gone! He was just gone, Grannie!"

Sarah was feeling a sensation such as she had felt many years ago, with an encounter she had with just such a stranger on a battleground. Alt-hough it was hard for her to speak, she was so overwhelmed with emotion, she forced herself to ask one more question of her little granddaughter. "Ruby, What did he say to little Jack?"

He said, "Rest now little Jack. I'll see you in thirty years."

"Say that again, Ruby," said Sarah, not understanding what the child said, or thinking maybe she had misunderstood. Emphatically the little girl said, "He said, rest now little Jack. I'll see you in thirty years." As Sarah looked down, she saw that her own tears were falling on the gently resting baby boy. Realizing they were holding up the wagon train behind them, she directed Ruby to make the horses go.

With the great horsemanship she had acquired on this trip, and taking the reins, Ruby said in her best cowboy voice, "Gidyup, you horses, Gidyup."

Sarah never mentioned what Ruby had told her to Clyde or Mary. Although Ruby talked about "a shiny man" to them, she never remembered to mention the message given to Jack.

Somehow, Sarah was glad.

AN INUMERABLE MULTITUDE

The weary family of travelers knew that there would be many people with the same dream they had. They had passed many on the trail to the Unassigned Lands. However there was no way the human mind could expect what they found when they reached the boundary line. That is, as close as they could get to the boundary line.

The largest crowd was on the northern boundary, which is where they were. The multitude that was milling around and camped at the very gate of the "Promised land" was vehicle to vehicle. It was horse to horse. It was wagon to wagon. It was ox cart to ox cart. They were all intermingled. There were people on foot, standing shoulder to shoulder. There were short men, tall men, and there were women, fat and skinny. There were all types from the rough trail rider types, to the dignified and well dressed. There were the rich, with their linen handkerchiefs held to their noses, to the poor, ragged, dirty and smelly. There were those that looked too young, and those that looked too ancient to even crawl in a wagon. There were angelic women making the run alone for the sake of their children with them, to those who looked like harlots from the bordellos. Camps were teeming on all sides of that Unassigned Land as it had been called.

The unbelievable crowds were in an array of mixed transportation. Their covered wagons and their surrey, was wedged between every inconceivable kind of transport. Some had made the most ludicrous carts out of inconceivable material. Clyde was astride his jittery horse that had made the wagon train trip well, considering it was such a new experience to him but this exuberant, excessively noisy crowd had the horse spooked. This was a concern to Clyde. He had counted greatly on this Hambleltonian breed for this chance to get a stake or claim.

Next to him was a man on a white mule. There were Indian ponies known for their speed. There were boney backed nags that it seemed a miracle they were even standing up. There were plow horses and mules. In the mix of it all, was John with his wagon and oxen. There, as far as you could see, were the throngs of people, as they waited in those last moments, all lined up at the border, ready to make the run into this miracle land give-away. Clyde thought of a scripture in the Gospel of Luke that said, "There were gathered together an innumerable multitude of people, insomuch that they trode one upon another."

This was the only opportunity of a life-time for many to have something of their own. Many hardy souls stood nervously among the mayhem around them, literally on foot. All were waiting for that twelve o'clock bugle and shots from the military guard into the air.

That morning, to their amazement, fifteen long trains loaded with passengers from Arkansas City, Kansas arrived at the border of the Unassigned Lands to wait for twelve o'clock noon. The train's overflow passengers were seated on the tops of the railroad coaches and others were hanging on the steps. When the time drew near for the starting signal, there were men standing ready to jump on the cow catchers.

There had also been loaded trains waiting at Purcell, in the Chickasaw Nation, with passengers bound for Oklahoma City, Edmond, and

Guthrie. A mass of humanity crowded to the borders to make what they considered the "run of their lives." The crowds were angry at the train's presence not knowing that they had been set to go no faster than the hordes could go. People were scrambling, pushing and shoving. The militia was lined up strong and nervously on the border.

No one was allowed to set foot on the new land until noon of that day. It was a multitude of madness. It was a multitude of hope. It would be for many, a multitude of despair. Many had turned their back on their past for a hope of a new future. Many had no past and were hoping to find a future. Many brave souls would stake a claim of a farm of 160 acres by the time the day was over. Others would be left, with dust on their face, eyes, and teeth, and nothing in their hand but defeat. Some got trampled to death in the race. A few died of a heart attack from the stress. Some celebrated with great jubilation before the day was out. Some cried with soul shaking sorrow with their past-life given up, and left with no future before them. Many that thought they won that day, had no idea what gut wrenching struggle lay before them in establishing a new life out of the unmerciful, untamed red dirt, prairie, and rock. This was what would be called "The Great Oklahoma Land Rush" in history. For this, the Ingrahm family had left all behind.

When twelve o'clock came, shots were fired into the air by the military guards, and bugles were sounded. The signal that the race for the claims was on! On the northern boundary, an indescribably huge shout of a congregation of voices arose from the anxiously waiting crowd. All at the same time fifteen long trains started puffing away down the track with their nerve-wracking bells ringing, whistles loudly sounding, and smoke bellowing from their black smokestacks. The trains had started their engines, even before the time for the signal to start, which had primed the waiting crowd to an even higher pitch.

Those on foot took off with the sound of the shots. Horses, with a kick of their rider's foot and a loud "Hah" lunged forward at a fast speed, with their riders leaning forward, getting ready for the ride of their life. Some recent immigrants yelled go to their horses in a language that those around them did not understand. Wagon teams felt a crack directly on their back they were not used to, and buggy horses were encouraged onward in a way that startled them, for their drivers were never this impatient. Every muscle in the runner's legs and body was straining, and as this huge dash of their life, of men, women, animals and assorted vehicles raced forward to locate free land claims, an event of unimaginable proportions was being carried out.

After all, the slow moving settling of the past had been bit by bit, little by little, in this great country, and now in the space of one monumental day by evening of April 22nd, 1889, thousands of people would be located in new towns and on homesteads scattered throughout the Oklahoma Country.

At the signal, the family followed the carefully made plans. Hopefully, Clyde would be the one who would surely gain a claim by speed. One of his two most treasured possessions were part of that plan. His two Hambletonian horses would serve on two fronts. He himself would on horseback take one, and on a dash for speed, he would quickly get to a claim. The other horse, also the same type of horse which was from the great line of horses that was bred for speed, would pull Sarah in the surrey and she would also seek a claim. Mary would put the children in the household wagon, seal up the back flaps tightly and drive it, with John following her closely, should she have a need with the children or help of any kind. They would head to the landmark that the family had been told to meet at. Clyde had known some "Sooners" who had lived illegally in the land before and was able to get the directions to a meeting place for them all that would be easy to find. This was to prevent getting lost and separated in the mayhem of what they knew would happen and also keep them out of the great fray.

There were things the family had not counted on; first of all, trainloads of people, who were long ready for this day to take part in this awesome event. Secondly unexpected, was Clyde's plan for his mad dash on horseback and also Sarah's light surrey ride were thwarted by one thing. Hambletonians were champion pacers. Not runners. No match for the sturdy horses that could run fast and with endurance were long accustomed to the rough clay and sandstone rock and prairie grass.

As the race had been going for what seemed an eternity to Sarah, ahead of her she saw a disastrous happening. A child had fallen out of a wagon as it careened and rocked back and then righted itself. Sarah saw the child fall as it happened. The animals and vehicles approaching the small girl were veering around her sharply. Sarah pulled her surrey to rest in front of the child to shield her from the racing swarm that would surely, if not alert, trample the little girl in the stampede. She got out of the buggy, praying the tremendous commotion running all around them would not spook her horse to run away. Running and bending down on her knees she quickly checked the crying child to see if anything was broken, not wanting to damage her further. Seeing that she only seemed to be scratched and bleeding from light wounds, she gathered up the screaming girl who looked to be about three, and ran back to the surrey and climbed up in the seat with her. Still speaking to the horse to hold steady she got the medicine bag out from under the seat and wrapped the little girls head with a linen homemade bandage to cover a place where she had scrapped her forehead. Just as she finished the child's wrapping, a large man ran up to the buggy.

"Is she alright?" asked the heavily breathing man as he peered at his crying child.

"Yes," said Sarah, "There's only a scrape on her forehead which will leave no scar. Just keep it oiled."

"Thank you so much Ma'am. I just knew she would be trampled. Thank God, you shielded her with your surrey. I got to get back to my wife and family. They're sitting in all this madness, trying to hold the wagon still."

Sarah said, "Get up in the seat and I'll take you both to your family." The man crawled up quickly and took his little redheaded girl who wrapped her arms around her daddy's neck and quit crying. Sarah slapped the reins over the horse and they took off so fast, it jerked the threesome sitting in the surrey.

Soon they came in sight of the wagon full of frightened children and the crying mother sitting in the wagon seat, holding a baby, and holding desperately to the reins. The man quickly got down from the seat with his child and looking for only a moment at Sarah said, "Ma'am, I will never forget you for saving my baby. I swear I'm gonna pray for you every day of my life. What's your name?"

As the horses and mules and wagons went by furiously, the man crawled up unto the wagon seat and put the little girl between himself and her mother. Trying to be heard over the noise he yelled, "What did you say your name was?"

"Sarah Elizabeth," she shouted back to him.

Giving her one more very serious look, he said, "God Bless you, Sarah Elizabeth!" He slapped the horse's backs and the wagon gave a jerk and off they went.

Seeing what speed the man took off in brought her back to reality and she realized that she too had a race to run. As she slapped the reins she wondered where Clyde was, and if Mary, John and the children were safe. She had never seen such pandemonium.

John's wagon, which would be their preparation for starting a new life, and prepared to open a food serving place for the new arrivals, was too heavy to be in the race for speed. Oxen have a mind of their own and running was not a priority with those stubborn creatures. They did not want to risk the life of the children, Jack and Ruby or Mary, so grouping John and Mary's wagons together was the plan for them to get to the safe meeting place.

The children had cried at the top of their lungs from the very start of all the noisy pandemonium at the beginning of the gunfire. Clyde's dogs who were tied in the wagon with them were barking continuously and Mary wanted to cry herself. The tumult around them in the mad race was indescribable. Then it was over! The pair had gotten their precious cargo to the safe place they had been told about and stopped the wagons to await Sarah and

Clyde's arrival after their race. So they waited. Their waiting seemed to stretch on endlessly.

In the evening of April 22nd, 1889, Clyde, Mary, Sarah, John and the children sat in the midst of the settled, choking dust feeling the biggest defeat of their lives together. They had made no claims. They had given up all behind them and now their lives seemed over. Their dreams lay in the dust of all that they had left for the dream of a new home in Indian Territory. They had not gained their promised land.

The most frightening thing of all, there was nothing to go back to. As they sat in their abject misery, with no homestead in this unknown land, their minds went to their former home where other people were living now. The unthinkable had happened.

When they regrouped, in stunned silence, not even able to communicate with each other, they looked at all that was going on around them, as the soldiers tried to keep order. They listened to disputes over ownerships. They wandered among arguing and fighting people who said they had claimed the same piece of land. They saw happy families, busily putting up their tents or guarding their claims protectively. There were many people just like them, who just stared vacantly at all the ownership disputes, and could not believe that in this great lottery of their life, they had lost. They had nothing. They had given up everything and they had not gotten a claim. The unthinkable had happened.

In the midst of their disillusionment, Ruby said, "Daddy, where's our land? Are we there, yet?" Then she added, "I'm hungry." Being brought back to reality, beyond her own pain, Mary realized it had been a long day and the children hadn't been fed.

As she brought out the food that had been prepared for this first day and assembled the little children around their meal, she noticed that people with their families were gathering around them; looking hungrily as they ate. A plan was started that day, much earlier, and certainly in a way that was not planned, but fast food service was started that first day. This family, who had always made serving their business, started serving through their unseen tears and heartbreak.

The military, that was there to make sure there was no one staying in the territory that did not get a claim, were hungry too. As people gathered around their little wagon, no one took –notice that they were there illegally. The family itself was too busy to realize they were illegally there. An old proverb says, "Ignorance is bliss."

As they busily fed what seemed like a multitude, Sarah said to John, "We are eating our seed, very quickly." She was referring to the food they had brought to set up a business when they moved to their new claim. "Yes," replied John, "We will need this food to live on until we find out what to do and where to go from here. The dried jerky is going fast."

Clyde was out with many other men, supposedly, looking for game at the moment. Mary knew Clyde well enough by now, to know he actually was off being alone on a prairie somewhere, trying to deal, just he and his horse, with the supreme disappointment of his life. It seemed to her that he had a way of disappearing at what seemed to be the ultimate time of Mary's need. She was baring a double heartache at the time, while her husband was trying to deal in his way with the failure of his ultimate "adventure." She worked busily meeting the food needs of their new customers and her little children. She would cry later, when everyone was asleep.

That day when they decided they would have to stop feeding hungry mouths, and move on, when Clyde returned from his hunt, a man and his wife approached the wagon.

"Pardon me," the gentleman said, "I'm looking for the owner of this establishment."

Sarah and Mary smiled at one another, thinking of the former boarding houses they had run. "We work together here," Sarah said, nodding to Mary and John.

At this moment John was looking very serious, as he was afraid that someone was on to the fact that they were illegally sitting in this place, conducting business. Maybe this was their land.

Sarah continued, "My son is out looking for wild game and this gentleman's name is John. My name is Sarah Ingrahm. This is my daughter-in-law, Mary."

"We are the Robertson's," the man introduced himself. "We have acquired some excellent land. We came with the thought that if we were fortunate to get what we wanted, and we did, we would be proprietors of a hotel. It will be a very good business as many people will need a place to stay in this new land," the man continued. Then a serious look crossed his face. "That was not your plan, was it?"

Sarah nodded her head no, as she heard a voice inside of her say sadly, "Not now, it's not." As she was listening carefully to what the man wanted to say, John with a smile on his face he did not mean, was thinking, "You stole our idea."

"My wife and I have been watching you since we arrived, and we are convinced, with a little training of course, you might consider coming and working with us in that area. Cooking is not one of our strong points, although management is, and we wondered if you would feel able to manage a kitchen in our hotel? You seem so well suited, and it seems you work very well together, and as I said, with some training, it seems you might be just what we would require to work in our establishment. I assure you the pay will be worth your consideration. It will be a large business and we could provide space as board for your family if you do not mind small quarters."

"Yes," Sarah said in a business like way, "We will gladly consider your proposition."

As the couple walked away, John did something she had never seen him do. He quietly winked at her and grinned. Sarah seriously considered doing an Irish jig, even in the absence of Clyde and his fiddle. Under her breath, but loud enough for John to hear, she said, "Thank you, GOD." John not saying it out loud, but in his mind said, "Me too, GOD!"

A LITTLE HISTORY PLEASE

Mountain View, Oklahoma

In the early days of the west, the railroads were responsible for the pioneering, development, and settlement of towns. Each expansion of a main or branch line was followed by promotion and sale of town sites, to serve as centers for farming and ranching and in turn provide resources for the railroad.

Early in April 1889, The Chicago Rock Island and Pacific Railroad completed its line 51 miles west from Chickasha, Indian Territory, terminating in the northern part of the Kiowa-Comanche-Apache Reservation, which was opened for settlement in 1901.

Crowds followed the railroad. Businesses such as newspapers and saloons began. Business was booming. On April 23rd, 1899, the first cattle shipped to the end of the line and were unloaded. There were 47 cars and 2,585 young cattle in good condition with 5,000 more on the way from Texas, where 30,000 more waited to be shipped. All were turned loose on Kiowa land.

The El Reno Development Company, consisting of prominent citizens of El Reno, some were railroad officials, arrived on May 8th, 1899 and began a town site. The depot, 144 feet long, was complete with platform, stationhouse, water tanks, and a very large turntable, where the engines could be turned around for their trip back east.

By June, the row of business tents on Main Street were being replaced with frame buildings, some being built over the tents, without a loss of business. Schools were set up for fall. The town flourished. On Indian paydays, Main Street was crowded with Indian's wagons, and in the fall was crowded with cotton wagons.

THE DAILY NEWS

The Opening of the Wichita-Caddo-Comanche-Kiowa-Apache Country

"Mom, John, come outside I want to read you something," Clyde said excitedly while poking his head in the back door of the kitchen.

John turned from his place at the old stove to see what Clyde wanted, hearing the excitement in his voice. Sarah, not looking up from beating potatoes said, "Not now Clyde. We are already late with lunch. Surely it can wait," she said.

Exasperation on his face, Clyde caught her eye, while nodding at the others working in the kitchen and said, "I need to see you both outside, now. There is something very important in the papers today."

The two left their chores to others and went out the back door where Clyde was already waiting with the newspaper in his hand. Sarah, while wiping her hands on her apron said in a slightly irritated voice, "Surely the newspaper reading for you and John can wait. We are running late with the meal."

Clyde, no longer irritated, with excitement in his voice said, "Please sit down and listen, both of you. You gotta hear this. It's the dream of a lifetime. Something we have hoped for."

As she and John sat down on the old bentwood bench side by side, they looked expectantly at Clyde to begin sharing what he wanted to share. John, up until that last statement, had wondered if someone they knew had died. "Listen carefully," Clyde said as he started to read slowly, almost word by word, one at a time while sitting down on his haunches. He read the first words slowly and then paused to let it sink in to his listeners. "LAST LAND OPENING IN OKLAHOMA TERRITORY. AUGUST 6th, 1901." He scanned both faces expectantly, waiting for any kind of expression or possibly a word.

"Oh no," Sarah said adamantly, standing up and turning to go back in to the kitchen. "Not again! Not on your life!"

"But Mom, wait, listen, its important," Clyde begged.

Standing on the back door porch, Sarah whirled around and with a stubborn look Clyde recognized as meaning definitely no, she said word by word, "I will not listen to any more of your schemes." She continued, "We gave up everything we had for one of these land deals, and never again. I backed down on the Cherokee Strip Run. I even finally stood back and let you do your Wild West Show thing, but I myself will have nothing to do with another land deal."

With large, innocent eyes, and not daring to say a word in this back and forth conversation, John's head bobbed back and forth to the two as they had their "discussion." He arose, thinking if I can just turn sideways as I pass Miss Sarah on the porch, I will slide in the door and be out of the battleground, and help Mary Edna finish lunch. I already know the answer to this one.

Clyde pleadingly said, "Please, John, sit down and Mom, just hear the article and I won't say a word more, please. I do promise you it is something that won't cost you anything and you don't have to give up this life right where we are. Just hear this article please."

As both stood there staring at Clyde with questioning eyes he said again, "I promise."

John, seeing Sarah remove her hands from her hips, and starting to move back to the bench, sat back down. She seated herself beside him, but only on the edge of the bench in readiness to get up quickly. She didn't want anyone to say she was unreasonable, she said to herself, but the answer was already "No." Taking a deep breath, Clyde somewhat relieved to have another chance, pulled a chair closer to the bench where they were sitting and started over.

"On August 6th, 1901 3,500,000 Acres of the Wichita-Caddo and Comanche-Kiowa-Apache Country Will Be Opened To Settlers." He looked up and quickly said, "This time there will be no race for claims."

Sarah looked up suspiciously at Clyde and said, "Now how is this going to happen with no race?"

"Just please let me read without interrupting and you will see, Mom," he pleaded.

"Alright, but hurry please, we are late with lunch and people will already be impatient."

Clyde continued with his reading. "A person who wishes to stake a homestead claim has to register at the Government Land Office in El Reno or in Lawton, Oklahoma. They are calling it a land lottery."

"Oh really," said John, scooting forward to the edge of the bench too. Being Chinese there seemed to be gambling in his ancestral genes. Clyde had his attention. Since time immemorial Asian men have liked games of chance.

Clyde stopped reading and started explaining in his own words. "When a person registers, he is given a card which has his name and address on it. Then they are going to place that card in an envelope and then it's sealed. They are going to be receiving cards at the land offices for fifteen days. At the end of that time all the envelopes are going to be placed in a large box and shuffled. Then the land officials will draw them out and number them. A settler can then stake his homestead claim in his turn according to the number on his envelope." Clyde, taking a breath saw interest on Sarah's face and was taking slight hope.

"What is this going to cost?" asked John. Then he added, "How many homestead claims are there in this last land opening and what are the rules if you get any land?"

"Let me read further. It's all here. It's really unbelievable. I read this article several times to make sure I understood."

"There are 130,000 homestead claims at 160 acres each in this last opening. Then there will be sale of lots in three county seat town sites for the benefit of the towns and counties."

Clyde paused before answering John's question on the cost, and drew a breath. He would not reveal his thoughts of course, because he was hoping for a group agreement as always had been done, but his mind was made up that he would not pass up this chance. He would do it alone.

He continued, "Under the United States Homestead Laws, settlers on public lands will pay from $1.25 to $3.50 an acre for a claim of 160 acres. Settlers in the unassigned lands to the Indians will be given their claims free, provided they pay a $14.00 registration fee at the time of settlement, make improvements on their claim within a certain time, and live on the land for five years." Clyde stopped reading and the silence was deafening. The three just sat there. Sarah was scowling down at the ground, saying nothing.

Clyde, whose heart always was toward the Indian said, "Let me tell you what will happen toward the Indians. From the Comanche-Kiowa-Apache reservation, a half million acres will be reserved called the "Big Pasture," since it was leased to cattlemen and brought some revenue each year to these tribes. It will be called the Indian's Grass Money. The Fort Sill Military Reservation is going to be enlarged to fifty-six thousand acres, and a forest reserve will be set aside in the Wichita Mountains. These will not be opened to settlers. Fort Sill will remain an army post and the forest reserve is going to be a wildlife reserve to protect the buffalo and wildlife.

"Well, there it is," said Clyde. "What do you think of that?" He sat back in his chair and drew his breath. Pausing, he waited. No one spoke. "Do either of you have anything to say?" Again there was the deafening silence. He waited.

"Yes, I do," said Sarah finally with her forehead puckered as were her lips. "Who is going take off to go register at the Government office and who is going to go up on the day of the lottery and who gets the unlucky job of minding the kitchen?" The Asian gambling man laughed in relief as Clyde jumped from his seat, picked up his mother and whirled her around, laughing also.

Sarah was slightly disappointed when she went in to find that the other help in the kitchen had gotten the meal on expertly without her help and the guests were already enjoying their coffee and dessert.

THE NEW TOWNSITE IN THE WICHITA
INDIAN RESERVATION

*"A very great vision is needed and the man who
has it must follow it as the eagle who has it seeks
the deepest blue of the sky."*
Crazy Horse
Oglala Lakota Sioux
1840-1877

The Rock Island Railroad that had played
such an important role in opening what had been
formerly Caddo, Comanche, and Kiowa country to
white land settlement had bitterly failed the Ingrahm family. As Clyde, Mary, and the children
walked beside the train at the Lathram Station Depot, they met Sarah and John who had been looking
again the opposite way, seeing if they had missed
their tent that was to arrive today at the very latest.
Among all the piles of lumber and various goods, it
was obvious that there was no tent with their name
on it. The lots would be open tomorrow and the
platform was covered with awaited supplies for a
multitude of new land owners. Many men and
women were loading their arrivals on their wagons.
They had waited daily but today was the last day
and the last train before the lot opening in the
morning. Their grand scheme of getting ahead on
feeding a hungry town just opening obviously was
not to be. Was all they had worked and sacrificed
for to be left in the dust of others who were totally
equipped for this day?

Sadly they gathered back at the wagons
laden with all they had brought to start their business. They had come so far to finally initiate their
plan and now they would have to wait on the tent,

not being sure how long the wait would be. As the day went on, they discussed together any alternatives they could think of. When the dark fell, their hopes felt as dark the black Oklahoma sky.

The morning of the new township dawned and overnight they had made a plan. This was no time to give up. Everything was at stake. They made the decision to work with what was available and do the best they could without the tent. They would start, while the other settlers worked getting their tents and storefront buildings up, on getting food ready to eat and serve it regardless of not having a tent. They had cooked outside on the wagon train, and they could do it again. They knew that trail drive cooks thought nothing of cooking outside and so they would cook and serve without a roof for the people to sit under. If God was with them, and it didn't rain, they could do it.

On that day on the birth of a new town, into the midst of all the confusion walked this determined group; a tiny, five foot tall woman, a Chinaman, the likes of whom most had never seen before, and a Wild West Actor and his family. Clyde's pretty little wife had a child on each hand. Most of the people stared momentarily and some even stopped their work to look.

As the people worked intently on raising the buildings or tents that would stake their claim for the time being, the aromas of food arose, and called to them as they were about their busy work. It was not as the little family had planned, and yet it was because they had no tent to put up, and because they were right out in the open visually, the whole "soon to be town" was being called early to the tantalizing smells that wafted through the air around them. As the aroma bid them come, they stopped their work and came. One by one and at different times the food lured them. These ex-Nebraskans were ready to take care of the hunger that the work of these new settlers produced.

Here they were, smack dab in the middle of this town-to-be and pandemonium reigned supreme! John had never cooked so much in his life it seemed. Never had the clamor to be served filled their day, as Sarah, Mary and Clyde had experienced this day. Continually hungry people were relentlessly crowding into their lot where they had set up the primitive tables to serve people. They knew it would be hard, but they were not prepared for this mayhem. It seemed every settler that had descended on this town being newly birthed needed food.

They had been among the fortunate to get a lot in what was one of the last places that had been the Oklahoma Indian reservations that would be opened to settlers. This little piece of dirt that had been at one time Indian Territory was actually theirs. They saw the wilderness become populated overnight with a new mixed breed of people, (plus one Chinese Man). The range was cut up into a town site and lots before their very eyes that the day before was prairie. Here they were in this newly opened country. They had longed for this day, and now the business they had hoped for was so primitive and overwhelming, they wondered what on earth had ever caused them to even consider this.

That first day, one long and wide strip of red dirt ruts and prairie grass was the main street of this little town that was to grow buildings into what would be a town. The family had known they were fortunate to get a lot in this thing that wanted to call itself a town. They knew it had been their good fortune among so many that wanted it, as so many, as had happened to them in The Cherokee Strip Run, had lost this miracle chance. Now they felt God had finally smiled on them, and try they would until the last bit of sweat.

All these people were strangers, milling around each other. What must they have thought of the strange family that had ridden into their midst. Small women were not that odd, but the man, her son, drew double-takes because of his Wild Western clothes and so did his pretty wife just because people like to admire beauty. It was the other stranger, though, that drew the unabashed stares. He was a rarity to most of these pioneers. Among all these strangers among strangers, a Chinaman, as he would be called in that day, definitely stood out. Ignoring adversity, this family walked in shoulder to shoulder in spirit and set up their restaurant business, in its primitive way in the unsheltered, red Oklahoma piece of land that was their lot. As John would relay to newspaper reporters later, "We cooked in the street."

What a nightmarish amount of people were scrambling and crowding each other to get a table and demanding service in these unfavorable conditions. The large tent still had not arrived on that first opening day, when Clyde pulled away during a lull to go check. So their "eating establishment" was to remain outside and open to the street. They served and worked in the glaring sun, in the midst of the blowing dirt, and they just prayed it wouldn't rain. The blue sky was merciful, for it was a dry spell. That was a small mercy in what seemed to be terrible luck. Hopefully the tent would be on the next train, which was to arrive tomorrow.

There were many tents going up side by side. Tents were the beginning plans of many in this "town to be" until they could get something better built. Clyde's family had one of those smaller tents the first day for their family. It had been used on their original trip when they first came to this land in the great land rush. It would at least be their shelter at night away from this throng of people, who had busily been crowding around them during the days, but still it was an unsettling thing to hear all the strange voices around them in the night. Here they were, shoulder to shoulder with strangers, having no idea what kind of people surrounded them.

This main street this first day consisted of all sizes of tents in the midst of hastily built wooden shacks that were thrown up for shelter quickly. Some just nailed together enough to claim "I'm here. This is my claim." The plan was to improve. Some didn't for a long time.

Sadly, some would just give up. This place set in this land of prairie grass and red earthed nothingness would be a town to those with a dream and willing to work, but how hard and punishing the work would be. How hard it was to start with nothing and unimaginably so! Most of the wooden buildings were no more than a sort of lean-to, just enough to protect your family for the time being, not just from the elements, but from this frightening looking mass of desperate, and sometimes suspect looking people.

There was a wide street that was to run down the middle of this imaginary town that was to be. You did not realize how wide it was because of all the masses of wagons, carts, and horses that crowded it. Many wagons were very crude things.

People had brought their dogs and they were mixed in the mayhem of those first days. Some of the carts were very homemade, built to carry what you would need to start a new life. Some had brought their cows or oxen to pull those wagons that carried the very last things they owned. Oxen were strong to plow the hard packed Oklahoma red dirt. In the midst of this menagerie there were mules braying their complaints.

The first settlers of these town sites always seem to huddle together out of the need for safety. So they build side by side in the little place they will call their town. They realize in that vast wilderness they have traveled through, there is much to be feared. They have seen the coyotes, wolves, large cats, and the prairie creatures that lurk in the tall grass. Always hiding in the grass and wilderness places are the snakes and the most feared of all was the deadly rattlesnake. There is no black, like the black of a prairie in which in the darkness of the night you cannot see what lurks there. The light of a fire and the glow of a lamp is the only respite from the terrible blackness engulfing the wary humans. In that blackness, the unimaginable lurked. With such a darkness surrounding you, the imagined was more frightening than what was actually there.

All prairie travelers had heard the wide-spread tale of a small child at the edge of the darkness being snatched away. As grownups tried to desperately follow the child's screams, they had to stop because they could not see in the blackness of the night. They could not follow the cry of the child as it obviously got further and further and the sound softer and softer until it was heard no more. As the tale was told to warn little children to stay near encampments, the story changed from the creature being a large wolf, to a bear, a large wild cat or maybe even a coyote.

To little Jack and Ruby there were small creatures they had not seen. Lizards and the horned toads were a new sight both strange and fascinating to them. They were warned about the painful scorpions.

One of the most fascinating things to the children was the prairie dog towns. It was an awesome thing to come upon one of these towns of little creatures. Small burrows of little hills were built together by the furry little animals, just as the humans do, as if they too need each other's company. They would sit on their burrows, on their haunches, as if visiting one another or looking around to observe what was going on. At the sign of man or predator they would suddenly disappear into their holes. The mounds holding their little burrows would reach as far as you could see, sometimes so vast that sometimes it seemed they went to the horizon. That's why they were called towns. Although the cute little animals themselves were harmless, their towns were not. The settlers had been told that livestock and horses could break their legs in these towns. Along with the slaughter of the buffalo by the white man, these towns would disappear too for the Natives valued them for their fur and the white man for target practice.

Because of the fear of the creatures that roamed the wilderness, the frontier towns seemed huddled together in the midst of this huge prairie. Of course, when the white man was first settling the natives land, the whites feared attacks and felt safety in building together. To the eye, the town seemed to abruptly end and suddenly became prairie. This was what would be the town site. The original town sites would be built around the railroad that was their lifeline to the outside world and that opened this country.

The town site would be picked in its location because of the train and its proximity to water. Lathram's water supply would be the Washita River which ran as a gently flowing, red tinged river, like the Red River it ultimately flowed into. The red soil of its river bed made it always take on this color. There would be times that this river that was considered a source of blessing would be a raging, swirling monster, angrily overflowing its banks and sweeping in all around it. Then as quickly as it came, it would recede back to its quiet, meandering role of being the town's water supply. It was a welcoming place of shade in the hot summers from mighty and giant cottonwood trees that no one knows are how old were lining each side. Many native peoples have swum in its ancient waters. Many buffalo, elk, deer and smaller game followed its banks on this river named after ancient hunting grounds. The white men would value the river's plentiful fish. The ancient ones talked about it as if it were a living friend and also a sometimes fearsome foe. It meant survival, but no one wanted to face the mighty Washita at flood time or be caught in its rushing flow.

This opening day, some serious minded business persons had brought in wagons full of water barrels in order to sell the precious liquid to the people. They were the local water company. Outrageous prices were charged to a thirsty people. Others made and sold small carts on wheels to put your barrel on to haul your water from the river for water wells were not easy to dig. They had to be dug in another day in time by the homebuilder. Anything that was for sale, and at that point there was little, other than from farsighted business people, was sold at an exorbitant price. Many had come with their home and their livelihood in mind, and would set up their homes in the back, that being the natural thing to do.

People were starting a new life, as was Lathram. As fate would have it the name of Lathram was not to endure for the little town, although the community would, for when the name that had been put on the depot was submitted to congress, it was rejected because Oklahoma already had a town by that name. For this day and this time it was a bustling dream about to birth and this community of people would survive under harsh and surprising circumstances. A name change and also a slight change of location would come, but that's another story.

The family continued it's never ending work as tired, hungry people lined up impatiently to get their meals when they felt they could take a reprieve from the hard and busy work that involved setting up a home and business.

The stew and the coffee, and the foods such as mush for breakfast that were prepared easily in the way that the family had to unexpectedly set up, had been a good idea and seemed to satisfy the customers.

Who would have thought that the first restaurant they set up in this little town site would have been prepared and served on the street? It was a stretch to even call it a street. They ran out of both bowls and room and so if people would bring their own bowls for the stew, they would fill them and let them take them home. Necessity made early "Take Out."

Very soon, desperately needing help, a man who had no money to buy food for himself or for his large family was asked if they wanted to work. He, his wife, and his teen age children thankfully started immediately and so both families benefitted. Of course, that was after they saw to it that the family was fed. Beans were boiled, potatoes were peeled and chopped vegetables held out, the pots were kept steaming and with the extra help they made it through the day and things were prepared for tomorrow.

Amidst the rattle, clatter, and squeak of wagons and horses, the hammering on wooden shacks, and the shouting of people trying to communicate with each other over all the noise the little family worked hurriedly with no rest until out of exhaustion and the need for more supplies, they closed. They sent the recruited family away, who asked if they needed their help tomorrow. They gratefully accepted and told them to be there bright and early to have their breakfast and start the process all over again.

They took down the long boards they had used for tables and laid them under the wagon, and the barrels that had supported them were put in a close little circle around the wagon. With their last bit of energy they put up the family size tent and Sarah, Mary and the children crawled in and exhaustedly fell asleep immediately, in spite of all the town noise that was still going on.

John and Clyde, guarding their new kingdom, crawled into the wagon to keep a watch on the precious and much sought after boards and barrels and attempted to sleep. Clyde would have to take the wagon for food at Mountain View in the morning at the first break of light. They had certainly made enough money today to stock up. Clyde smiled as he thought of that. Then he thought of the time it would take him to get back. He pondered that a minute and then he smiled again. "The soup will have to be a little thinner tomorrow," he thought.

As they thought of all the things to do, in the midst of all the noise that was still going on, he somehow drifted off into a deep, exhausted sleep. Somewhere, in the very early hours of the morning, while yet dark but with a full moon, John hearing a noise under the wagon, reached to his side. Nudging Clyde, he sat up and saw a dark figure reaching under the wagon. Clyde pointed the rifle that had been at his side at the shadowy form that froze when he knew he had been detected. He was still holding the end of a piece of board. "Wait, Clyde," John said. "It's just a kid." Clyde paused, and with the gun still aimed, snarled, "Get out of here and you come near my lot again and I'll kill you!" The teen dropped the board, turned and ran. The two relaxed, sitting back against the wagon.

"John" asked Clyde, "don't you think now that we've moved to Indian territory, that you might get a gun? You know with robbers, and cowboys, and angry Indians and all that?"

John grinned and patted the steel sleeping companion beside him. "Naw", he said, "I'll just use my "devil knife". It's always been good enough."

Looking at the wicked looking machete knife, Clyde grinned and said, "I've never seen you use that 'devil knife' as you call it, but it sure scared a lot of people in the Wild West Show. It was amazing how you could change characters with that evil looking knife and a lot of hair in your face."

"Scaring has always been enough for me." John said with a grin.

Clyde said, "There's a full moon and plenty of time till morning. I'm going to get a head start on the day and head for Mt. View. Why don't you take your bedroll and your 'devil knife' and sleep here on top of our fancy restaurant. I'll go load the wagon with supplies."

As Clyde took the wagon out of the "town" somewhere in the background he heard the rinky-tink sound of a piano and laughter. Men were singing a rowdy barroom song with an off-key woman. Someone had already started his saloon business this early in the morning in the new city.

Out in the surrounding tall grass, eyes of the hidden prairie creatures looked with wonder and fear. What was this new thing of humans and noise and buildings that was invading their territory that had been theirs alone? Sadly, other brown eyes, these human, wondered the same thing.

THE TENT ARRIVES AND A TOWN ARISES

The much anticipated tent to temporarily house the pre-named Olymphia Restaurant arrived. As the resilient family had done before, they enlisted some hungry people willing to work for food to raise the big white canvas covering and it was up in extraordinary time. With foresight they had purchased a very large tent that would hold many people. It would not hold as many as the bare lot they had been serving from, but it allowed the pandemonium to be stopped somewhat, and limited the number of people expecting service all at one time. The two children were given the job of doorkeepers, sitting right inside the tent door. How they relished that and people seemed to enjoy and respect their roles for the most part. Their job was to politely tell the people waiting when there was room to come in. It kept the children in sight and busy.

There was a line outside the door at all times. They had installed the same boards as tables on the wooden barrel bases. People, busy building and setting up their new lives, and short on food supplies until gardens, crops and produce grew, were glad to smell the food that bid them to stop and take a rest while they ate.

As time progressed, and people got their own households going, a one street wooden shanty-tent town arose. Things were going well for the little family. They developed a routine that worked and the tent had made their endeavor a bit easier.

At least they were adjusting to the routine of feeding a whole town. The family who had been helpful at first in helping run the primitive restaurant were still helping out and were doing a dependable job. Sarah and Clyde felt good to be able to help a family that was in need. They were building a friendship that would last.

Those that came with their dream to build a mercantile and dry goods store were getting their small shipments of supplies in and so the fledgling town was learning to adjust to its minimal way of life. The most popular place in the little optimistic town was the Lathram Railroad Station where the daily arrivals brought resources to make life more bearable. The Rock Island Railroad was responsible for this miracle in the prairie.

A limited amount of food supply was arriving and people were learning how to get a water supply. Water could be bought from those enterprising people that supplied it. Some would take their barrels to the Washita River for themselves to get their own supply. Digging wells was a time consuming, back breaking effort that would have to take place later. One good effort that would be made in time, was a well dug in the center of the down town area for public use. The Livery Stable, Feed Store, and Lumber Company did well. Businesses to help resurrect a living out of a raw frontier were the enterprises to have and there were those that had the wisdom to start that immediately as did the little family from Nebraska.

In three months' time, with the help of hungry town folks again, The Olymphia Restaurant was built. They restrained themselves from calling their new building The Olymphia #2. In actuality, it was probably painful to look at this present primitive restaurant when they remembered the establishments that they had held in Nebraska. However, life seems to progress gradually and since they started cooking first on their open lot, then moved to a tent that sometimes whipped in the Oklahoma wind, this was a welcome thing to behold. The plain, wooden building with a porch in the front was fortunately right in the middle of where all the building activity was. It was a joy to them when "THE OLYMPHIA" was painted in huge words across the front of their building.

In looking back on when they were serving in the street, they knew they could have gotten no better advertisement than those first days when the town was desperate for any kind of food and this little family had come through. They were right out in the open and so the town knew them and who they were. Even those who didn't eat their food had learned to recognize them.

The community had learned to trust the man John, even though he was the first Chinese man many had seen. They had learned to accept his simple, but filling food, and also the smile that was always there for them on their worst hardscrabble days. They came to accept and not even notice the apparel of the man Clyde who wore either his Wild West clothes or his Spanish American Uniform and hat and his pretty wife, Mary with the slight British accent. Their two children, Jack and Ruby would soon be adopted by the township as part of the scenery as they ran and played with their dogs and other children in the busy little frontier town.

As the Olymphia building went up, the citizens had a taste of the family's real cooking and not just what they could scramble up in a make-shift tent. They used the recipes they had honed in their days in Nebraska. By then, they had made friends with the business people of the new town site, as well as with others who would become regular customers. It was the same routine they had always had. The temptation went out to all along the little prairie street as the smell of John's mouth-watering doughnuts and cinnamon rolls drifted through the air after their building went up. For by then the stove was installed and the street was filled with the wonderful smells of hot cinnamon and sugar.

As had been in John's early introduction to the white Nebraska settlers, before they knew his name, he had been spoken of as "the Chinaman." Later, as he was spoken of he might be referred to as "Chinaman John." Somewhere along the way his name became either simply John or by those who never were fortunate to know him closely "John Chinaman." Rarely to his face though.

With the new Olymphia, breakfasts had gone from mush to the more satisfying eggs and other specialties. Sizzling meat frying, stirred the senses and palates of those that were busy working and made it hard to keep people's minds on getting their businesses going. The ever ready smell of coffee simmering was always putting out its siren call to those needing a break from the work being done. The tent had worked as a primitive introduction before the real restaurant had gone up and for what seemed to the family a step-down from what was their past, for now the primitive wooden restaurant seemed a wonderful thing.

What did it take to get this new town blooming right out in the middle of what had been an open prairie in an Indian reservation? It was sheer optimism, resilience, resourcefulness, zestful eagerness, raw courage, and an overcoming spirit.

What joy they must have experienced as they sat under the shade of the trees they had planted and admired their accomplishments while listening to the winds softly blowing through the leaves.

What accomplishment they must have felt as they serenely observed the little kingdom they had built, and they remembered the nothingness it had been. How victorious must those emotions have been as they surveyed the work of their hands and saw the enduring imprint left on what had been to them a great prairie wilderness They had helped bring forth a town.

Only to the white man was nature a wilderness and only to him was the land "infested" with wild animals and "savage" people. To us it was tame, earth was bountiful and we were surrounded with the blessings of the great mystery."
BLACK ELK, Oglala Lakota Sioux 1863-1950

A TOWN ARISES

In the late of the day, after the restaurant had been built, the family was sitting on the boarded porch in front of the restaurant just before sunset on a peaceful Sunday, their day of rest. The family and John were reclining on the benches that Clyde had made to seat some of the overflow customers.

However, the benches had become a place where some of the Indians gathered and sat at times, much to the delight of Clyde. On those days they came to town with their families, not in feathers and buckskin riding ponies as the white settlers had imagined. They brought their families in wagons. For the most part, the men had adjusted their ways to the white man's dress, aside from the brightly colored feathers they put in the bands of their hats. However, in the winter, their brightly colored blankets were always seen. They came on those days for their various days of trade.

This day the family was admiring their little town, remembering how barren it had been and recalling what had come out of nothing. The children were playing and laughing in the red dirt road that was now the street of a town. The object of their fascination was a new puppy that their parents had allowed them to keep from a litter born to people down the street. A furry, round, little mixed breed, it was pulling furiously on a short little rope that the children took turns tugging. As they gazed at the wide dirt expanse that wasn't called the main street of Lathram, because it was the only street of Lathram, they marveled at what happened suddenly at the decree of a government.

It had seemed that overnight, and surely it seemed so to those that had roamed this Indian prairie, that in the midst of this wilderness an invasion of locust-like people had come and in almost in the blink of an eye, there stood a town looming out of the prairie grass. Swiftly, the invasion came, even before the buildings arose. It was no more a tent and shack city, as they looked down the wide street that was on either side of The Olymphia. The wooden buildings looked very much alike, except they varied in size. Side to side, they stood, all resting flush against the board walk to keep the pathway open and city folk out of the red Oklahoma mud and muck that rain, wagons and horses and mules produced.

Things had gone up swiftly to meet the needs of these adventuresome people that had left civilization. It had been so hard, and yet they did not realize how much more fortunate they were than those that were called early settlers in this expanding of this vast country. This town had the railroads breaking through the open land. Precious stock and merchandise had come to fill their shelves, and the needs of the people. Also those iron rails brought people. Elsewhere and for the earlier pioneers, and before the railroads there was nothing except what they could bring in their wagons.

Now as Sarah, Clyde and Mary looked upon this town that was theirs, they were pleased with what they saw. Work and time had taken care of so much. It had all mostly come from nature, however nature does not give up her treasures freely. Extremely hard work had brought forth this town they were looking at. Women had done what was formerly considered man's work. Children did their share, and even more so, out of necessity. Small children became babysitters of even smaller children, while both parents labored to survive and make this community called Lathram happen.

How often this was repeated in this vast country named America. How wisely had those that were the natives that came before in their simple ways had gently taken from the good earth what it so generously had given to them! Would these new landowners be as wise now that this earth was theirs?

How things had progressed. Wells had been strenuously dug. Gardens had been laboriously planted. Wood had been chopped for firewood. Wood had been brought in for building. Coal could now be brought by rail for their potbellied stoves.

How hard it had seemed and yet so quickly it happened and now they were looking with pride at what they saw this pleasant evening as they quietly sat and surveyed their domain. As they looked down their little frontier street they saw the bank. There before them were the mercantile and dry goods stores that provided everything from food stuff to calico. The town had a meat market.

They saw the hardware store, from which the tools it took to dig the hard earth had come. So much from their time in history had come from the iron and steel revolution that allowed this town to progress. From a man named Carnegie it was born. It was even from that man that the great steam engine, that some of the tribes called Talihina (Iron Horse), would bring these things on its steel rails, such as their plows and shovels. The iron and steel to dig much needed water wells. Not to be named for Indian names as most towns were in this Oklahoma land, it may have been providential that this town would later be named for the man Carnegie who was responsible for the steel revolution that made all these outreaching frontier towns possible.

There was the feed store and livery stable. There was the blacksmith, so needful to this time. There were the wagon makers and wheel menders and canvas sellers. These and other stores were lined up on each side of the street. Then on the outer parts of the town were the little farm homes away from these storefront buildings. Further on out were the farms without which none could exist, that eventually would be the backbone of this great nation, without which no nation could exist.

The family sat peacefully and relaxed, enjoying their Sabbath Day. They had been going to the Presbyterian Church in Tecumseh before they left Nebraska. Now there was just one little fellowship of like-minded people here in their little town and it was a pleasant thing to gather together. Whoever went to it seemed to think it was of a different name, but the gentle fellowship was the same, as they sang the old familiar songs of faith known to all in that time. The little simple fellowship of believers shared each other's needs, and helped one another. The old Holy Bible seemed to read the same. It was enough.

The next morning Clyde decided to make a trip to the post office. He woke early and told Mary of his intention. "I'm going early so I can get back to the restaurant so I can help. I won't take long. I'll be back before anyone knows I'm gone. Mrs. Batton, the postmistress, has opened early for me before. She and her husband are always up early, anyway." With that he hitched up the team and he was off down the road toward the river.

"Be watchful," Mary shouted after him. "You know how the Washita can be after we've had a big rain." Clyde drove the team on as if he didn't hear.

Surely, he thought to himself, the rains been gone long enough for the river to have gone back down. This has been one big drawback to where the town of Lathram had been located. The towns on the north of the river, and yet the depot and post office are on the south. Of course, we didn't know the cantankerous ways of the ole Washita when we built. The big guys should have asked the Indians. When they saw what we were doing, they probably wouldn't have told us that what we were doing was not good anyway. I bet they laughed in their tipi's.

The more he thought about it, he laughed out loud! I wouldn't have told us either, if I were them, he thought. He laughed for quite a while. "Guess the jokes on us," he said aloud.

Clyde continued his silent conversation with himself. That Washita sure gets ugly when it rains. Mighty ugly! Of course, the Indians probably say it's mad at us. I never understood why the Post Office is built where it is. I do understand that because the government wanted to take land to run trains anywhere they wanted to run them, they made up that law called "Eminent Domain." Said it was ok as long as it was for the people's good. Guess it depended on what good it was talking about and what people. So that makes the train depot on government land. I understand that. Some say, though, that the little cabin that the Post Office is in is on Indian Territory. I even heard it was owned by an Indian man and that the white family

who live there are just renting it from him. None of
it makes sense to me!

I don't understand a lot of things, as Clyde
continued to dialogue with himself, but I do know
we should have built on the south of the river. We
wouldn't be having the mess we're having trying to
get to the Post Office and the train. Maybe the river
is mad at us. I couldn't blame the Indians for thinking so. This was their last reservation.

As Clyde drove the wagon up to the place
where Lathram forded the river, which usually was
at its lowest a trickle, he was surprised that the water was deeper than he expected. He stopped the
wagon and looked at the red flow which seemed
murkier than ever. It always did get murky right
after a fresh rain, from the sand getting stirred up
from the bottom. Sand tends to move with the river
if it's flowing fast. It was flowing swiftly, but it
wasn't too deep, Clyde concluded. There had been
times he had seen what looked like chocolate whirling water, hurtling large logs and trees down its
murky river course and this was nothing like that.
He decided to go on across to the Post Office. He
slapped the lines over the horse's backs and they
hesitated a moment. He slapped again and they
stepped out into the flowing water. Following his
guidance, the pair walked across the water that was
now swirling around their feet. Suddenly, from
around the bend, a small branch came flowing
swiftly down with the current and crashed abruptly
into the horses. The horse on the right received the
blow, which was not heavy, but was startling, and
he reared up with a loud whinny. This caused the
horse on the left to shy over. The fording place in
the river that the people used was a really deep river
place, as most of the river was. A tall sandstone

ledge rose up however, out of that deep river bed which made a narrow ridge-like road that could be crossed. However, on either side, was a dangerous drop off. Clyde spoke loudly to the horses and they managed to step on to the shore just as the current caught the wagon that was behind them and drug the wagon to the left, resting the wheel exactly on the left edge of the sandstone. Clyde, from his high seat leaned over looking at the wheels, front and back. He knew the wheels lacked only a centimeter for the wagon to go over the edge of the rock ledge pulling the wagon over into the deep, fast moving, monstrous hole of water, and only God knew what would happen to the horses.

The horses were standing on the bank, showing distress, as the wagon seemed to be pulling against them in the water. With every nerve screaming in his body, Clyde sat very still and spoke to the pair with the calming voice they were used to. Speaking softly the names they knew usually meant stroking, rubbing, and a carrot was coming, he comforted them, hoping they weren't noticing his quivering voice. After a time, the signs in their body language he knew so well, said they were calming down. With a sudden loud voice beyond anything he had ever used, he yelled "Giddy Up" and slapped the lines sharply. With a jerk, they pulled forward, and the wagon lunged suddenly unto the bank and unto the dirt road with them. Now Clyde was yelling "Whoa" as loudly as he could. When the team came to a stop, he had a change of plan suddenly.

He wasn't sure what else that old Washita had in store upstream, so after soothing his horses for a while, he turned the team around, drove carefully the obedient pair over the sandstone ford, and headed back home.

When he got back home, he gave each horse two carrots, and went to work in the restaurant. When Mary inquired, he said there wasn't any mail.

Excerpt from CARNEGIE OKLAHOMA, The First 100 Years

Busiest town on the Rock Island

"Carnegie's history is the story of hard times, of good times, of economic success and of failure, and economic depressions like most settlers discovering the new country.

The railroad played a vital part in the development of Carnegie, in 1870 the government would authorize only one railroad into Oklahoma from the North. There were three vying for this chance. Government officials decided the "prize" would go to the first one that reached the Oklahoma border. This touched off an exciting race. Springtime brought torrential rains causing swollen streams which had to be bridged, flooded valleys had to be graded and sodden prairies had to be crossed. Anything went from luring away working crews from one another and actual fighting battles between crews to circulating false information and wining and dining public officials.

Finally, at noon, on June 6th, 1870, the first train reached the line and touched the soil of Oklahoma. The winning railroad became the Missouri, Kansas, and Texas, called the "Katy".

An immense volume of cattle was shipped on this line. Coal mines were developed and coal was shipped via the "Katy".

Meanwhile, an east-west line known as the Atlantic, and Pacific was being built and in 1871 it met the north-south Katy line. This line stalled somewhat until 1882, which saw some further building. This line was purchased in 1897 by the Frisco. There was more expansion which involved land grabbing schemes, but finally became a through line. These railroads had a great influence on Oklahoma development and soon town and cities sprang up almost overnight along every branch line. The railroad was a means for many settlers to bring their family belongings, and livestock to homesteads being opened up in this new country.

The years from 1900-1907 were a time of rapid expansion into Oklahoma. Oil added to the fury of this development. Oklahoma headed the lists of oil states in this era. One-third of all new construction in the nation was in Oklahoma.

Many parts of Oklahoma were opened by land runs, but the Wichita Indian Reservation, comprised of the present counties of Caddo, Comanche, and Kiowa was opened by lottery. The Indians were given the privilege by the U.S Government to select any allotment of 160 acres in these lands. All land not selected was allowed to be filed on by white persons if they held one of the lucky numbers at the land drawing held at Lawton and El Reno. Any white person who drew a lucky number and selected a tract of 160 acres and filed on it was required to live on it, for a period of five years and make improvements thereon. This included plowing, building fences, or erecting buildings. They must also pay $1.25 per acre to the government before obtaining a patent to the land from the U.S. Government.

It was then that Mr. Straight drew a parcel of 125 acres north of the Washita River. He improved the land making way for a township called Lathram.

In the early 1900's, the east-west line was purchased by the Rock Island, which constructed a branch line from Chickasha to Mangum, building a depot near the site of the present town of Carnegie.

The station was called Lathram after the township on the north side of the Washita River.

The Lathram town site grew quickly, and businesses and homes were built. The town post office, a single log cabin, was located on the south side of the river in the home of Sarah Batton, the first postmistress. Mr. and Mrs. Batton lived on Indian land belonging to Pau-tau-die-ty.

With the town situated north, and the depot and post office south of the river, the townspeople had occasion to cross the Washita frequently. The ford was a little below the present dam. There the river emerged from its deep, muddy bed to flow over shallow sandstone, jagged and full of holes. It was comparatively safe, unless one got too far east with the current, but some always held their breath when crossing and thought surely this time part of the wagon would be left behind. Many times high water made the ford dangerous or stopped travel entirely.*

When the name Lathram was submitted to congress it was rejected because Oklahoma already had a town by that name. Mrs. Batton then suggested "Carnegie" in honor of Andrew Carnegie. The name was chosen in hopes that "The Richest Man in the World" would donate his wealth to the town as he had done to charitable causes. Today he is remembered for his generous gifts of music halls, educational grants and nearly 3,000 public libraries. By the time of his death in 1919 he had given away over $350 million (over $3 billion today).

Despite the man's rag to riches story in the steel industry in America, the town of Carnegie never received a dime from the Scotland native. However, the name was approved by the government and the new site had a name."

*Many years later, Sarah's great granddaughter played on the large sandstone rock there by the dam. That would be Jan Harding the storyteller. Also her future husband, Noel Don Chapman, of Alfalfa, fished there at times with his father.

Excerpt from CARNEGIE OKLAHOMA, The First 100 Years

"The Olympia Restaurant was managed by Mrs. S.E. Ingram, mother of Clyde Ingram. Mrs. Ingram came from Nebraska in 1900 and located in Mt. View until the opening of the town site. John Lum Seow, the Chinaman, was her cook while she lived in Nebraska. The day the town lots were sold, their tent had not arrived and John out of necessity was forced to cook in the street to feed the hungry crowd. Mrs. Ingram sold to Henry Cates in the spring of 1904 and in the fall of 1904, the restaurant was destroyed by fire."

Meal card for the Olympia Restaurant

The Olymphia Restaurant, Carnegie Oklahoma
Top Row Far Left: **Sarah Ingrahm,**
Top Row fourth from the left: **Lum Seow (John)**

Also noted: Mrs. Shaffer, Dr. Shelton, Phil Doyle,
Clyde Batton, Tom McGuire, Mr. Brown, Jeff Wilson, and
Henry Campbell

Land Certificate Issued to Clyde Ingram dated 1906
And signed by President Theodore Roosevelt

THE OLD OKLAHOMA HOMESTEAD

"**Whereas** *Clyde F. Ingrahm of Caddo County Oklahoma has deposited in the GENERAL LAND OFFICE of the United States a Certificate of the Register Of the Land Office at El Reno, Oklahoma whereby it appears that* **Full Payment** *has been made by the said Clyde F. Ingrahm according to the provisions of the Act of Congress of the 24th of April, 1820, entitled "An Act making further provision for the sale of the Public Lands," and the acts supplemental thereto, for The South West quarter of section four in Township five, North of Range Thirteen West of Indian Meridian in Oklahoma containing one hundred and sixty acres according to the Official Plat of the Survey of the said lands, returned to the GENERAL LAND OFFICE by the SURVEYOR GENERAL, which said Tract has been purchased by the said Clyde F. Ingrahm.* **Now know ye,** *that the United States of America, in consideration of the premises, and in conformity with the several Acts of Congress in such case made and provided,* **Have given and granted,** *and by these presents* **Do give and grant,** *unto the said Clyde F. Ingrahm and to his heirs, the said Tract above described; To have and to hold the same, together with all rights, privileges, immunities, and appurtenances, of whatsoever nature, thereunto belonging, unto the said Clyde F. Ingrahm and unto his heirs and assigns forever.*

*   **In testimony whereof I, Theodore Roosevelt, PRESIDENT OF THE UNITED STATES OF AMERICA,** *have caused these letters to be made Patent, and the seal of the GENERAL LAND OFFICE to be hereto affixed.*

GIVEN under my hand, at the CITY OF WASHINGTON, the fifth day of February, in the year of Our Lord one thousand nine hundred and six, and of the Independence of the United States the one hundred and thirtieth.

BY THE PRESIDENT: Theodore Roosevelt Recorded Oklahoma: Vol.169, Page 208"

Clyde purchased a piece of property south of where the restaurant was established that would be later called a little farming community named Alden. He moved his family there and established a new farming life in 1906. This was another beginning and a new "start from scratch." More than likely, the expression "starting from scratch" probably started with the word homesteading because life literally started with digging and scratching a living from nothing out of the bare ground. The family purchased this piece of rocky property that was just outside the foothills of the Wichita Mountain Range. Actually, this was a good piece of land for grazing and ranging.

Early pictures of this place they called home show a wooden, unpainted, small house of the primitive style you see in many of the pioneer pictures. The family, standing in front of the building, were wearing the attire of the many pioneers you see in old photos of those days. The drab cardboard pictures always add to the poverty look of all pictures of those early pioneering days that have survived to modern days. The clothes Clyde wore in this photo certainly didn't measure up to those of the Nebraska days when he looked very debonair in his photos. Nor were they as exciting as the wild-west costumes that he and his cousin wore in their

Wild West Shows. The family's attire on the Oklahoma homestead looked as all old pictures that you see in history books of the prairie people in 1906. The clothes conscious Mr. Ingrahm looked pure prairie farmer settler in the surviving photos of that day, other than a few photos in which he liked to wear his Spanish American War uniform.

In that photo, they had added to the two children, Jack and Ruby that had been born in Nebraska, It was another little girl, named Blossom Larraine. Seemingly, the family was given to nicknames, for this child was called Midge all her life. All the girls in the family were small, and it's assumed that's how that name came about.

From left to right: Mary Ingrahm (pregnant with Margueritte, the storyteller's mother), Blossom Larraine, Ruby, and Clyde

Hiding under Mary's blouse is another baby girl. That's Margueritte, the storyteller's' mom. She would be born in 1907, the year that the territory of

Oklahoma would become a state. That child would be called Charlie by the family because of her love for a horse they had by that name. On scanning the old photo closely you will see a black and white cat peering in the old house window and of course, the Ingrahm family would always have a dog. The shack and the clothes point out that their Oklahoma life was a bit of a step down from their previous life, which was the experience of all beginning pioneers.

On Clyde's piece of land they would farm and raise sheep. All people of the land would have cows and goats for milk, along with chickens for meat and eggs. My mother remembered her mother Mary shooting the heads off chickens for supper. Men of the prairie and wilderness lived by their guns. At one time in Oklahoma there was elk, Wichita antelope, plentiful deer, and wild hog. Of course there was small game such as raccoon, possum, rabbit and squirrel. There was wild turkey, prairie chicken and quail. Indians had eaten the prairie dog and used their fur to make small articles.

Also, the pioneers had to use their guns to protect their livelihood from predators, such as panthers, wolves, bears and coyotes. As the Indians, they probably relied heavily on corn, pumpkins and squash. There were wild plums, grapes, blackberries, strawberries, dewberries and huckleberries, all growing wild.

As to the plains buffalo, which the white man had depleted in the time this family moved there, it was to this very area of the Wichita Mountains range that the endangered buffalo would be shipped back to, of all places from New York City from a zoological park in 1907 to establish a wildlife reserve and refuge by some farsighted men. Bless those people.

There are records of Clyde Ingram bringing loads of broom corn into the town, later when broom corn could be shipped by rail. Also, there was a broom factory among the early businesses of Carnegie. In that area around Carnegie broom corn was a popular crop being raised by the local farmers. It was hard work and a hard crop to grow. Even now, the economy in this area is sustained by cattle grazing, hogs, poultry, cotton, wheat and peanuts.

As far as raising food to feed a family on this rocky land, they did much as the Indians did before the settlers came.

The children went to a school near their home place called Cache. So named because French explorers found an Indian cache of food hidden on that creek and named it Cache Creek. That is the French word for what would be to us a hidden stash. There are records that Clyde Ingram was on the Cache School Board.

On that old farm, there was much excitement in living that life of that primitive time. Some was good. Some was bad, as was an exciting story that was almost tragic. This is a story that was very, very dear to me about my mother Margueritte. It was repeated over and over at my own childhood request, as many of the stories in this book were, by the people that had experienced them.

The family was engaged in burning corn stalks when Margueritte, or Charlie as she was called, was around the family project. Suddenly some tall grass caught on fire. As the family was battling the grass fire the dry, paper like cornstalks started to burn like paper. The flames whipped around seven year old Margueritte. They were crackling and snapping on either side of her. The flames licked at her legs, caught her cotton dress on fire and went up her back. She was choking and suffocating in the smoke. Her father grabbed her and rolled her as her mother wrapped her in a wet cloth she kept nearby during this chore in case the fire got out of hand. The fire smothered, she was carried into the house where Sarah was working. The child was black with cinder and soot. It was a terrible sight for the family to behold. She had been severely burned. The fire had burned to the spine in one place. Sarah, being a nurse, administered what help medically she could do. Apparently, it was very serious.

I'm not sure how word got to John at Mt. View, where he was working at the time, but the message came that she was nearly dead. John went immediately to the local mercantile to buy a beautiful piece of silk material for the child's burial. Then he walked and sometimes ran, the heart pounding 15 miles to Alden, sorrowing all the way. This was the baby of the family and dear to his heart.

My mother would tell that the only thing she remembered of that time was lying in bed in terrible pain, as her mother sat by the bed, sewing. Obviously, she recovered for she lived to tell me the tale. When Marguerite was an older child and heard the story of John's journey to her bedside, she then knew that her mother Mary had been sewing that special burial dress John had brought the material for. Apparently God had another plan for my mother and that dress probably became a Sunday-Go-To-Meeting dress. That story will live on in my family. Often, as a child, I would say to my mother,

"Tell me the story of "John and the Fire." John is still my great hero.

Being a daughter of Margueritte, who cared for John in his older days, I have my remembrances of John's gifts of kindnesses to me as a child. When I would have something simple like the flu, he would make the downtown trip to Carnegie and he would come back with African Violets. Special in my remembrance was a polka dotted piggy bank to make me smile. When I think of my John, I see him walking with his hands behind his back, and having gotten to know people from Asia later in my life, it seems to be a way with older Chinese men.

Of course, at that time I never suspected that John was put in my life in his later years for a special reason, and that knowing an Asian man would serve a special purpose. Because of John, who might have been the only Asian man in that early territory, the word Asian would never be foreign to me. For in later years, in my married life, my husband and I would adopt a literal house full of Asian children.

Other stories of childhood tragedies were related in the early years of that Oklahoma era in that area in which they homesteaded. One is remembered to this day. There was a small community store where a rain barrel was kept outside to catch precious water. A small child fell upside down in the barrel, drowning. To this day, that place is called "The Dirty Shame" because of remarks that were made of the child's death by the people of the area.

Also, in the area a family tragedy involving children my mother told was that some parents had left their children alone for some reason. While they were gone, the children found a gun. A small child was accidently shot and killed. When the parents returned, the children told them that an airplane had flown over and "shot Little Willie." A sad story for an early age of airplanes; easily discerned by adults not to be true.

The area my great grandmother and her son homesteaded is full of rich recorded history --going back to the original natives of the land and mentioned by the Spanish and French explorers of that area when they took note of and recorded the existence of the natives. The hard, rocky land they homesteaded was not far from the Wichita Mountains, which is a treasure trove of tales of animal and Indian lore. This haunting land, in which my forefathers first put down Oklahoma roots, lies in the southwestern part of Oklahoma. A distance from where their little place lay, the Wichita Mountains rise in the midst of and it is surrounded by vast prairie land. A trip, even today, to this mountain area near Lawton, Oklahoma and you can readily see a land out of the olden days where Indians would choose to dwell.

Sod houses were no new things that pioneers brought to these prairies. Even now, in that area of the mountains, timber is small and scraggly because of the dry climate. Mesquite, Oak, Black Jack, and Cedar are the main trees of the area. Lovely Red Bud bloom brightly in the spring and near the plentiful lakes and waterways, stately Cottonwoods spread their welcoming shade. Early Indians in these parts of this country were earth house dwellers. In history books, we named them earth-house people. These people used a building frame of heavy timbers. Over that a layer of sod was laid. A hole was in the center of the roof so fire smoke on the earth floor could escape. Mounds of these houses are still in existence in Oklahoma with pottery, hoes, and spades buried under the collapsed ancient dirt. The earth house people, the cave people, had disappeared and other tribes of Indians were living in Oklahoma before the first explorer from Europe came to this country. Of course, we know of the Wichita Grass Houses and tipis of skins and then after the demise of the buffalo, canvas was used in later days. These were still there when my settler ancestors came to that place. The Wichita Indians were the descendants of these people. In 1939 one of the Wichita houses was still standing in Anadarko, Oklahoma, in Caddo County which was one of the reservation lands my ancestors moved to.

The Caddo Tribe, closely related to the Wichita, is also believed to descend from the earth house people. The Caddo had many religious ceremonies, conducted by Medicine Men, which they performed in connection with growing corn. They sang many songs in these ceremonies in which they asked the Great Spirit to give them health and prosperity, long life and happiness. They were a peaceful people. They occupied the country to the east of the Wichita.

The Apache of the plains and western Oklahoma country lived by hunting of the buffalo. For this reason they named a river that sometimes meanders, and sometimes is a mighty torrent, that flows into the Red River, the Washita. The Washita is a Native American name for "The Hunt." They followed roaming herds of buffalo from place to place. Into this place of so much Native American history, my people came. Animal and Native American lore is abundant there.

The names still remain in the Wichita Mountains to this day. There is Black Bear Mountain, where the last known bear habitat of that area was. There is Elk Mountain, so named because of the abundance of Elk that supplied the early natives of this country. Eagle Mountain was so named for it was a nesting place of the great eagle. Its feathers were greatly valued by the Native Americans. Was Devil's Mountain really haunted, as said? The early natives thought so. Panthers roamed that area. Did wild horses run in Wild Horse Creek Canyon? Who does not know of the thundering of the massive buffalo herds that ran over this area? Coronado wrote of "hump backed cows" as far as they traveled this land.

What of the white men that have walked this land, that are judged only in the light of history by their deeds? What of this Sheridan who named the Fort Sill for a friend? In later years he said the answer to the "Indian problem," was to slaughter the buffalo. He and a famous soldier by the name of Lieutenant George Custer, who actually carried out a slaughter of Native American men, women and children called the "Battle of the Washita," would later come to an area now named Fort Cobb after a fort that was established there by General Sherman. General Philip Sheridan accompanied him with 2,000 men, 4,000 horses and mules and 300 wagons loaded with a month's supply of provision to the fort near the Washita River. It is recorded that General Sherman said that at that Fort there was an encampment of 3,000 Kiowa and Comanche with their herds of literally thousands of horses grazing out the grass on the range for miles in all directions. An excerpt from one of General Sheridan's reports related that, "My camps of Indians extended along the river for about twenty miles, on either side of Fort Cobb, and this was necessary to give grazing to their great number of ponies, amounting sometimes to 200 owned by one Indian."

This fort was moved to become Fort Sill near the Wichita Mountains. The large group of soldiers on that move stopped to rest on that march at Cache Creek, which is located near the property the Ingrahms were to homestead.

Theodore Roosevelt hunted in the Wichita Mountains in 1905, probably while my grandfather was working in his broomcorn field, two years before my mother was born in 1907. It is said he came to hunt wolves. Interestingly enough, my Grandfather Clyde was involved in a little war that involved Roosevelt and his Rough Riders in Cuba a few years earlier. I doubt if he came and looked him up when he was in his broomcorn field while he was in his "neck of the woods."

Winfield Scott had a mountain in the range named for him in 1852. Mt. Scott is a beautiful scenic mountain that as a man makes the twisting journey around it up to the very top, and looks out over a gorgeous view all around, he can envision "Indians" lurking behind the huge boulders, waiting with his bow and arrows of a day gone by. It is said that they used the mountains for headquarters for their raiding. It would be quite a hide-out before the roads were built. To climb that mountain you would have had to climb huge round boulders.

What of the Native Americans that have visited and lived in this nearby Wichita range? In the Wichita area, Quanah Parker cut slashes in a Post Oak Tree. There is a Hunting Horse Hill named for a Kiowa Warrior who was later a scout for the United States Army. There is a Sitting Bear Creek, where Satank (Sitting Bear) attempted to escape from army captors near a creek and was killed in 1871.

There are names which tell the passage of time and changes of lifestyles for the old War Chiefs. There is Tahoe Creek where a Kiowa Apache chief made it his choice to settle land along that creek.

There is a prison cell, in the Fort Sill compound, which you can visit, where the famous war chief and medicine man of the Chiricahua Apache, Geronimo was held for a time. As a prisoner of war he was exiled there in 1894. He engaged in farming there. When he was released he remained in the area, when he wasn't traveling as a celebrity. His fame grew and he appeared at national events such as the 1898 Trans-Mississippi, International Exposition in Omaha, and the 1904 Louisiana Purchase Exposition in St. Louis. In 1905 he rode in President Theodore Roosevelt's inauguration parade. Geronimo received money for his appearances at such events and even sold autographed pictures. It was told by the old-timers, Clyde Ingrahm being one, that he made a living from selling post-card pictures of himself on the streets of Lawton, nearby the Fort Sill base. He, his wife, and daughter are buried in the cemetery on the Fort Sill base. Other very famous Indian Chiefs are buried at the cemetery, also. The base and the nearby mountain and wildlife refuge make for an interesting history trip. Nearby Medicine Park, a town made from cobblestones is a sight seldom seen. Mt. Scott will take you back to another time and place in history and will give you a tremendous view at the top.

Somehow, though, this Oklahoma girl's mind always goes back when I visit these beautifully scenic places, to the late 1800's and before

when the Native Americans lived in these places before they were invaded by the early settlers.
However, I am descendant of a family of these settlers. This was the role given to my family.

Storyteller's note: My Grandfather, Clyde Ingrahm said that he was told by an old Chief named
Eagle Heart, that he only regretted killing one white
man. He said that during some kind of confronta-
tion he threw a little girl up in the air so she would
land on his knife. He said that as she was coming
down, before her body hit the knife, she smiled at
him.

While we feel the shock value of that story told
to my Grandfather and we judge him savage, consider if someone came to your house where lived
your precious little family, saying "Get out, this is
my house." Consider they slaughtered your whole
town, both women and children.

Ruby, Blossom Larraine, Jack, and Margueritte Ingrahm, 1911

THE SCOUNDREL

Grannie was so excited, she was actually giddy. They had gotten the word that the three relatives she loved most, aside from her brothers themselves, her nieces were coming down to the Oklahoma property. They were "coming down to the sheep ranch", as the Nebraska relatives called it. What welcomes were given when that new black car pulled up that dusty old country road and into the yard, and those past middle age ladies crawled out excitedly. No one remarked on Grannie's looks for she was showing her age. It was 1927 and she was pushing 90. It had been a long time since they had seen her. They didn't expect her to come running out of the house to greet them as she had, though. They were amazed at how she got around at her age. Never ever being big, she looked very fragile to them. Clyde had hinted in a letter that she seemed to be losing a little ground in the stamina area that she had always been known for. That was actually the reason for this visit. Of course, she didn't know that. Sarah was a much loved and remembered Auntie, having made visits to Nebraska, and they had decided to make the long journey, for they thought her time might be passing.

On her trips to Tecumseh she had managed to stay quite a little while each time and "get her visit out" as they called it. When she had gone up to Nebraska, all the old timers would be told she was coming for a visit and many gathered around this lady that once was a central part of the Nebraska area, as all the Stantons were in those early days. Although she proudly kept the name Ingrahm in remembrance of her husband, she was part of the Stanton clan that was so prominently part of those early Tecumseh days, if for nothing else than for the fact there were so many of them. Not only had she been gracious in those old surrounding communities to all, but she was interesting to talk to, for who would know more about all the old stories of that town and its past than the lady who lived right in the middle of it all; where all came and did business. She was not given to gossip, because she had experienced the pain of whispers behind her back about her missing husband, yet she wasn't deaf to all that had been talked about in those years of hotel life, and plenty was talked about in those hotel parlors about life in Tecumseh, Elk Creek, and Sleepy Lane and all the surrounding areas of Johnson County. There were few other pastimes when the days were long and wintery cold days too bitter to go out. She had heard it all.

This visit would be no different. The old family times would be gone over, even though everyone knew them by memory. The same old stories would be told, as if they had never heard them before. The funny family stories would be funnier than ever. They would sit around the table, laden with good old country cooking, talking, laughing, reminiscing and sometimes wiping away tears. That always happened when they talked about Sarah's poor sister, their Aunt, Mary Anderson, whose only daughter Grace had her head blown off accidentally when she was around eight, while one of her brothers was cleaning a shotgun. Poor Mary had spent her life in the State Asylum in Lincoln. The sons Victor, Axel, Orson, Anson, and Gordon were so traumatized by the ordeal that they seldom had ever talked about what happened to the only girl in their family.

Sarah, never really known as a talkative person, told a lot of funny or interesting tales on her brothers and sisters as they sat at the table. It seemed she was reliving her past. She regaled the nieces with stories from both childhood and adulthood. They listened with great interest. She talked about Michael, named after their father. She told stories on Jane, Ann, and Mary as little girls. There were funny stories on Jerome and Frank that had their sides splitting. She told of how mad their mother, Catherine was when she overheard the boys Jerome and Michael using some of the words that the mule drivers used who hauled the barges when they lived on the Erie Canal. They found a new use for the soap bar. While on the subject of her parents, she told them something they had not known. Michael Sr. and Catherine had actually eloped to America. At first they lived at a place called "Irish Ridge Settlement." She told how the family went by Canal and covered wagon to a place then called Shintown that would later be called Galesburg, Illinois. That's where Clyde had been born.

"Right before the Civil War," she told one of the women who was listening so raptly, "Jerome as a very young man was carrying water to the Illinois Infantry that was mustering to go to the front. It was at Shintown, Illinois where our father, Michael Sr., died when thrown from the wagon when he was hauling a load of hay," Sarah said.

Then the generally quiet Sarah, triggered by those who represented the Nebraskan life, started to share happenings that had occurred in her hostelries, as they were called back then. She spoke of the original place she purchased as a young widow called "The Smith's Head" thinking it would be a place that she could give Clyde and herself a home and make a living. She relived happenings at the later owned *Caledonia House.* She talked of *The Centennial* which she had built herself and what a major project that was. She reminisced about the 1885 reception she held in that place. Her eyes shone as she told how they had dancing and had fine suppers in the evenings and how Clyde had started playing the violin those nights for the patrons, although he was only twenty. At that point all eyes shifted to Clyde, who was listening raptly as the others were, in his old faded farm clothes and his ever present Spanish-American hat.

The tears in the eyes of the Tecumseh visiting nieces were there because this little fragile wisp of a woman with such joy in her eyes at the reminiscing of the glories of days gone by, was now not only so feeble, but was wearing a dress made out of a feed sack. A pretty feed sack, but a feed sack never the less. As they looked and it seemed her eyes glowed with her story, she was as regal as any queen with her silvery hair as a crown. This woman had lived a life of adventure none of them would ever experience, nor did they want to. To them it seemed this was a woman, that the world should know, and that she would be destined for the history books. A woman, who with her lone faithful son, and an Asian man who felt he had owed her his life, and through her great faith, had conquered life and lived it like no one they had known in their so called prosperous family.

That day she told them fascinating stories none had heard of the parents of this whole tribe of Stantons. Later, this group of visitors knew it as such a good and timely thing. These were things left for family memories to be passed down for their generations to come.

As little work as possible would be done those days, because company had come and it was a holiday. This was special company. It was family. Of course, as they talked, old John walked into the room with a large platter of his doughnuts that he had prepared in the big kettle outside. The girls, looking at each other and laughing, told him that they wondered in the car on the trip down if he still cooked and how they would love to have some of his special doughnuts.

This was a festive time for Clyde too, because old folks like to talk about old times. They asked him questions about the Land Run and about The Spanish American War. They were most interested in what it was like to come live among the Indians. They remarked they had been disappointed because they hadn't seen any. Clyde told them he was sure they had, but they just dressed like everyone else now. It was his joy to tell it all. They saw that the old play-acting that had been the old Clyde in the boarding houses had not left as he took them through his animated stories, delighted that they wanted to hear. Then when the nighttime came, out came the old fiddle, and the singing began. Time went by swiftly, and soon it was the day before the company was to leave.

On that day all of Clyde's festive feelings left with a jolt, and in his heart he welcomed the guests to leave. One sentence and thoughtless conversation unwound and shattered his world and destroyed everything that he had ever believed that made up his world. As happens, it was innocently said.

As John and Clyde were attending chores outside, one of the nieces accompanied them. She was asking Clyde about Sarah's health and mental soundness. "It seemed," she said, "that she is doing extremely well for one her age." Clyde agreed with her saying they tried to keep her from the extreme activity she used to thrive on by giving her hand work to be done. "Her mind is a good as it ever was," he assured her.

As they continued their conversation, John opened the gate of the chicken pen, and went in closing it behind him. He carried a container of water and a half-empty sack of chicken feed. Bending over, he poured water from the can into the chicken's water container. Then he poured the bag of feed into the far corner of the pen. As the chickens ran to the corner for the feed, he picked up a rake leaning against the henhouse and started to rake the ground they had vacated.

The well-dressed lady, looking out of place on the old homestead, said to Clyde, "Did Sarah ever get her mind right about Zebulun? The family worried about her for a long time, you know. You being as small as you were you couldn't possibly remember at the time that awful thing happened."

"No, I didn't," Clyde replied, "But Mom told me much later that it hit her pretty hard and it took a little help from the Lord to get her over it. As you say, I was too young to remember anything. I don't even remember my Father at all, but only what Mom has told me."

The niece, chattering on said, "I do remember my Dad and all the brothers talking about how Aunt Sarah wouldn't let herself realize the truth about him leaving you both and stealing that money. Then my uncles started talking about knowing he was a scoundrel before she married him and that the whole town knew it. Uncle Frank said it worried him because she refused to believe the truth and preferred to believe he was dead. 'She needs to get hold of reality,' is what I overheard him say."

John with his back to them where he was raking the ground, stopped what he was doing, dropped his head looking down, and was just standing there motionless. Clyde was standing quietly, staring at the back of John's head. There was a strange roaring in his ears.

"Well, I guess that's all water under the bridge now, as they say," the clueless lady said. "Hearing all the facts that Sarah recalled to us from back in our folk's childhood around that table, it's plain to see there's nothing wrong with that lady's mind. She had to have told herself the truth about that sorry man a long time ago."

Looking at what John was doing, she suddenly changed subjects and said, "What kind of chickens are those, John?" She paused, waiting. Then she tried again, "I've never known what you call those black and white chickens." Standing in the heavy quiet and seeing no one was responding to her, she excused herself, awkwardly going back to the house saying, "I think I'll go and see how to pack the doughnuts John made for us to take in the car with us to eat on the way home."

Clyde whirled around and walked hurriedly into the barn. John stood with his head down for some minutes. Then leaving the pen and shutting the gate behind him, he followed Clyde into the barn. Clyde was standing with his head and face against his folded arm on the wall, sobbing. John walked up close to Clyde from the rear, and simply lowered the top of his head against his heaving back, saying nothing, as if he was trying to absorb the hurt.

Clyde was not sure if he was crying for himself for having his lifetime hero desecrated and destroyed, or for his poor mother who was deserted with a baby by a man who was a scoundrel. When the shock of it was over, it would cause him to love and respect her even more for the wonderful job she did in raising him alone. Now though, there was nothing but the gut wrenching hurt and shock of his lifetime.

Sarah Ingrahm with nieces and nephew

John, Sarah, and Clyde with visitors from Tecumseh

Sarah Ingrahm age 90

GOODBYE TO A FAITHFUL FRIEND

When your time comes to die, be not like those
whose hearts are filled with the fear of death, so
that when their time comes, they weep and pray for
a little more time to live their lives over again in a
different way. Sing your death song and die like a
hero going home."
TECUMSEH

John stood outside the little house belonging to Sarah, as Clyde was spending time by her bedside. John was taking some much needed time outside. He stood under Sarah's old giant cottonwood tree within its wonderful shade. It was the only big tree on her small property. This was Sarah's favorite summer place in the years that her health had been failing. She, who had never been still, now enjoyed sitting quietly in the heat of the day and watching the bird sanctuary she had created. She brought out daily bread crumbs and water to her leafy arbor for the feathered creatures. She loved looking at her southwestern plains country. How she loved it's gently rolling hills and its flat grass lands that rested at the base of the rocky Wichita Mountain range that had been named for the Indian tribe that had made Nebraska a far off memory. She had heard when she first came here back when the century turned, that the Indian name for this Caddo County meant "Chief." Some had said it meant "Life." It had been that to her.

All she had been very sure of was that in 1901 when the Federal Government allotted the Kiowa, Comanche, Caddo reservations and sold the surplus land to white settlers, she was fortunate to become a part of this land that was called Oklahoma Territory. When her last granddaughter was born on this land, down the road at Clyde's old homestead in 1907, this land of Oklahoma became her state and no longer just a territory.

She had seen this vast grass land turn into cotton land. She had seen not only grazing land, but corn, wheat, alfalfa, peanuts, and broom corn spring up with hard work and sweat. She loved these red gypsum hills and these red bed plains. Cache Creek, just a short distance away had been her grandchildren's swimming hole.

Of late, she had, because of necessity, given up the independence she had always insisted upon, for the inability to help herself had been increasing. She had been getting weaker. John had moved in with her for it was getting harder and harder for her to care for herself alone. It was obvious the last week or so she had been failing and her strength was going fast.

John had spent his Oklahoma life after they had sold the restaurant, living his own life and employing himself, and yet coming to the homestead where the family needed him when crops needed tending. He had worked in surrounding communities as a cook, but when the family had farming needs he would join them there. Here at the last, in his older days it had been a good thing that he had been here to help Sarah and Clyde. This was a need of all needs now to help their much loved matriarch. Clyde and John were making sure she was never alone now that she had become bedfast and was obviously in very serious condition.

He thought back to the time that she as a young woman, had taken him in and cared for him so gently until he was on his feet when he had been a complete stranger. Now here he was, as she was at the age of ninety, returning the favor so to speak. What a heartrending thing it was because now after their long life together, she was totally a family member to him. One with whom he had spent so much of his life. She was, and had been since that time so long ago brought to her doorstep, his dearest of all friends, with the exception of Clyde. Neither he, nor her son, could imagine life without their beloved Sarah, but he knew that her time seemed to be passing.

Clyde walked out of the small whitewashed clapboard house and joined John under the shade of the tree. Tears were running down his face, unashamedly. "John," he said to his old companion, "Mom wants to talk to you." Pausing for a minute he said, "She's going John. She's so weak." Then he started to sob. "She told me goodbye."

The seventy-two and eighty-two year old men embraced each other while crying together. Then Clyde said, "She doesn't have much time, I don't' think. Her breathing is so labored. You better go now because she's asking for you."

John removed himself from Clyde's embrace, pulling a wrinkled handkerchief from his old brown, worn pants. Thoroughly wiping his face outside the door of the house, he paused a moment trying to compose himself. He then entered the house and went into the familiar room where Sarah was lying under her hand sewn quilts. Her breathing seemed more labored than ever.

He spoke her name. "Sarah, did you want to speak to me?"

She immediately opened her eyes, looking into his face, as the old man had seated himself in the old chair resting beside her bed. It surprised him because for some time now she had kept her eyes closed and he had not been sure if she was aware if anyone had been there.

She feebly lifted a pale, thin, wrinkled hand toward him and he took it gently. How soft it was. Her eyes fluttered open, looking at him a moment, and then closed again. He sat there holding her hand. He watched her face, which now seemed the dearest old face in his world. His eyes were glued to what seemed to him in that moment like that of an angel. How pale and soft she looked. How he loved this one who had taken him in and had cared for him as a son.

He felt it was important to hear what it was she wanted to say. He tried again saying, "Did you want to say something to me, Sarah?" Waiting a moment, he waited for her response.

Again, her eyes fluttered open, looking directly into his old brown eyes. He looked at her expectantly waiting. Her eyes lingered on his face. Still she said nothing, but he waited still.

She closed her eyes again and the hand he held softened its hold on his hand. Still he held on to it, not releasing his gentle grip. It seemed she was asleep or not with him now. Still determined, he waited knowing time was important.

Again, she looked at him. With great effort, she whispered something to him. Not hearing her, he bent his head forward, nearer her face. "What?" he said. "I didn't hear you, Sarah."

With her eyes fixed upon the old man's eyes she opened her colorless lips. With much effort she said in a raspy whisper, "Please take care of my Clyde. He'll need your help."

With eyes filling with tears, the old Chinese man said, "I will Sarah. I promise I will. You know that I will. He's my little brother."

She smiled and looking into his eyes, she said in a whisper, "I love you sweet John." Before he could respond, her eyes closed and her grip loosened limply from his hand. She never spoke another word.

Suddenly John was aware that there was a brilliant light on the other side of Sarah's bed. A beautiful man in a white robe stood there with a smile more glorious than any he had ever seen. Sarah too smiled as she opened her eyes and smiled at the stranger. She stretched her hand to Him in welcome. John had the feeling she was going to get up to greet Him.

A sudden recognition burst upon the old man's mind. He had seen this beautiful apparition long, long ago in a hotel room in Tecumseh, Nebraska, when a strange lady with the now lovely name of Sarah was tending to his wounds in a darkened room of that inn. He had barely been able to open his eyes to see in his weakened state, but there He had stood in a corner of the room, as if watching the nurse's careful attention to his battered body. He had thought on it later, after he had recovered and had decided it was a hallucination.

Now as he watched the glorious stranger reach forth His hand to Sarah, she immediately reached further for him, and after that reach, her arm then dropped suddenly to the bed. As John watched in amazement, he saw the life had gone from that frail little body.

Standing there frozen, looking at his beloved little friend, he heard a whisper float through the air. It was real. It was tangible. It was spoken aloud and yet so softly sweet no human could whisper it. Although the apparition was gone, he heard the gentle words, "*Well done, good and faithful servant.*"

After the words ceased and John stood in silence a while looking at Sarah's lifeless body, he went to the door and called for Clyde. They both stood at her bedside, a long time looking at the little shell that once held something so beautiful to them.

They laid her tiny body in a little plot of ground that was used by the little community of settlers in the area close by as a burial ground. It was nearby this place where they had homesteaded. They had no idea then, that it would someday be named "The Old Settler's Cemetery."

Sometime later, the two old friends went to pay their respects to that grave, as they often did. They were both hot and sweaty from fieldwork as they crawled out of the old black truck. They began the walk to Sarah's grave and began to do the upkeep work they religiously did around her gravestone.

"I been thinking about something," said Clyde to his old field buddy. He leaned on his weathered old hoe handle. He needed a rest anyway, he thought as he brought up this well thought on subject to John.

"About what?" said John, who was on his knees, picking weeds from around Sarah's grave. He continued the struggle with the stubborn Johnson grass that to his mind had no business on an Ingrahm grave. Anytime he saw this weed, it was an interloper in his mind, even though he wouldn't know what the word interloper would mean. He hadn't gotten that far in his English dictionary of words yet.

Wiping the sweat from his forehead, with an already wet handkerchief of a doubtful once white color, Clyde said, "Well, I'm tired of working myself to death and I've been thinking about leaving the old farm and going to the city and living like city folks do. Would you be ready to do that with me?" He had said it almost as one sentence as if he had to get it out quickly as if John would interrupt him in shock.

John, with a surprised look on his face, stopped picking weeds and looked up at Clyde, mid pluck. "You mean move into Carnegie?" the startled old man asked. After a pause, John continued, "I ain't never ever thought about such a thing. I just thought I'd probably just fall over in one of these fields one of these days and be buried here in this graveyard." He then said, "Besides, I couldn't ever just **not** do nuthin!" He still remained in his kneeling position, looking up at Clyde, waiting for his reply.

"Here's what I've been thinking," said Clyde. "I've been thinking about it ever since Mom died. I think we are both due a rest now. We could sell the farm to those people that are interested in it, and get us a simple little house in town where the grocery store and post office is. It would be on a little piece of land where I could plant nothing but rose bushes, and as for you not being able to do nothing as you say, you could plant all of the vegetable garden you wanted."

By this time John was excitedly on his feet. "Yeah," he interjected, "And we could have a few chickens if we got a place on the edge of town. I doubt if they would let us keep a cow, but we'd be right near a grocery store. They even have store-bought bread there and we wouldn't have all that long drive to the post office to hear from and write your Nebraska relatives."

"I've wanted to do this even before Mom passed, but I knew she loved this old rocky grazing land out here and I knew I couldn't leave her alone as old as she was." They had started the walk toward the truck to go back to the old home place as they continued their conversation. "Truthfully," Clyde said, "I would have said something before now, but I wasn't sure what Mom would think even after she died. If she'd want us to move from here, I mean."

John stopped in the middle of the graveyard and looked at Clyde. "Listen, Clyde," he said soberly, "Sarah always talked about how happy a place heaven would be and she was sure that's where she would be after death. She was sure of that Bible of hers and sure of that fact too. If that's so, and I'm sure it is too, she would want you to be happy on earth, just like she is there now. I really think she would like to think of you moving back to the place we all started back when it had been Indian Territory and we had a start in making that little town of Carnegie. That's where our Oklahoma life started. I think she would be pleased if you moved there. She worked so hard when you were a boy, and even after you were a young man to see you were happy and had a good life. Why wouldn't she like to see you happy and able to rest and just enjoy life?"

The two old men started to the old battered truck again to travel up the road they had known many years ago as a wagon trail before they knew cars. Clyde felt that old excitement start to bubble up again. He was going to have a new adventure, at his age! He was totaling all the past up in his mind, and all his life-time adventures. Amazed that at his age, he was to have another, he thought back on the past.

One by one he listed them. Something he had never done before. He had been a part of, and grown up in, that frontier town in Nebraska named Tecumseh. He had made that old Oklahoma Land Run in 1889. He had seen action in that Spanish American War. He had been a part in opening of that first town in what had been that old Caddo-Comanche, and Kiowa Indian Reservation in 1901 and he had seen Oklahoma become a state.

Now he was going to see what that word he had heard about for so long was. The one he never thought he would ever be a part of. That elite group he had heard about before as the *retired*. Best of all, he thought, he would be retired in that old town he had worked so hard in to make out of an Indian prairie of grass and dirt. As he walked along he did a quick hop in the air in excitement; a very high hop for a man his age.

Old John grinned and thought to himself with the only cuss word he ever used only on very special occasions. "Golly Damn, I'd like to jump in the air too!" Then he had another secret thought that made the old man laugh to himself. "If I did, I'd probably fall flat, break something, and then we wouldn't get to move to town." So with a smile on his face, and his hands clasped behind his back, he continued his slow, measured walk back to the truck.

John and Clyde in front of the Carnegie house

John and Clyde

NEBRASKA MYSTERY TRUNK UNCOVERED

In the 1930's an old building was being torn down in Tecumseh Nebraska. It was in the part of what had been considered the old historic district where early Tecumseh had been pioneered and established. Town historians had recorded the building was a boarding house that was established in the 1880's.

As the demolition had started on the ancient old building, an alert construction boss noticed a door under a stair case had come open. Having gone through the old building before the destruction had started, he had not seen the door, and being curious, went to inspect what was behind it. On inspection he discovered an old black trunk from another era. Lifting the old lid, it had obviously not been opened for many years. When looking inside, he felt there was treasure there he best not touch.

Telling the construction workers not to go near the stair case, he left the building to find the owner of the building. When the old trunk was examined by the owner, he notified the person that had been considered the town historian. As a result of the discovery, the trunk was transferred to a museum. The trunk and its contents rest in a large glass case to be seen by visitors.

Should someone visit that museum, they might see in that glass case, a story from another century of living people from the past. The contents are carefully displayed with no explanation.

You will see, carefully displayed in the center, a Federal Soldier's Uniform with medals lying on the uniform jacket, just as it was found. You will notice among the medals there is a medical insignia.

In the glass case, is an old cardboard photograph from the Civil War era, showing a young, tall, handsome man and an attractive petite woman in what seems to be a wedding dress. They are posed in what would be a typical wedding picture of that era. There is a second cardboard picture of a tent with some unknown Civil War soldiers sitting in chairs in front of it. There is a small tag in front of the picture identifying the central bearded man as General Ulysses S. Grant.

The case has a few other articles displayed that had been found in this trunk of the past. They are personal things that had been stored, but would mean nothing to anyone of this day, except for their antiquity.

There is one most poignant article. It is a short letter. Many pass by and don't take the time to read it. It is written in a man's hand. It is almost as unreadable, as doctor's handwritings are in this modern day. To those that do stop, this is what is written:

January 3, 1868
My Dear Little Sarah.

I write this letter to tell you how I love you. Sometimes for some reason, those special words are not spoken often. So I write these special words to you now. How blessed we are to have had this love. Many never experience such a thing. Having lived our early marriage lives through the living reality of the Civil War and of death all around us made our lives together seem more precious. Now that we no longer daily see war, how little problems seem, and so it is a precious life we have lived. How sweet our little son has become to me in these last days.

I have tried to explain to you the restlessness in my spirit in these last days and the desire to get away from the physician's role. There has always been the cry for something different. It is more than I had strength to tell you, for I did not want to hurt you. It seems I have always had this restlessness in me. It was a call to a new adventure. I want you to know it has nothing to do with any lack in you. As I write this letter, I am not sure where this inner need will take me.

There is a purpose for this letter I write to you on this day, my Love. I will place it in the bottom of my trunk of special things. It will be hidden away in that place, and should you read this, it will be because I will no longer be with you. I want it to be my last message to you. I seem to be able to write my feelings, better than I can speak them. I seem to be one that speaks his love with my hands.

I have so treasured you and cannot speak of the great love in my heart for you. It is good to know you will read these words, should something happen to me. My heart's desire is that you know there has never been any lack in you as I describe this restlessness in me. This call to a new adventure is a lack in me. Never blame yourself.

Stay strong as you are my little Sarah. You were meant to do great things.
Forever, Zebulun

P.S. I'm sorry I could never live up to the meaning of my name "The House of Honor." You loved it so. It's my hope our son will."

Storyteller's Note: Sarah could never bring herself to go through the trunk, and so never saw the letter.

SIXTY-THIRD YEAR.

VERY EARLY SETTLER HERE

MRS. SARAH INGRAHM DIED AT HOME IN OKLAHOMA.

Served as Nurse Throughout Civil War—Was Pioneer Hotel Keeper in Tecumseh.

Mrs. Sarah Ingrahm died at her home on a ranch, near Alden, Okla., on Friday, January 17, 1930, at an advanced age. She had been very well for one of her age, yet had been declining for years. Tecumseh relatives were advised of her death by a telegram from her son, Clyde Ingrahm.

Mrs. Ingrahm's maiden name was Elizabeth Stanton and she was born in Oneida county, N. Y., 18—. Her girlhood was spent in that state, where she secured her early education, and, when Sarah was fifteen years of age, the family moved to Knox county, Ills., where her schooling was continued. At the age of twenty years she was married to Dr. Z. W. Ingrahm, a physician. A year later the Civil war broke out and both Dr. and Mrs. Ingrahm enlisted for service, he in the Eighty-third Illinois infantry, and she as an army nurse in the same regiment, and both served during the entire war. During

MRS. SARAH INGRAHM.

her service as army nurse, Mrs. Ingrahm cared for many sick and wounded soldiers, and as the regiment was made up largely of men from her home community, she was well acquainted with and interested in the most of her patients. Among them were the late Joseph W. Buffum, Wallace W. Jones, and others, early-day Illinois men who later came to Nebraska to settle. For the longest period of her service Mrs. Ingrahm was stationed at Fort Donaldson, Tenn., and she was also at Fort Henry for some time. Since the war Mrs. Ingrahm had always been an active member of the Women's Relief Corps and greatly interested in all Grand Army of the Republic activities, at least during the years of these activities and her younger years. In less than three years after the war was over Dr. Ingrahm died near Davenport, Iowa, where they had established their home, leaving his widow and one son, Clyde F. Ingrahm. After the death of her husband Mrs. Ingrahm returned to Illinois where she made her home with a sister, Mrs. Olive Anderson, for a time. A few years later her mother, the late Mrs. Michael Stanton, and her brothers and sisters came to Nebraska, Mrs. Stanton taking a homestead south of Tecumseh. In the year 1870 Mrs. Ingrahm and her sister and husband, Oliver Anderson, also came to and settled near Mayberry, in Pawnee county.

In the year 1875 Mrs. Ingrahm started a boarding house, on a small scale, in the old Andrew Head residence in Tecumseh, and she met with such success in the business that she moved to a frame business building owned by a Mr. Myers, on the west side of the square, conducting the business in the second story of this building. Later Mrs. Ingrahm bought the old frame hotel building, on the site now occupied by the farmers feed yard, at the corner of Clay and Second streets, which was the Caledonia hotel and which she operated as a first-class hotel. This hostelry will be well remembered by early settlers, for it was the headquarters not alone for many home people but for the weary travelers enroute throught this new country as well. In the year 1882 the increased business Mrs. Ingrahm was enjoying, and the growth of the town and surrounding country, made it necessary for her to build a larger hotel, and she secured the site opposite her old-time location and built a part of what afterwards became known as the Arcade hotel, now in operation. Mrs. Ingrahm remained in business here until the year 1900, when she retired from work. After giving up the hotel here Mrs. Ingrahm accompanied her son and his family to Oklahoma, at the time many claims were thrown open there, and the son took a claim, and he and his family lived upon it for many years. Mrs. Ingrahm had continued to live there with the exception of frequent visits to old Johnson county, to see her brother, Jerome Stanton of Elk Creek, sister, Mrs. Jane Freemole of Tecumseh, deceased, numerous nieces and nephews and many friends. Mrs. Ingrahm greatly enjoyed the visits to Nebraska and the meeting of old time friends. Many of the people of Tecumseh and Johnson county can recall numerous interesting things that transpired in the early day, when Mrs. Ingrahm was engaged in the hotel business here, and these early settlers got great satisfaction out of their reminiscent moods and visiting with the pioneer woman. Mrs. Ingrahm had been honored by both the Grand Army of the Republic and the American Legion post of Tecumseh, each one presenting her with a nice emblem of their organization. During the late World war Mrs. Ingrahm pieced a fine quilt, which she gave to the local American Legion post soon after it was organized, and which the Legion boys sold for the splendid sum of $115.00. Tickets were issued and the quilt went to Dr. J. M. Curtis of this city, the post being named for his soon, Kenneth A. Curtis.

The funeral and burial were at Alden, but we are not informed as to particulars.

287

TECUMSEH NEWSPAPER OBITUARY
VERY EARLY SETTLER HERE
MRS. SARAH INGRAHM DIED AT HOME IN OKLAHOMA

Served As Nurse Throughout The Civil War –
Was Pioneer Hotel Keeper in Tecumseh

Mrs. Sarah Ingrahm died at her home on a ranch, near Alden, Okla. On Friday, January 17, 1930 at an advanced age. She had been very well for one of her age, yet had been declining for years. Tecumseh relatives were advised of her death by a telegram from her son, Clyde Ingrahm.

Mrs. Ingrahm's maiden name was Sarah Elizabeth Stanton, and she was born in Oneida Co., N.Y. in 1840. Her girlhood was spent in that state where she secured her early education, and when Sarah was fifteen years of age, the family moved to Knox County, Ill., where her schooling was continued. At the age of 20 years she was married to Dr. Z. W. Ingrahm, a physician. A year later the Civil War broke out and both Dr. and Mrs. Ingraham enlisted for service, he in the 83rd Ill. Infantry, and she as an army nurse in the same regiment, and both served during the entire war. During her service as army nurse, Mrs. Ingrahm cared for many sick and wounded soldiers, and as the regiment was made up largely of men from her home community, she was well acquainted and interested in most of her patients. Among them was the late Joseph W. Buffum, Wallace W. Jobes, and other early day Illinois men who later came to Nebraska to settle. For the longest period of her service Mrs. Ingrahm was stationed at Fort Donaldson, Tenn, and she was also at Fort Henry for some time.

Since the war Mrs. Ingrahm had always been an active member of the Women's Relief Corps and greatly interested in all Grand Army of the Republic activities, at least during the years of these activities and her younger years.

In less than three years after the war was over Dr. Ingrahm died near Davenport, Iowa, where they had established their home, leaving his widow and one son Clyde F. Ingrahm. A few years later her mother, the late Mrs. Michael Stanton, and her brothers and sisters came to Nebraska, Her mother taking a homestead south of Tecumseh.

In the year of 1875 Mrs. Ingrahm started a boarding house, on a small scale, in the old Andrew Head residence in Tecumseh, and she met with such success in the business that she moved to a frame business building owned by a Mrs. Meyers on the west side of the square, conducting the business in the second story of this building. Later Mrs. Ingrahm bought the old frame Hotel building on the site now occupied by the farmers feed yard, on the corner of Clay and Second St. (The Centennial House) which she operated as a first class hotel. This hostelry will be well remembered by early settlers, for it was the headquarters not alone for many home people but for the weary travelers enroute through this new country as well. In the year 1882, the increased business Mrs. Ingrahm was enjoying and the growth of the town and the surrounding county made it necessary for her to build a larger hotel, and she secured the site opposite her old time location and built a part of what afterwards became known as the Arcade Hotel, now in operation. Mrs. Ingrahm remained in business here until 1900, when she retired from work.

After giving up the hotel here Mrs. Ingrahm accompanied her son to Oklahoma at the time many claims were thrown open there, and her son took a claim and he and his family lived upon it for many years. Mrs. Ingrahm had continued to live there with the exception of frequent visits to Johnson County, to see her brother Jerome Stanton of Elk Creek, sisters Mrs. Jane Freemole of Tecumseh, deceased, numerous nieces, nephews and many friends. Many of the people of Tecumseh and Johnson County can recall numerous interesting things that transpired in the early days, when Mrs. Ingrahm was engaged in the hotel business here, and these early settlers drew great satisfaction out of the reminiscent moods and visiting with the pioneer woman.

Mrs. Ingrahm has been honored by both the Grand Army of the Republic and the American Legion Post of Tecumseh, each of them presenting her with a nice emblem of their organization. During the late World War Mrs. Ingrahm pieced a fine quilt which she gave to the local American Legion Post shortly after it was organized and which the Legion boys sold for the sum of $115.00. Tickets were issued and the quilt went to Dr. J. M. Curtis, of this city, the post being named for his son, Kenneth A.C. Curtis.

The funeral and burial were at Alden but we have not been informed of any particulars.

Personal Remarks by the Storyteller
The Wild West Show

There is a wonderful aged brown picture that is from the old days that is a keepsake of one of the adventuresome things that my grandfather took part in. It is an old cardboard type picture that was made in the late 1890's or early 1900's that has survived his partnership in a Wild West Show. Sadly, there is no picture of John's part in the show, but there is a wonderful picture of a cousin that is posing wearing a rugged western type costume and posing with bows arrows, knives, and guns and all that was used in the theatrical performance.

In the late 19th and early 20th centuries, Wild West Shows flourished, especially Oklahoma Wild West Shows, because Americans thought of Oklahoma as the Wild West because it had been Indian Territory. At that time many of these shows reproduced the frenzied 1889 land rush into Oklahoma Territory and Clyde and John were certainly experts on that subject since they made that run. Oklahomans took pride in their roughhewn past.

The Wild West Show occupied an important role in Oklahoma history. There was always horsemanship and trained dogs doing routines in the smaller shows.

The shows presented stirring Wild West History, adventurous and likeable people, patriotism, and tolerance. The adventurous white men always made friends with the beautifully feathered red men who rode their horses so magnificently in mock battles. Then the flag would fly through the arena on galloping horseback and all would end in peace and harmony.

It's not known what Indians took part in Clyde's show, but in that era many Indians engaged in such activities to make money and it was a lucrative business for some.

The word passed down through the family was that Cousin Victor Anderson used the name Yellowstone Vic in this show. Granddad's cousin was apparently the real deal. In Sarah's early widowhood years she stayed in the home of her sister Mary who was married to Oliver Anderson. So apparently Clyde had quite a playmate in his cousin Victor, who was known for his riding and roping. They were both born in 1865, making them the same age and that's probably how Clyde learned some of the things he knew. They may have practiced that Wild West play in their younger playtimes together. Children have their heroes and that may have been what developed their later endeavors in that thing called Wild West Shows.

Realizing all was not play then in a day when young boys carried guns for the family table food and horses were the mode of transportation, it's understandable that young boys practiced and copied some of the novels that would come out in that day glorifying the "Wild West" heroes such as Buffalo Bill Cody.

Much of the information I have shared has come from much toil of a daughter of one of Sarah's brothers. She, among others, has shared much genealogy with our family. I will share some of the knowledge she passed on about this showman cousin who was known as Yellowstone Vic:

"He traveled with Buffalo Bill's Show in the U.S. and Europe. He did movies in Hollywood. One I remember was "Pride of the

*Prairie." Another is "Rose of the Rio Grande".
In later years he traveled with Golmar Bros.
Circus, Campbell Bros., and Ringling. When
he came to Tecumseh my family usually went
to see him. He did fancy roping and shooting.
He also did a knife act, outlining his wife,
Blanch Ring's body. She, in turn, stood on her
head and shot an apple off his head. In very
late years they appeared in state fairs, and
county fairs. Vic went back to the circus
where he died."*

Nettie Fernley

A wooden handled bell belonging to my
Grand-dad, with horse teeth marks on the handle
portion of the bell, exists to this day. Apparently,
they had a horse or pony that was trained to ring
the bell at some point with his mouth in the act. It's
easy to envision some of Clyde's dogs performing
tricks to the sound of the bell. Mary was a sharpshooter and that was a marketable thing in that
day, especially in females. John when being inter-
viewed on his ninety-eighth birthday by a
newspaper mentioned the show but, it's not known
specifically when this occurred in their lives. He
mentioned they traveled around with their own
show. Another thing I cannot imagine is that the
lovable old John mentioned he played the role of a
Wildman in their show. Unbelievable if you knew
this sweet man as I did.

Letters from some early day relatives say
that Clyde settled down because of having a family
but that Yellowstone Vic went on to make a success
of that occupation. However, Grand-dad Clyde had
an eccentric side to him always, because in the
1940's he was still wearing his Spanish-American

Cavalry hat. He obviously was his own person. It's really hard to put together the idea of a skilled violinist who could play beautiful concertos, toe tapping Irish jigs, sang with a sweet tenor voice with a combination Spanish American Cavalry rider and cowboy, who just happened to own hotels and helped found new towns in new territories. No wonder my Grand-mother Mary was always confused.

A restaurant I frequent has an old reproduction of a Buffalo Bill Wild West Show poster that is quite a colorful thing to see with its cowboys, Indians, and buffalos doing all their maneuvers. I always like to stop and look at the picture and imagine my family past, but should the restaurant be crowded, I just smile as I walk by.

Clyde Ingrahm on the Right
Possibly from Clyde's Wild West Show days, but the date
and identity of the other person unknown

Yellowstone Vic Anderson Postcard
Addressed to "Aunt Sarah", Carnegie Oklahoma

Clyde F. Ingrahm Rites Were Friday; Burial At Alden

Services were in Pitcher's chapel Friday for Clyde Ingrahm, one of Carnegie's first businessmen after the opening of the town. Rev. Brodace Elkins, pastor of the Methodist church, preached the sermon and burial was in the Alden cemetery. Mr. Ingrahm died at 8:15 p.m. Tuesday of last week. He had been in failing health for five years.

Clyde Francis Ingrahm was born in Illinois Nov. 6, 1865. When he was 2 years old his parents moved to Tecumseh, Neb. He was married to Edna Rainey in 1896 and they came to Oklahoma in 1901.

Ingrahm served in the Spanish American war, was a member of Co. I, Second Neb. Regiment. He enlisted Jan. 27, 1899 and was discharged June 5, 1901 with the rank of QM sergeant.

When Carnegie was founded, Ingrahm operated a hotel here. His companion and cook was John Seou, Chinese, who survives his employer.

Later Ingrahm located on a farm in the Alden community where he lived until 1936 when he and John moved to Carnegie where they have batched since.

Ingrahm was made a Mason in 1918 by Carnegie Lodge No. 294 and was a member at the time of his death.

Survivors are three daughters, Mrs. T. H. Henderson, Houston; Mrs. C. A. King, New Jersey; and Mrs. Marguerite Houp, Waxahachie, Texas; 10 grandchildren and seven great grandchildren.

Mrs. Henderson and Mrs. Houp and her two daughters, Mrs. Juanita McElroy and Miss Jo Ann Houp were here for the funeral.

Clyde' parents were Dr. and Mrs. Z. W. Ingrahm, both Civil War veterans. Dr. Ingrahm served as a physician and Mrs. Ingrahm served as an army nurse during the entire war. Dr. Ingrahm died three years after the close of the war. Mrs. Ingrahm, the former Sarah Elizabeth Stanton, came to Oklahoma with her son and made her home here. She died at Alden Jan. 17, 1930.

The Carnegie Herald, Wed. Aug. 17, 1949

Clyde F. Ingrahm Rites Were Friday;
Burial At Alden

Services were in Pitcher's chapel Friday for Clyde Ingrahm, one of Carnegie's first businessmen after the opening of the town. Rev. Brodace Elkins, pastor of the Methodist church, preached the sermon and burial was in the Alden cemetery. Mr. Ingrahm died at 8:15 p.m. Tuesday of last week. He had been in failing health for five years.

Clyde Francis Ingrahm was born in Illinois Nov. 6, 1865. When he was 2 years old his parents moved to Tecumseh, Neb. He was married to Edna Rainey in 1896 and they came to Oklahoma in 1901.

Ingrahm served in the Spanish American war, was a member of Co. I, Second Neb. Regiment. He enlisted Jan. 27, 1899 and was discharged June 5, 1901 with the rank of QM sergeant.

When Carnegie was founded, Ingrahm operated a hotel here. His companion and cook was John Seou, Chinese, who survives his employer. Later Ingrahm located on a farm in Alden community where he lived until 1936 when he and John moved to Carnegie where they have batched since.

Ingrahm was made a Mason in 1918 by Carnegie Lodge No. 294 and was a member at the time of his death.

Survivors are three daughters, Mrs. T.H. Henderson, Houston; Mrs. C.A. King, New Jersey; and Mrs. Margueritte Houp, Waxahachie, Texas; 10 grandchildren and seven great grandchildren.

Mrs. Henderson and Mrs. Houp and her two daughters, Mrs. Juanita McElroy and Miss Jo Ann Houp were here for the funeral.
Clyde's parents were Dr. and Mrs. Z.W. Ingrahm, both Civil War veterans. Dr. Ingrahm served as a physician and Mrs. Ingrahm served as an army nurse during the entire war. Dr. Ingrahm died three years after the close of the war. Mrs. Ingrahm, the former Sarah Elizabeth Stanton, came to Oklahoma with her son and made her home here. She died at Alden Jan. 17, 1930.

Clyde Francis Ingrahm
Birth: 1865   Death: 1949

The Carnegie Home Place

*"Prepare a noble death song for the day you go
over the Great divide."*
TECUMSEH

How hard it was to walk away from that
old cemetery that day. This cemetery that was so
near to the place they had homesteaded and where
they had made early memories in a land so primitive
and hard.

Without Clyde, how quiet was the house
that they had moved to and spent their last years in
town! There was no more the sound of that sweet
violin or the lively Irish jigs that made John's old
feet tap. There was no more the singing of that old
sweet, but shaky tenor voice. There were no longer
roses, brought in daily for a touch of beauty from
the beautiful bushes that Clyde so lovingly planted.
There was no daily reading to him of the news by
his old friend out of the *Time Magazine* or the weekly
Carnegie Herald.

There was no more walking together with
Blackie and Whitey, their two Scottie Dogs. There
were no more little jaunts to the beautiful city park,
so near the house, to enjoy the coolness under the
giant Cottonwood trees in the hot summer. He remembered with a smile, Clyde taking his violin to
the park and the children dancing to the Irish jigs
that he played. Then they would try to follow them
home, for John always had candy, and they would
have to tell them not to leave the park. What a respite that beautiful old park was during the summer.

They remembered that place before it became called a park in the early 1900's.

There was no more sitting in the yard in the late evenings together, listening to the beautiful tom toms of the Kiowa Indians as they gathered near the banks of the Washita, flowing near their house, where they held their yearly holiday pow wows. They would be in their beautiful feathers doing their hoop dances, their stomp dances, their war dances, their round dances, and the squaw dances way into the night. The tom toms would be their lullaby as they would go to sleep on those summer evenings, just as they would be mine later. Although, it was now in the late 1940's, those ancient songs of the prairie people lived on, in that old familiar yard, with the fragrant smell of the roses, they would remind each other of the times they had traded with the Indians. They spoke of the old settler and Native American friends they had made and the stories they had told them. They had spoken to them of how hard it had been for the natives of this land to adjust to their culture as the new settlers were coming in to their territory. It had seemed like a locust infestation overnight. How they had lived as hunters and the white man required them to bring food out of the ground. What hardships they had endured. Clyde and John talked about the outlaws and their stories. They still had an old picture of a dead Jesse James that they had bought for a pretty price.

They reminisced of many things that they relived of the early pioneer days in Nebraska and Clyde talked of his childhood there. John talked of his arrival at Sarah's hotel and the wagon ride that brought him to her doorstep. They remembered the great Nebraska blizzard of 1888 and how the ice blew through the air in the deadly wind and they remembered how men and cattle died in a matter of minutes when exposed. How many times they talked of the excitement and disappointment of the time they made the Great Oklahoma Land Run. They talked of the settling of their small Oklahoma town Lathram, and also the homesteading of the old farm south, now at the place called Alden. They laughed when they talked about these last days they had spent where they were now as "gentlemen of leisure" in this old house in this town no longer called Lathram, but now called Carnegie. They laughed because when they came to this retirement place they found that having worked a lifetime they could not sit still. As they looked out on the old road in front of their house they lived in now, they remembered it was not far from the place where they as early settlers forded the Washita in wagons when it was high. Now the new automobiles drove down that old road now named Cedar Street but not frequently. It wasn't a popular part of the town, now that it was old. The building of the old dam right up that road was quite a deal when that happened because Carnegie got electricity. What a stir that caused even when it wasn't for a full day like it is now. It was built in 1911 and the electricity came in 1912. They had already moved on south of town then, to the old homestead. It was good that they had sold the old Olymphia though, because there was that fire that burned part of the town and the restaurant with it in 1904.

So on and on they talked of the times past, the good and bad, but ever the past, for that is what old people talk about. They are not sure if they have a future and it seems now they are not really recognized by the people of the now. It is as if no one even sees them now or has any interest in anything they might know or want to talk about. How could they have had anything interesting in their lives that could have happened, the people of the now seem to think, and so it is they never listen to their old unexciting, true life stories. "Yet, they make movies about them, and go pay money to see them," they said. "I bet we could tell them some tales they wouldn't believe," Clyde would say. Then he would get quiet and not talk for a while when his mind would wander to the firing squad he was forced to be on in the Spanish-American war. He never spoke about that – even to John.

Yet when the old people are gone, the people of the now wonder. They wish they had asked. For they want to tell their stories to their children. Afterwards they see that these old stories were their family stories too. So it has always been.

How still was that old Oklahoma house now without Clyde! How John still thought of the woman that had showed such kindness to him almost as if he were a son, even though she had been gone all those years.

Now, just as he and Clyde had made a yearly pilgrimage to Sarah's grave at the old cemetery, he would make that trip to two graves now. It was such a lonely pilgrimage now. Every year he wished there would be Clyde's roses blooming for him to take to his old friend's grave.

THE OLD SETTLER'S CEMETERY

Could you see that old cemetery, one day a year a taxi cab would drive up and the driver would get out and open the gate. More feeble and bent every year, an old man would struggle to get out of the back seat of the car. The taxi man was accustomed to the yearly trip, for Carnegie was small and there was but one taxi. Slowly, you would see the old man and his flowers make his way to the back of what was to him, hallowed ground. That whole area was. They had ridden horses, driven buckboards and wagons and finally primitive cars in this country they had lived in. Officially the obituary for Clyde had called this burial place they had known so long as Apache, Caddo County, Oklahoma, U.S.A. Those that lived out there had just called it the "old cemetery" back then.

The closer he got to one hundred, the harder it got to make the journey. At last, as the Taxi driver watched, the slight old man would stop at the two graves, side by side. It was just as they had been through life, these two old friends of his.

The Military Stone that was given to those who fought in the Civil War was on one grave. It was a white marble soldier's stone with the words:

SARAH E. INGRAHM
MATRON UNITED STATES ARMY

Nearby, on the other granite stone was a Mason Insignia.: The words engraved:

CLYDE INGRAM
1865-1949

Clyde's name had been misspelled, but actually both names were, as names were often changed for the early settlers to blend in with the culture and become more pronounceable. The old man knew that a place next to his friend had already been arranged for him. He had already decided that he only wanted the name John on it. It was the lone name he carried most of his life.

Clutching his flowers to himself, suddenly not even aware he was holding them, he became lost in thought. Where did his mind go? Did the last century parade before him?

Did his mind travel back to his start in China? Did he see a small boy deposited on the rough coastline of a place called San Francisco, California? As his mind wandered over his life as a businessman there, did he wonder what his fate would have been had he remained there? Would he have married? Maybe had children? Would he have lived in a Chinatown, not being the one and only "Chinaman"?

Surely as he looked at that first marble grave stone, he envisioned the face of the kind woman who welcomed him as a stranger into her home and nursed him from his severe injuries in that old Tecumseh hotel.

Did his mind go back to the days when he worked as a cook in her four boarding houses and he became fast friends with her son? Did he remember the early pioneer time in that town of Nebraska? What were his thoughts of his slow emersion into a non-Asian culture?

Surely, were he reliving their lives together, he would remember the wagon journey they made together to that place that had been the Cherokee Strip that Clyde's grand-children were studying in their history studies now.

As, he looked at that grave, did he go back to a time mentally that they walked shoulder to shoulder into a town that only existed in the mind of brave adventurous people that would later be called Carnegie, Oklahoma? A time they dared to be among all those clamorous people who were starting their Oklahoma life that first day? Was he remembering what it was like to try and feed a hungry mob of people in buckboards, who had no more than a deed in their hand to a piece of dirt property, and a need for a belly to be filled. Now it seemed crazy that although their tent had not arrived they opened that restaurant in a town in the midst of a bare dirt lot.

Then as his mind turned to the grave of Clyde, he must have thought of all the years they had worked side by side in these frontier lands that yielded no existence easily and how together with Mary from nothing they had to build life itself. How real that seemed now as he stood back in the place they had struggled near these graves bordering the foothills of the Wichita. Life had been as hard as the rocky hills were themselves. It was only a few miles from this cemetery where they scratched out a living on that hard land. Sheepherding, a few dairy cows, chickens, planting corn, broomcorn and hunting had made their survival. He remembered Mary working from before dawn until after the last lamp went out every day. Hauling water was such a chore. No lights. The food preparation was a constant thing for the family. What a trooper she had been. She just did was expected of a prairie woman. There was the raising of four children, and the death of the one later in life who was their only boy. Clyde had lost his Mary as they lived on that land, but he had really lost her heart when he volunteered to go to the Spanish-American War leaving her alone with two small children.

Just a short piece away, as they say in the country, from that homestead, the indomitable Sarah had moved and died at an old age. The whole land he was standing in the middle of now, held so many memories.

Out of it all, looking back some would call it settling the frontier. The Indians had another name for it, but American History would call these settlers pioneers. John didn't see that though. He, looking back would call it a great adventure with his adopted family. These were the ones who didn't call him Chinaman John, but just plain "John."

As the cab driver restlessly watched the old man finally lean over and place the flowers on the two graves, he wished he would hurry up. He wanted to get back to his business. Never thinking the old man was spending these brief minutes with the only family he had ever had, he looked impatiently at his watch. The town's only Taxi was probably losing business.

The taxi driver almost got out when he saw the old man stumble a bit as he left part of his flowers near one of the graves, but he caught himself on the white gravestone and straightened himself up. Turning to his left, he walked the few steps to see his old friend Clyde.

Leaning over his grave, he placed the assorted wildflowers he knew that he would have liked down, and said, "I wish they could have been your roses, my friend." The taxi cab driver saw him take a handkerchief from his pocket and wipe his face. He softened a little, forgot his watch and leaned back in the seat of the taxi still watching.

Slowly John turned back, starting what to him was a long journey back to the taxi cab. The driver had gotten out, opened the gate, and helped the shaky old man into the back seat and shut the car door. Getting in, he turned the car and drove up the short gravel road to the highway where the sign said "The Old Settler's Cemetery" and stopped to make his turn. The car with the passenger that had first come to this land in a covered wagon turned, then quickly accelerated, heading toward the place that he had helped make a town in 1901.

As John leaned back in the car, he thought about the fact that it would be another year before he would come back. He didn't know that his body, which had outlived so many other men's, would start to wear out, and this would be his next to last visit to that old cemetery.

Excerpt from The Carnegie Herald, 1953
Lum Seow, 98, Gives Away Fortune in Kindness

John Lum Seow, 98 year old Carnegie resident is a philanthropist who has given away a fortune. Not money – human kindness.

Seow isn't one to talk about his charity. He would rather tell about the time he chased Turk Bebee, Rosco Schooling, and Clyde Pitcher out of the Hartman hotel with a butcher knife for cutting his hot pies.

One has to contact Seow's near friends to write a story about his kindness. Like how he would take poor children off the street and outfit them with clothing at a department store. The pint-sized American has a heart bigger than the country where he was born.

The fifth member of the Carnegie Herald's "91 Club" was born April 22, 1855, in Canton China. The United States and Carnegie got a break when a California uncle brought Seow back to the U.S. in 1864, following the death of his mother.

I was sea sick during the whole 30 day voyage" Seow recalls. "I ate only one full meal".

After 30 years in California, asthma** forced Seow inland to Tecumseh, Neb in 1894. He registered at a hotel and the woman behind the desk was Mrs. Sarah E. Ingrahm. From this meeting developed a friendship that was continued thru the years.

Seow came with the Ingrahms to Oklahoma territory and made the run in the strip in a surrey. They didn't get any land so traveled on and homesteaded 12 miles south of Carnegie.

Grandmother Ingrahm opened a café in Lathram and Seow was the cook. He remembers they opened the eating establishment for three months in a tent before moving into a new building. They traded with the Indians for cooking utensils. All the old-timers remember Seow's cooking.

Among his treasured possessions are his tattered naturalization papers and membership in the Chinese Masons. He won't send the papers off to get them replaced. He's making sure they don't get lost. Seow became a citizen in 1899, after making application in 1894.

"I'm an old Republican," Seow chuckles. "Been one all my life. The first president I voted for was McKinley."

In 1930, Mrs. Ingrahm died. Before her death she asked John to look after her son, Clyde. The two batched together until Clyde's death four years ago.

Clyde kept john up on world events by reading Time magazine to him. And Clyde wouldn't let anyone take care of him but John.

Clyde's daughter, Mrs. Margaret (sic) Harding looks after John in the four room house on the northeast end of town. However, John still does his own cooking and takes care of his garden in the back yard.

His quarters are in one room where he has his bed and cook stove. He still makes a daily trip to the post office and chats with friends. But he has slowed down the last year and spends a good deal of his time in bed.

"I don't know why I live so long", John says. But he has a formula for a long life. "Don't go crooked. Go straight, and don't owe nobody".

Altho Seow can't read English, he's a regular subscriber of the Herald. "I owe for the paper," John says. "I always subscribe to it during the fair and I was sick this year. You'll have to wait until the fair next week."

He is a member of the Presbyterian church, and he never misses placing flowers on the Ingrahm plot at the cemetery each Memorial Day. He makes the trip in a taxi.

One time Seow walked from Mountain View to the Ingrahm farm to bring silk to make a dress for Margaret (sic), then 7. She had caught on fire in the field and John thought she had died and he wanted her buried in a nice dress.

Another friend tells about the time he would go out and clean house for a newlywed, and how he would go out in the country and visit.

"He would stop at every house along the road", the friend recalls, "and chat with all the kids and their parents".

Seow's one request when he dies: "I want plenty of flowers at my funeral."

"Don't put too much in the paper," he cautions the reporter. "My friends might think I'm going crazy."

Besides being cook, farmer and all around worker, Seow played the part of a wild man in the early days. He and Clyde had a dog and pony show and would tour the country in a wagon. Seow would pull the hair down over his eyes and jump at the crowd with his long butcher knife.

He still has his trusty butcher knife. "I might have to go back to work again," he laughs. He uses it to cut up his vegetables for canning. Then he gives them away.

Seow says his friends don't drop around like they used to. "They might think I'm dead", he laughs.

The highlight of the year for Seow is Election Day. "The fellows would always give me a cigar that day at city hall. " Seow says, "But I didn't get a smoke off of them this year."

Seow's eyes light up like Chinese lanterns when company drops by. A visit to the garden is a must, and john points out how his garden is doing. He is famous for raising garlic. On the culinary side, John's specialty is doughnuts. His friends say they stay fresh for a week.

Runaway boys probably remember Seow. He would keep them at his house until they cooled off and then they were ready to go back home.

"Don't write so much", Seow repeats.

From China to Carnegie, Ninety-eight years old. Seow has truly distributed a wealth of kindness.

**Storyteller's note: Outside of the family, John was always reluctant to tell the story of the traumatic incident that brought him to Sarah's boarding house.

Excerpts from The Carnegie Herald, April, 1955

STATE OF OKLAHOMA
OFFICE OF THE GOVERNOR
APRIL 18, 1955
Dear Mr. Seow:
Mutual friend of ours have reminded me that you will celebrate your 100th birthday April 22. Knowing of your many contributions to Oklahoma and the nation throughout a full and helpful life. I feel you deserve the highest possible commendation.

I am familiar with your personal philosophy of hard work and honesty. I know also of the helping had you have always cheerfully extended to others.

There is an old Chinese proverb which I feel suits you very well. It says "Great men never feel great; small men never feel small".

For 100 years you have lived up to that definition of greatness. May this birthday anniversary be your most pleasant one.

Sincerely,
RAYMOND GARY
Governor of Oklahoma

PROCLAMATION
Whereas our friend and fellow citizen by choice, Lum Seow will celebrate his 100th birthday Friday, April 22 and

WHEREAS he has lived an upright life among us for more than 50 years, being kind and helpful, an uncomplaining worker, proud of his citizenship of the United States.

NOW THEREFORE, by the power vested in me as President of the Board of Trustees of Carnegie, Oklahoma, I do hereby declare Friday, April 22, 1955 to be "Lum Seow Day" in Carnegie and further name and appoint said Lum Seow Honorary Mayor for the day.

PRESTON N. HOLBROOK, President of the Board
Attest: B. E. Grissom, City Clerk

THE WHITE HOUSE WASHINGTON
April 18, 1955
Dear Mr. Seow,
I am indeed happy to join with your host of friends in extending warm and cordial congratulations on the occasion of your one hundredth birthday anniversary on April 22.

From all accounts the honor being paid you on your Special Day is truly deserved for your deep and abiding interest in your fellow man and your many acts of kindness have served as a source of inspiration to all who know you. I do hope that you take the proper amount of pride and comfort in this circumstance!

It is my earnest hope that the years ahead will hold an abundance of peace and happiness for you.

MAMIE DODD EISENHOWER

Excerpt from The Carnegie Herald,
April 20, 1955

Carnegie's 100 Year Old Citizen, Lum Seow,
Made Honorary Mayor for Day

Friday is "Lum Seow Day" in Carnegie and it couldn't happen to a nicer fellow. Lum Seow will be 100 years old April 22 and that day he will serve as honorary mayor, chat with friends downtown and tell them about his birthday cards from President and Mrs. Eisenhower and Gov. Gary, have dinner with some of his old friends and watch the Carnegie high school band march and play in his honor on Main Street.

"I don't know why I live so long," Seow chuckles. He also has a formula for a long life: "Don't go crooked. Go straight, and don't owe nobody."

Lum Seow was born April 22, 1855 in Canton, China. He arrived in the United States during the Civil War and arrived in the Carnegie area by way of California and Nebraska shortly after the turn of the century. He became a US Citizen in 1899.

Seow will lunch with old friends at 1 p.m. in Norman's Café. Director Pat Malloy will bring the band downtown shortly after 1 o'clock.

"I'm an old Republican," Seow says, "Been one all my life. The first president I voted for was McKinley."

It will be Mayor Lum Seow, Friday, April 22. His honor probably will give away the town because he is a fellow with a heart as big as China.

Open House Sunday

Old friends and new, neighbors then and now are invited to an informal reception and open house in Mrs. Harding's home at 224 East Cedar Sunday afternoon. The time is set from 2 p.m until 4 o'clock. "We cordially invite anyone in the community who wishes to come and visit John," Mrs. Harding said.

He will display his many birthday cards including those from the President and Governor Gary and his most prized possession: his faded and worn naturalization papers.

John, as pictured in the Carnegie Herald as "Mayor for the Day".

THE OLD OKLAHOMA TRUNK

Clyde and Mary's youngest daughter, Margueritte, soon moved to Oklahoma to care for John, the one who had cared for her family, when his health was failing. With her, she brought her daughter, the Storyteller, who lived out her fifth grade to senior year there. They stayed in that small house, taking care of John on that old dam road.

Margueritte had such a respect for Sarah, in what she had remembered of her, she would not allow any of her grandchildren to call her Grannie, which was the name Sarah had been called. My mother said she could never live up to that name.

When faithful old John died, it was Margueritte who opened an old trunk that told the story of his life and memories. What were those mementos memories of?

The black cue, which had been cut off so long ago, but carefully saved in perfect condition, represented the land of his birth, which America and its people never let him forget by the name they called him, even though he had not seen it since he was a small boy.

There were a woolen hat and gloves, hand knitted, representing Sarah's love for him as a second son in the icy Nebraska winter. There was an old deed that belonged to Sarah's mother, Catharine Stanton that was from Nebraska from the old homestead. It was dated 1883. There was a small white punch card that said OLYMPIA RESTAURANT, Mrs. S. E. INGRHAM, proprietor. Carnegie, Oklahoma. GOOD FOR 21 MEALS. There were honorary certificates to Sarah E. Ingrahm from both the Grand Army of the Republic and The American Legion Post of Tecumseh, Nebraska. There was a funeral remembrance card by the name of Sarah Elizabeth when she was laid to rest and with it a packet that once had been flowers from her grave that was so old the contents had fallen to dusty powder.

Also there was Clyde's hat that was a reminder of the Spanish American War, which was the only time they were separated and a time John lent his arm to guard Clyde's family in his absence. There was an army insignia from Clyde's old uniform. Included was the bell with one of his show horse teeth marks from one of his "wild west" show days that was a reminder of a man's fabulous talents, that didn't always go the way a mother wanted. There was a yellowed deed to land that Clyde had obtained for a homestead in Oklahoma before it became a state. It was signed by Theodore Roosevelt. There was the town obituary of Clyde Ingrahm who had died at 84 years of age.

Another memory in that old trunk of the old time Wild West Show was the frightening knife used by a kindly Wildman named John, who tried to help make a family a living. The old flour sack with the Three Musketeer Bars in it represented his love for children and his desire also to tote groceries and toil for a family he loved all his life long. She also found the letter certifying that he had joined the Tecumseh Presbyterian Church in 1899 which represented his faith in God.

Certainly not last, was something he always kept out on display was his American Naturalization papers dated 1899. The congratulatory cards from Mrs. Eisenhower and Oklahoma Governor Gary were symbols of the long life God gifted an extraordinarily humble man with a productive long life in an adopted land. There were two *Carnegie Herald Newspapers* with front page headlines, and articles about him when he had reached 98 and then 100.

A little green enamel teapot spoke of the delicious donuts he always whipped up for a visitor, and was a memory to all those who knew and remembered him. Green tea was always on his stove. It was his daily beverage. Almost his entire diet was white rice. Dieticians today might be skeptical and if it affected his height, which could have been only genetic, is not known but it did not affect his longevity.

When John was one hundred and four years old, he would go back to see his old friends at the cemetery. This time he would stay with them. Margueritte saw to it that he was laid to rest in that long ago purchased place, next to Clyde and Sarah.

Should you ever be near the beautiful ancient Oklahoma Wichita Mountain Range, near old Fort Sill, at a town named Lawton, Oklahoma, journey on north about 30 miles and you will come to a little place of the past called Alden. If you come to a town called Carnegie, you've gone too far, although that is the town Clyde and old John died in, and with Sarah's help they helped many other hardy pioneering souls establish. Should you go too fast, you might miss the cemetery. Should you be alert, and not let your mind imagine the buffalo grazing, and the Indian braves riding their ponies instead of paying attention, on the right side of the road you will see a small sign saying "Old Settler's Cemetery." Stop by and see my relatives. They always love to have company. It gets lonely out on the prairie.

Should you visit the "Old Settler's Cemetery", you will find many personal family stories lying behind that gate, under that sod. They all have stories to tell, for we are all stories in the making. Should you pass all the other stories, go clear to the back of that cemetery to the right and you will find my Great Grannie Sarah, my Granddad Clyde and my Beloved John.

Oh yes, one other thing needs to be explained. Margueritte, my mother, saw to one other thing. She was the last one left there and so it fell to her to have John's gravestone laid. It seemed so fitting that they be placed shoulder to shoulder in death as they were in life. I'm not sure if Miss Sarah or her son Clyde would have approved of his epitaph, but those that knew the man and knew his heart would have agreed that it was the perfect thing for a man that decided he owed his life to a family, and literally gave it. It reads:

JOHN
HE LIVED TO SERVE
APR 21, 1855
JAN 20, 1960

JANUARY 27, 1960   NUMBER 51

Death Claims Lum Seow, Carnegie's Oldest Citizen

Lum Seow, a native of China and Carnegie's oldest citizen, died Wednesday in an Anadarko rest home after being bedfast since September 31, 1956.

Seow, well-known throughout the area as "Chinaman John," was born in Canton, China, in 1855 and would have been 105 years of age had he lived until April 22. He came to the United States when nine years old. He lived with an uncle who had a mercantile store in San Francisco, and later was given a half interest in the store.

Later Lum Seow became ill with asthma and in 1894 moved to Nebraska where he met Mrs. Sarah Ingram, mother of the late Clyde Ingram and grandmother of Mrs. Marguerite Harding. He cooked in a cafe for Mrs. Ingram and when the Ingrams sold their cafe and came to Lathrom (Carnegie) when the country opened in about 1900, Seow came with them.

He worked as a cook for the Ingrams here for many years and when they purchased a farm three miles south of Alden he went along to help with the farm work. In 1919 they moved to Raymondville, Texas, returning here in 1922. They again moved to Texas until 1937. Clyde Ingram and Seow returned here in 1937 to remain.

Seow did odd jobs on the farm, pulled bolls and was an expert gardener. He also worked in cafes here and in Mountain View. He became a citizen of the United States in 1899.

On his 100th birthday residents of Carnegie paid special tribute to him by naming him "Mayor For A Day." He received congratulations from President and Mrs. Eisenhower and from Gov. Raymond Gary. The Carnegie band paraded in his honor and openhouse was held. "Don't Go Crooked—Go Straight" was the motto he lived by.

Services were held here Saturday at 2:30 p.m. at the Pitchee Funeral chapel. Burial was in the Alden cemetery.

LUM SEOW

Rock Island Asks Close Of 21 Depots

Rock Island stations at Fort Cobb, Gotebo, Bridgeport, and Apache will be among 21 in Oklahoma to be closed and the services of their agents discontinued if a request made Monday to the Oklahoma Corporation commission is approved. Stations at Carnegie, Mountain View, Hydro, Geary, Hobart, Anadarko and 15 others on the line would be retained under the proposed plan.

The railroad maintains the business transacted at the stations they are requesting authority to close requires an average of only one to two hours work a day by the agent, and points out the 21 agents on duty at the stations are paid for eight hours a day.

Other stations listed for closing include: Billings, Calvin, Comanche, Goodwell, Granite, Hardesty, Hitchcock, Jefferson, Renfrow, Kremlin, Ringwood, Rush Springs, Ryan, Verden and Waukomis.

Accounts handled by the stations to be closed would be handled by 21 stations left in operation on the Rock Island lines.

Railroad officials are petitioning for relaxation of a labor contract that prohibits any agent at one station from performing the duties at another station. The railroad contends one man could perform duties at two stations more efficiently and economically.

Officials contend the proposal would reduce operation costs in Oklahoma by $100,000 annually.

Carnegie Herald, January 27, 1960

"DEATH CLAIMS LUM SEOW, CARNEGIE'S OLDEST CITIZEN"

Lum Seow, a native of China, and Carnegie's oldest citizen died Wednesday in an Anadarko rest home after being bedfast since September 31[sic], 1956.

Seow, well-known throughout the area as "Chinaman-John", was born in Canton China in 1855 and would have been 105 years of age had he lived until April 22. He came to the United States when he was nine years old. He lived with an uncle who had a mercantile store in San Francisco, and later was given a half interest in the store.

Later, Lum Seow became ill with asthma and in 1894 moved to Nebraska where he met Mrs. Sarah Ingrahm, mother of the late Clyde Ingrahm and grandmother of Mrs. Marguerite Harding. He cooked in a café for Mrs. Ingram and when the Ingrahm's sold their café and came to Lathram (Carnegie) when the country opened in about 1900, Seow came with them.

He worked as a cook for the Ingrahms here for many years and when they purchased a farm three miles south of Alden he went along to help with the farm work. In 1919 they moved to Raymondville, Texas, returning here in 1922. They again moved to Texas until 1937. Clyde Ingrahm and Seow returned here in 1937 to remain.

Seow did odd jobs on the farm, pulled bolls and was an expert gardener. He also worked in cafes here and in Mountain View. He became a citizen of the United States in 1899.

On his 100ᵗʰ birthday residents of Carnegie paid special tribute to him by naming him "Mayor for a Day". He received congratulations from President and Mrs. Eisenhower and from Governor Raymond Gary. The Carnegie band paraded in his honor and an open house was held. "Don't Go Crooked, Go Straight" was the motto he lived by.

Services were held here Saturday at 2:30 pm at the Pitcher Funeral Chapel. Burial was in the Alden Cemetery.

A MYSTERY SOLVED

In the early 1980's Margueritte Queen, the granddaughter of Zebulun Wheeler Ingram, ran a Veteran check to see if the Civil War Stories were true on her Grandfather. This information, to the family's great surprise, was on the record she received back.

Zebulun W. Ingham
Served In War: Aug. 10, 1862 – June 26, 1865
Unit Served G,83 Ill. Inf,   Pension No. xc-2479-756
Date of Birth: **Oct. 12, 1837**   Date of Death: **Mar. 30, 1915**
Veteran Lived In Home For Soldiers Montgomery Co. Tennessee
NAME OF WIDOW OR CLAIMANT: **Lydia Ingham**
Place veteran lived after service: Lafayette Co. GA

AFTERWORD

To The Settlers of This Land

Wagon trail travelers, land runners, claim-stakers. Sod busters, hayseeds, weather beaten shack dwellers. Water haulers, well diggers, burning sun field workers, burned and blistered. Freezing and shivering food providers, raw and calloused handed child bearers, and noble caregivers. Family protectors and lonely homesteaders. Those who forever carried the pain of buried children or loved ones on lonely prairie wagon trails, and rode away, never to return to their desolate forsaken graves. These were the ones that gave us our start in this land. These were the ones who populated this land. From lonely farms, to now bustling cities.

To those that laid new foundations great honor is due for their courage. A beautiful statue memorial called "The Pioneer Woman" in honor of the pioneer women of Oklahoma stands in Ponca City, Oklahoma. It is a statue of a woman. The woman, wearing a sunbonnet, is holding the hand of her lone son. How can I not think of my great-grandmother, Sarah Ingrahm, who alone raised her son in that era when I view that statue? The story-teller's son and great-great grandson of the pioneer woman Sarah Ingrahm, was born in that town.

To all the women, who endured alone, whether by death of a husband, or a husband that had to leave the lonely homesteads looking for work, while they took care of and raised children, I believe that statue is dedicated. I give honor to all the pioneers, both men and women, for their courage that gave us this great country.

That statue was erected in the year of 1930. The year Sarah Elizabeth Ingrahm died on a piece of Oklahoma land, at the age of ninety.

Jan Harding Chapman

From the Storyteller

On our trip back to Texas from the Carnegie Oklahoma area, after visiting some of our dearest friends, the Larry Chapmans, we passed the "Old Settler's Cemetery". There we passed the graves of my ancestors.

A few miles away lay what had been their property. As always we start to drive leisurely along that part of our journey before we head for the stretch of highway south that will lead us to the muddy Red River and our Texas home. My husband drives slowly for me to view, just as I allow him to take his time exploring his old beloved boyhood home area. It's a place near the small town of Carnegie where I spent my childhood. His memories lie in a community that lies eight miles away from Carnegie in a place named Alfalfa. It has ever been his delight to tell people who inquire about what place he is from in Oklahoma to say "Alfalfa". They generally laugh, but almost always say "Where's that?" Having taken the bait, he gives his old punch line "Between Corn and Cobb." They laugh, thinking he is kidding. It is a truth, though. Strangely, in a room full of strangers, they might not remember his name, but before the evening is over they will remember the man who is from the town of Alfalfa, between the towns of Corn and Cobb.

Often on these trips, we will take a leisurely journey down the Alfalfa road that leads to his old homeplace. We will see the old windmill that stands not far from where the childhood home he shared with his parents and 8 siblings. We will meander further down by the lake that has overtaken much of the land that used to be neighboring farms. We will drive by the Horn's family farm, where the owner of that place, whom my husband loved dearly, taught the value of a good work ethic. We will pass by another Horn farm, that if passed at the right season, will be beautifully in bloom with many colorful canna plants. Finally we will drive by the old Alfalfa schoolhouse, now deteriorating, from which my husband made friendships that last to this day.

Alas, the name of my childhood town is not as romantic as some of the surrounding towns named after Native Americans, nor funny like Corn, Cobb, or Alfalfa, but a name filled with memories of a small, safe place to have grown up in. We drive the streets and roads surrounding Carnegie slowly, as the past comes alive again, only in our minds.

As we slowly drive further south, we know that the old hill that my grandmother lived on with her son will look the same. It will be that same old piece of ground my grandfather tilled the soil with my grandmother, who was then his lover. It will be the same old rocks that my mother showed to me as a child, telling of her memories of playing house and using the large stones as tables and chairs just as children play today.

There will be up there, no one knows where on that vast piece of land, a place where there is said to be an ancient Indian grave. It is a place that beads would wash out from their hiding place whenever it rained and can still be found to this day. When my mother was young in the early 1900's, the beads were brightly colored. Now they are snow and dirty white.

Now, as our car winds that old highway, I look with expectation to see the old familiar Oklahoma land of my mother's childhood memories. I am totally in shock beyond belief at what I see. Could my ghostly relative companions from the past now see their old home land that they had settled, they would cry out in terror, not knowing what it is they behold. What thing is this that looms in the twilight horizon? The total unexpected shock caused me to utter a cry that startled my husband, as my eyes beheld the sight before he did, and I cried out, "No!"

As I gaze across the old familiar horizon, I see rows and rows of giant wind turbans and I, having no right to the new Oklahoma land that this is now, still utter my shock as if some travesty has been done to sacred ground – to all that I considered almost holy to my ancestor ghosts of the past.

Again, the thought of my family's old settler's home came to mind. If they could only see those ghostly looking wind turbans scattered over that hill, as they would have huddled together with their little family, what would they have thought?

What wonder would the old Indian buried up there under those rocks contemplate before him were he to have a brief moment fast forward in time to view the fearful sight of those gigantic looking monsters lifting their huge, rotating arms in the sky. I could imagine him standing nobly, as the men who seemed almost as centaurs as they were astride their prairie ponies in that day and age, on that land, beholding such a sight.

The rancher and his wife, who bought that old farm place in 1986 after other families since, and made a ranching operation for their family of that land, could never have envisioned the property with my family on it, in the days of wagons. Not now, with its beautiful ranch home and those awesome wind turbans softly singing lullabies to baby calves across that low mountain range.

From the time of my ancestors to ours, how miraculous has been the change. From the time of the 1900's, in which my early settler family struggled to survive, to now has been the laying aside of horses to cars and supersonic jets. In so short a time, the pony express to the telegraph and now to a world wide web of communication. Food at your fingertips on that very ranch now from what will soon be an outdated microwave oven. How my people labored all day long, every day, just in hope to have their family fed. In the last century, technology has taken off. How knowledge has increased in these last days! As the inventor of the telegraph said "Look what God has wrought".

The relative ghosts of the Oklahoma territory will always be alive in my mind. They live in the misty clouds even back to the Emerald Isle. They still live in The Great Dragon Land of China. They live from The Great Lady in New York Harbor to an early immigrant America with their thick accents. They travel from taking barge canals on the Erie Canal and covered wagons. They live from a great battleground that separated this nation, to a prosperous land of peace. They live in the blizzards and beauty of Nebraska to the southwestern Indian plains of Oklahoma.

From a feisty little woman who bravely supported a son alone in an early America, to that son who played Irish jigs as he adventured to all the places his heart called him to. From the curious name of "Chinaman John" to a wild frontiersman named "Yellowstone Vic". These are my people. My children's people.

Those hardy people, those settlers, those pioneers and the people of whom I speak, and I too, will soon be gone. It is my hope to pass their memory on to my children and my grandchildren so that the memories of these people might remain alive.

There is a powerful scripture that says "The power of life or death is in the tongue." It will be up to them, my children's children, if these memories live or die.

References

CARNEGIE, OKLAHOMA THE FIRST 100 YEARS, Scoonmaker Publisher Weatherford, OK 73096

ALONG THE BANKS OF THE WASHITA The Story of a Town by Whitham D. "JIM" Finney copyright 1976

THE WICHITA MOUNTAINS – E. Buford Morgan copyright 1973, Second Printing 1994 by Texian Press, Waco, Tx.

OUR OKLAHOMA by MURIEL H. WRIGHT Copyright 1939 – Co-Operative Publishing Company

AMERICA'S HISTORY, Second Edition copyright@1993 by Worth Publishers Inc. 33 Irving Place N.Y., N.Y. 10003

THE CARNEGIE HERALD – WEDNESDAY, DEC. 16, 1953 "Lum Seow, 98, Gives Away Fortune in Kindness"

THE CARNEGIE HERALD - WEDNESDAY, APRIL 20, 1955 "Carnegie's 100 – Year- Old Citizen, Lum Seow, Made Honorary Mayor for Day"

THE CARNEGIE HERALD – WEDNESDAY, JANUARY 27, 1960 "Death claims Lum Seow, Carnegie's Oldest Citizen"

TECUMSEH NEWSPAPER – SIXTY-THIRD YEAR "VERY EARLY SETTLER HERE—MRS. SARAH INGRAHM DIED AT HOME IN OKLAHOMA. Served as Nurse Throughout Civil War—Was Pioneer Hotel Keeper in Tecumseh." (Lengthy article on Sarah's life)

Made in the USA
Monee, IL
02 June 2022

97371867R00204